WŁADYSŁAW REYMONT

THE REVOLT OF THE ANIMALS

THE REVOLT OF THE ANIMALS

A Fable

by Władysław Stanisław Reymont

Translated from the Polish and introduced by
Charles S. Kraszewski

First published in the Polish as *Bunt* in 1924

This book has been published with the support of
the ©POLAND Translation Program

WŁADYSŁAW REYMONT

THE REVOLT OF THE ANIMALS

TRANSLATED FROM THE POLISH AND INTRODUCED
BY CHARLES S. KRASZEWSKI

GLAGOSLAV PUBLICATIONS

CONTENTS

WŁADYSŁAW REYMONT
(1867 – 1925)

OH, THE HUMANITY. ON WŁADYSŁAW REYMONT'S *REVOLT OF THE ANIMALS*

Charles S. Kraszewski

POLAND'S ORWELL

The second of Poland's six Nobel laureates in literature, Władysław Stanisław Reymont (1867–1925), is not an unknown quantity outside of his homeland. Translations of *The Peasants* [Chłopi, 1904–1909], which won him the Nobel in 1924, and his earlier *Promised Land* [Ziemia obiecana, 1899] have been available in English since 1925 and 1927, at least.[1] The same cannot be said for his last novel, *The Revolt of the Animals* [Bunt, 1924]. Besides its serialisation in the year of his death, there have only been three editions of the novel in book form printed in Poland: the 1924 edition of the pre-war firm of Gebethner and Wolff, that of 1934, brought out in Warsaw by the 'Wydawnictwo Tygodnika Ilustrowanego' [Illustrated Weekly Publications], and, most recently, that of Wimana (Gdańsk: 2018).

The timeframe is eloquent: two printings (or three, if the periodical serialisation is counted) before the Second

....

[1] By Knopf in New York, both works translated by M.H. Dziewicki.

World War, which put an end to the independence of the resurrected Second Polish Republic, and one in 2018 — two decades after the resumption of Polish independence and the crumbling of Soviet hegemony in East-Central Europe. For, as the editors of the 2018 printing note on their flyleaf:

> The novel is the Author's personal reflection on the Russian revolution, and a critique of its ideology. Although he looked with distaste on unfettered capitalism, a distaste he expressed in his *Promised Land*, the results of falling into the other extreme terrified him. On this earth, all Utopias will remain unrealised ideals. Despite the best initial intentions, every attempt at imposing Utopia, especially through revolution, will end in the same fashion: in the deaths of hundreds, thousands, even millions of mostly innocent victims. It's no wonder that throughout the years of the Polish People's Republic, Reymont's *Revolt* remained on the index of forbidden titles.[2]

The novel, which Reymont subtitles *baśń* — a fable, or fairy story — centres on Rex: a powerful, mastiff-like dog, raised on a manor, who, after outliving his use and being brutally expelled from his human Eden by the family following his master's death, arrives at the revolutionary idea of leading the animals out of human bondage. He will take them on a trek far to the east, inspired by the songs of the cranes that wax lyrical about a paradisiacal land where human foot has

[2]   Władysław St. Reymont, *Bunt* (Gdańsk: Wimana, 2018), rear leaf.

never trod, where the pastures abound with fat grasses and sparkle with pure springs of water. How this will play out, the reader will see in due time. However, the very concept of an animal fable — a poetic genre known since antiquity — turned to a consideration of socialist revolution and totalitarianism cannot help but call to the reader's mind a more famous novel, also subtitled 'a fable' — George Orwell's bitingly brilliant *Animal Farm* (1945). With rather disarming forthrightness, the editors at Wimana are quick to point this out, a few lines farther down from the above citation: '*The Revolt* preceded by more than twenty years the publication of G. Orwell's *Animal Farm*. Perhaps, if not for that blacklisting, it might have become a worldwide best-seller of its genre.' The cynical reader might well ask why no translator reached for *The Revolt* in the fifteen years of relative peace and prosperity following the initial publication of the novel, before the Nazi/Soviet invasion of Poland in September 1939 put paid to all such secondary concerns in the country as literature; why a full English translation is only now appearing, nearly an entire century after the book's first appearance, whereas Orwell's novel was translated into Polish almost immediately after the publication of the English original, at the end of 1946, in paper-scarce London.[3]

....

[3]   George Orwell, *Folwark zwierzęcy*, trans. Teresa Jeleńska (London: The League of Poles Abroad, 1946). As far as *1984* is concerned, the first printed version in Polish was the translation by Juliusz Mieroszewski, published in 1953 by *Kultura* in Paris. However, as Beata Dorosz notes in her article 'George Orwell's *1984*: The Polish Chapter in Light of the PIASA Archives,' *The Polish Review*, Vol. 61, No.

One might say, 'because *Animal Farm* is a better book.' There is no riposte that I, the translator, or anyone intimately acquainted with literature, can make to that. But: are there really better and worse books? Is Evgeny Zamyatin's *We* 'better' than *1984*? Or is *1984* better than Koestler's *Darkness at Noon*? Is there any sense to saying that Roger Waters' magnificent reworking of the Orwellian theme on Pink Floyd's *Animals* (1977) is 'better' than Ray Davies' cheeky and hopelessly idyllic 'Animal Farm' from the *Village Green Preservation Society* (1968)? One may prefer The Kinks to Pink Floyd, or vice versa; Orwell to Reymont, or Reymont to Orwell, but do rankings of 'better' and 'worse' apply in art? Is Raphael a 'better' painter than David Hockney? Is Picasso's photographically naturalistic *First Communion* (1906) better, or worse, than his *Portrait of Dora Maar* (1937) which plays havoc with perspective and colour? Perhaps it's best to set aside all such evaluative comparisons, and approach all artworks, including these two books, on their own ground. What was the author trying to do? Did he succeed?

Polish critics, both before and after the war, were none too effusive in their praise of the final fruit of their Nobel-winner's pen. In 1938, writing in *The Slavonic and East European Review*, Wacław Borowy spares but one descriptive sentence to the novel, telling enough in its avoidance of assessment. He calls it 'a sort of contemporary *Roman du*

<hr>

4 (2016), pp. 57-66, it was the poet Jan Lechoń who first made a radio-play translation of the novel, which was aired by the Voice of America in November, 1949, and hence within a year of the printing of the original English text.

CHARLES S. KRASZEWSKI

Renart, in which [Reymont] attempted to picture the tangle of present social ideas.'[4] In 1926 (and thus just two years after its publication), Roman Dyboski, translator and professor of English literature at the Jagiellonian University, saw the genesis of *The Revolt* in the context of contemporary history: the Polish-Soviet War of 1919–1921, in which the victorious Polish Army under the command of Józef Piłsudski stymied Soviet attempts at exporting communism to the west 'over the corpse of white Poland.'[5] Dyboski writes:

> Reymont deals with the monstrous phenomenon of Bolshevism under the allegorical guise of a story of revolt in the animal world (*The Revolt*). This suggests to the literary specialist an interesting comparison with the Latin poem of the medieval English poet John Gower on the great peasant revolt of 1381 (*Vox Clamantis*), but it is in itself too full of the natural excitement of the Poles over the terrible things happening next door to them, to claim attention as a lasting literary reflection of the great political drama enacted before our eyes.[6]

....

[4] Wacław Borowy, 'Reymont,' *The Slavonic and East European Review*, Vol. XVI, No. 47 (January 1938), p. 443.

[5] So proclaimed Soviet General Mikhail Tukhachevsky (who not long after suffered an ignominious defeat at the gates of Warsaw, which led to the ultimate Polish victory): 'To the West! Over the corpse of White Poland lies the road to world-wide conflagration.' Citation from Norman Davies, *God's Playground: A History of Poland*, Vol. II: '1795 to the Present' (New York: Columbia University Press, 1982), p. 396.

[6] R. Dyboski, 'Żeromski and Reymont,' *The Slavonic Review*, Vol. IV, No. 12 (March 1926), pp. 560-561.

It is something like the writer's mind caught *in flagranti*, Dyboski seems to imply, and if Ezra Pound's definition of literature as 'news that stays news' is to be accepted, Reymont's *Revolt of the Animals* was, a mere five years after the Polish-Soviet War, as dead a letter as the newspaper reports of the military campaigns yellowing away in the archives. Closer to our own day and age, Jerzy Kwiatkowski, a literary historian specialising in the interwar period, expressed his assessment of the novel in terms reflective of the prevailing political climate of the Communist People's Republic of Poland. Speaking of the novel in the context of 'science fiction,' which often in the twenties 'constituted a satire on and warning against the "materialisation" of the new, post-war society and — a Communist takeover,' he writes:

> Reymont's *Revolt* (1924) has the same aims. It is a sharp pamphlet directed against the revolution, conceived as an 'animal fable,' with a catastrophist tone in the spirit of Florian Znanecki's writings. [...] *The Revolt* strikes the reader with its bluntness, its concrete nature, its artistic consistency. Still and all, it is a satire; it is shallow and luridly exaggerated. The tastelessness of its idea (presenting the 'revolt of the masses' as a revolt of beasts) blew up in the author's face, as it limits the possibilities of analysing the phenomena it condemns.[7]

....

[7]   Jerzy Kwiatkowski, *Literatura dwudziestolecia* [Interwar Literature] (Warsaw: PWN, 1990), p. 206. I am far from suggesting that Professor Kwiatkowski (1927–1986) was towing the party line here. As an insurgent who fought for his country in the Warsaw Uprising, he had more familiarity with Soviet perfidy than Reymont, who lived

This assessment seems harsh, indeed. For even if *The Revolt of the Animals* is intended as a 'warning against a Communist takeover,' and if Reymont is decidedly opposed to Rex's revolution — any revolution — he does not demonise the animals or their leader. Rather, he shows just as much sympathy and understanding to them and for their just grievances as he does to the peasants and workers which populate his earlier, more famous books. It is hard to read a passage descriptive of man's viciousness, such as we find in the first chapter of the book, when Rex climbs onto the porch to visit with an old friend:

'Rex, Rex!' the parrot screeched in joy from her golden hoop.

'I was looking for you,' he growled, climbing up on a chair, as he used to do. They had been friends for a long time. She fluttered down on the armrest and, flapping her wings, began to tell him all sorts of news in her squawking voice. But before he got a chance to confide in her, the dachshunds rushed in, baying, and behind them, the lady of the house, the little master with his blunderbuss, and a whole mob in their train.

'Run, run!' gasped the parrot in terror.

....

in a time when Poland successfully resisted Communist incursions from the east. However, like all writers of all political stripes in Communist-controlled Poland, in his publications, Kwiatkowski had to choose his words carefully. He died before his country regained its independence, and the above assessment appears unchanged in the newest edition of his book (PWN: 2012, p. 248). It would have been interesting to see if he would have altered his wording, had he lived into the present era.

It was too late. The furious woman rushed over at him and screeched:

'Out! Out! Out of my sight, you filthy thing! You bloody mutt! Out!' And right then he felt the teeth of the dachshunds sink into his legs, while painful thumps rained down on his back.

Frenzied with insult and pain, he grabbed the wretched little dogs and tore at them mercilessly, paying heed to nothing now, neither screams nor jets of water nor thrashing staves.

'Run! Run, Rex, run!' the parrot continued to screech.

At last, he tore away from the attacking mob and, with a lionlike leap, cleared the terrace and landed on the lawn. But before he made it to the thicket a shot rang out, and something like a hot handful of gravel bit into his left flank. The cruel impact was such that he was thrown headlong, but soon, gathering together what strength he had left, he leapt amongst the low firs. A second shot boomed. Tiny branches rained down upon him, like dead, green tears. He waited no longer, but, crawling through the parkland back into the yard, near the barns, he squeezed into a kennel, where he fell down, fainting with pain.

Even harder to read is this passage, a little later on when, harassed and whipped, and frenzied with anger at the animals' treatment at the hands of his former protectors, the budding canine revolutionary witnesses a particularly chilling episode of human sadism:

A bloodcurdling cry was then heard, and they saw the donkey run up in panic to throw himself on the dung-hill.

'The master's whelp's splashed him with boiling water! It all but took off his skin.'

With a horrid, mournful bellow, the donkey rolled in the cool muck, while a pack of boys, with the young master at their head, ran up to continue their fun, pelting the beast with stones and knocking at his legs with staves.

One would have to be heartless not to be moved to anger and pity at such a scene. And most people, I venture, in reading Thomas Hardy's heartbreaking lyric 'The Mongrel,' in which a man deceives his dog into leaping into the harbour during a strong undertow, drowning the beast to save a few pence in taxes, are full of understanding when, at last, the dog realises what his 'god' has in mind for him:

> Just ere his sinking what does one see
> Break on the face of that devotee?
> A wakening to the treachery
>   He had loved with love so blind?
> The faith that had shone in that mongrel's eye
> That his owner would save him by and by
> Turned to much like a curse as he sank to die,
>   And a loathing of mankind.[8]

....

[8]   Thomas Hardy, 'The Mongrel,' pp. 25-32. From Thomas Hardy, *The Complete Poems* (New York: MacMillan, 1982). The poem

Yet when we come across cruelty, we call it 'bestial.' When we hear of a horrific atrocity, we exclaim 'That's inhuman!' How wrong we are. To paraphrase Hardy's American acolyte, Robinson Jeffers, there's nothing *more human* than gratuitous cruelty and sadism. Animals do no such things. Whether or not Reymont would agree with the philosophy of Inhumanism that the great Californian worked up over his half century or so of poetic creativity we'll never know. However, *The Revolt of the Animals* is no flat essay, no B-western with black and white hats to identify the villains and the heroes. If — in the context of the novel — Reymont takes the side of man's society against the revolutionary hordes of the hoofed and horned, it is not that he is blind to the wickedness of humanity. Consider the one human being judged worthy by the animals of accompanying them on their trek — the cast-off, bastard waif Dummy (no given name is mentioned; his nickname — *Niemowa* — is derived from his speech impediment). No one knows how he showed up one day, as a baby, on the kitchen stoop of the manor; the hard charity of the toffs was such as to make us wonder if it mightn't have been better not to take him in at all, but rather to expose him, as in the bad old days of the ancient Greeks, than to feed him just enough to keep body and soul together, to beat him, to make fun of him, to treat him like one of the animals (remember the donkey?) who are his only friends. There is a telling scene in the second half of the novel, when, poking through the smoky ruins

....

was originally published in the collection *Winter Words in Various Moods and Metres* (1928).

of a town abandoned by its human inhabitants after the passage of the angry sea of animals, Dummy finds himself in a smashed toy store:

> Ranging around the store with his eyes, he suddenly shivered in holy fear — as if he'd stumbled in front of an altar. There was a large wardrobe set with reflective glass panes, and on its shelves there were dolls of different sizes and costumes. There were bears, ruddy ones and white ones, horses, jumping-jacks and, besides these, piles of swords, guns, drums, horns, and thousands of other wondrous things that he was seeing for the first time. He blessed himself and rubbed his eyes, unable to believe this great good fortune. He devoured all these miracles with feverish eyes, breathless and afraid lest it all dissolve like the mist. He stood there gaping, moved to the core, astonished, tears flowing down his cheeks.
>
> 'O dear Jesus, how pretty!' he sobbed out in a voice thick with ineffable joy.

Do we need any further proof of man's evil? It takes a revolution of the animals to introduce a child to toys. At the risk of citing something out of context, Robinson Jeffers once said 'I'd sooner, except the penalties, kill a man than a hawk.'[9] Yep. You got that right.

....

[9]   Robinson Jeffers, 'Hurt Hawks,' II: 1. In Robinson Jeffers, *Selected Poetry* (New York: Random House, 1959). The poem was first collected in *Cawdor and Other Poems* (1928).

I may as well come clean.

It may be no surprise to you, but I'm a little inhuman myself.

I don't eat animals.

I wasn't always like this. Like most humans, I grew up eating *Fleisch* (I'm using the German word consciously here). I remember — as an adult already — laughing at an advert of a New York steakhouse which featured nothing but a knife and the (witty, I thought, at the time) caption *Horrifying vegetarians for over fifty years.* Little did I know that, before long, I would be among the horrified.

Most people who stop eating meat, after being raised on it, will have a story explaining when, and why, it came about. Mine has nothing of the dramatic about it at all. It was at the Norfolk Zoo. They had a section called 'The Virginia Farmyard,' or something like that. It was a place where all the animals domesticated by man were featured. It didn't occur to me at the time, but, actually, I was wandering amidst all of the animals you find on the farm in Orwell's novel, or on the manor grounds of Reymont's. At one point, I walked into the sty. There was a low wooden barrier — a few horizontal planks nailed onto posts — beyond which slept the hugest pig I'd ever seen. This hog was immense. I bet if I stretched out next to it (no, I didn't!) he wouldn't be much shorter than me, and I'm over six feet. I don't quite know why — it wasn't a *mystical* experience — but as I leant there on that low barrier, gazing down at that gigantic porcine shape, I was mesmerised. And suddenly I said, *Why would I want to eat you? Why would I want to kill you, and eat you?* It wasn't a petting zoo; the pig was not turning somersaults or nuzzling up for a treat or pushing his huge head close to be scratched; he was asleep. Maybe it was just that vulnerability of his, lying there on his side, his huge, barrel chest inflating and deflating with each breath, his ear twitching away a fly… the sound of a sudden snore so similar to mine (I'm told) when sleeping on the beach I suddenly grunt against my palate… It was a living creature. A mammal. An intelligent creature. And I'm going to put it to death — a rather cruel death, in the case of what some people call with flippancy 'the other white meat' — just so I can lay some bacon across a patty of ground *Fleisch* cut from another mammal sacrificed to that god my stomach? Nope. And from that time forward, I stopped eating meat. I'll eat fish, but not mammals. No, thank you.

There's some hypocrisy in this, I suppose. From one perspective, you might say I'm not only inhuman, I'm unnatural. Reymont would probably think so, as I'm about to show you.

I was writing the above lines on a hot, sunny afternoon, on a sandy beach in south Florida, looking out from time to time at the turquoise waters of the Atlantic. Suddenly, the water began to crackle with a swath of tiny plops — as if a pinpoint cartoon cloud had suddenly let loose a downpour some ten yards long by five yards wide. It was mullet and other small fry, leaping desperately out of their element, just to plunge back down and then, turning my gaze to the right, I saw why: three or four long dark shadows just under the surface of the water, with dorsal fins resembling those of sharks — tarpon, patiently swimming northward, gathering an early lunch. And then, one of those huge brown pelicans — beautiful birds — hovered above the water to make one of their dramatic plunges after another living creature, soon to be just dead, fresh, *Fleisch*. And finally — was Somebody trying to tell me something? — there went a hawk, winging his way to a perch somewhere in the direction of Collins, with a silvery fish in his claws, tail still sweeping left and right — What else was he supposed to do? Reymont, or you, reader, might ask. And of course you're right.

I'm not an imbecile. But I bet it's not only me who looks away from the screen when the wolves finally catch up with the sick buffalo. How can David Attenborough describe that so calmly and mellifluously? And I know it's heretical, but I've never been a big fan of the Old Testament. All that blood. All that *animal* blood spilled on altars, sprinkled on the people, daubed on door jambs. Don't even get me started on Abraham and Isaac. But if there's one part of the Bible I do like, it would be Isaiah. For example:

> The wolf shall dwell with the lamb: and the leopard shall lie down with the kid: the calf and the lion, and the sheep shall abide together, and a little child shall lead them. The calf and the bear shall feed: their young ones shall rest together: and the lion shall eat straw like the ox. And the sucking child shall play on the hole of the asp: and the weaned child shall thrust his hand into the den of the basilisk. They shall not hurt, nor shall they kill in all my holy mountain, for the earth is filled with the knowledge of the Lord, as the covering waters of the sea. […] The wolf and the lamb shall feed together; the lion and the ox shall eat straw; and dust shall be the

serpent's food: they shall not hurt nor kill in all my holy mountain, saith the Lord.[10]

Sure, but that's *God's holy mountain*, not Florida. Yet, isn't this how we'd all like it to be? Some of the most moving parts of *Animal Farm* are when everybody — every species — runs off in solidarity to help the popular Boxer:

> About half the animals on the farm rushed out to the knoll where the windmill stood. There lay Boxer, between the shafts of the cart, his neck stretched out, unable even to raise his head. His eyes were glazed, his sides matted with sweat. A thin stream of blood had trickled out of his mouth. Clover dropped to her knees at his side.
>
> 'Boxer!' she cried, 'how are you?'
>
> 'It is my lung,' said Boxer in a weak voice. 'It does not matter. I think you will be able to finish the windmill without me. There is a pretty good store of stone accumulated. I had only another month to go in any case. To tell you the truth, I had been looking forward to my retirement. And perhaps, as Benjamin is growing old too, they will let him retire at the same time and be a companion to me.'
>
> 'We must get help at once,' said Clover. 'Run, somebody, and tell Squealer what has happened.'
>
> All the other animals immediately raced back to the farmhouse to give Squealer the news. Only Clover re-

---

[10]   Isaiah 11:6-9; 65:25.

mained, and Benjamin who lay down at Boxer's side, and, without speaking, kept the flies off him with his long tail.[11]

And again the objections: 'Where's the realism in that? This is a novel! Remember what your dog did when he caught that woodchuck and gave it a good shake? And the way foxes will bring back live prey for the kits to "play" with until they learn how to kill? What does St Robinson Jeffers have to say about that? And the bird-feeder out back? How the cowbirds chase off the sparrows and the jays the cowbirds, the squirrels the chipmunks and…'

And that's exactly the point. If there is a programmatic novel here, it's not *The Revolt of the Animals*, it's *Animal Farm*. As splendid as that novel is, it is *only* a thinly-cloaked commentary on human society. The animals — except for the central committee of the pigs and their NKVD cadre of dogs — get on well with one another, as the great majority of the duped citizens of people's democracies will, all the while the big shots get fat, never having to ration. Towards the end of the novel, the pigs begin taking on human airs to such an extent, that the *hoi polloi* gathered at the window during the summit-banquet of the chiefs of (renamed) Manor Farm and their human neighbours, looking in at the feast 'from pig to man, and from man to pig, and from pig to man again; [already found it] impossible to say which was which.'[12]

....

[11]   George Orwell, *Animal Farm / 1984* (New York: Harcourt, 2003), p. 71.

[12]   Orwell, *Animal Farm*, p. 84.

In *The Revolt*, whatever its metaphorical content, animals are animals. They don't read, they don't build windmills or brew beer, and — what is conceptually even more interesting — they *act* like animals: children of a nature proverbially, and truly, red in tooth and claw:

> Like an oak buffeted by a strong wind, the bear swayed this way and that, torn from all sides by the fangs of the frenzied horde. He gave no thought to escape, defending himself with the valour of despair, but he could now feel the teeth sunk deep inside him. His sides were torn, as were his thighs; his ribs broken from falling to the earth again and again, yet he always spun to his feet with the last remnants of his strength, covered in wounds and tattered, the blood pumping out of him, his eyes clouding over in death — but he fought on to the bitter end. Suddenly, in a flash, when the bear had risen to his feet for the last time, Rex threw himself at his throat. Both tumbled to the earth and the rest of the pack piled on. They whirled in a tangled ball of claws, heads, horrible wounds and howling, tumbling over the turf from one side to the other, spurting blood, striking against tree, bush and stone, marking their furious progress with the bodies of the slaughtered and gravely wounded.

There is no reason for Rex and the dogs to kill the bear, who had been merely crossing a clearing with others of his kind. But you might say there is: they are acting exactly as a pack of wild dogs would act in a situation like this. Rex, the domesticated animal gone feral, who was castigated by the wild creatures earlier in the book for his heedless slaughter of animals at what — according to the 'rules of the wild' — were inappropriate times, here performs a — natural — feat that is recognised by all: he has knocked off the king of the woods, the predator at the very top of the food chain, and from now on, he will be recognised by all as the successor monarch. The king is dead; long live the bloody king.

It is behaviour just as natural as that witnessed by Dummy, after his banishment, one winter night, when he sees animals wild from time immemorial doing what comes naturally to them:

> He caught sight of some strings of shadows slipping towards the river. At the very front raced a gigantic stag who, pinning back his antlers, flew on with the last of his strength, stumbling more and more until, having reached the steep bank, he paused there and bellowed in despair. The wolves then caught him up and now wild howls of triumph tore the air. But then the stag tumbled down the bank, and with giant leaps reached the marsh, through which he tore with all his might, sinking here and there. He extracted himself again and again and hurled himself with all the might of despair until, at last, he plunged breast-deep through the thin skin of the ice. Before he could clamber out of that, the entire frenzied pack fell upon him. A furious battle ensued. The stag pulled himself out of the mire, defending himself with his antlers, pummelling the wolves with his hooves, and then escaping anew. Falling into the marsh, he fought to the bitter end until at last he fell, torn apart by the fangs.

Curiously enough, Dummy does a very *human* thing. He is filled with pity for the stag. He anthropomorphises the beast, sees a heroism in his fighting to the bitter end, and his heart goes out to the underdog (no pun intended). 'You bastards!' he screams toward the pack of wolves, angry at their ganging up against the one animal they naturally prey upon, and he pulls out his revolver and fires into the whirling mass. In short, he does exactly what wildlife photographers and filmmakers do *not* do, as much as it breaks their hearts (I'm sure) — he intervenes, as a human, in the natural processes of the wild. And that is wrong. Just as wrong as Orwell's pigs' exploitation of everyone else on the farm, once they learn the ways of man. And so, despite its nature as a political fable, *The Revolt of the Animals* is an eminently realistic work, which shows animals acting like animals, before and after their 'liberation.'

We will have more to say about Dummy in a moment. He is a character such as we do not find in *Animal Farm*, where men are mentioned, but only in the impersonal terms of the programmatic political metaphor the book is. Jones is the overlord who pushed his workers too far. The farmers on both sides of 'Animal Farm' are by turns the demonised mortal enemies of all 'animalkind', and helpful allies in reciprocal parasitism, when a modus vivendi is reached with the pigs, who forget the principles of Animalism as soon as it becomes profitable to do so. Dummy is a human observer, who looks at the animals from within, having been accepted by them — later to be cast off.

But he is no hero. Indeed, there are no heroes in this book. It is important that Reymont chooses dogs as his protagonists, for thus he plays with our natural sympathy for these friends of ours — by showing them acting cruelly — just like men. 'He shall be left alone, naked and defenceless, like a puppy torn from the teat and thrown into the ditch,' Rex exclaims at one point of his triumphant battles against man. Now, this is one more dig of the author's at the well-known cruelty of man: that the simile would even occur to Rex is proof of how man's cruel behaviour (drowning 'unneeded' litters) was *de rigueur*. But, to return to Dummy, even more chilling is why this old friend of Rex's will be banished: he was becoming more popular amongst the animals, exhausted as they were at the long march to a happy future which seemed ever farther away, the farther they progressed. It was Dummy who took control of the situation during a sudden, ferocious storm and saved the animals from destruction, something that the animals — including the canines — were unable to do (thus proving man's natural superiority); even in his 'treason,' moving about from herd to herd and urging them to abandon the trek, to return home, Dummy exhibits a reasoning power of logic that is beyond the grasp of the animals. Oddly enough, in this, Dummy, the token human among the animals, shows himself to be a more *natural* creature than Rex and the other true believers. He sees the true lie of the land, whereas Rex and his 'party' are chasing chimeras, whether they know it or not. And so, why is Dummy expelled? Because Rex and the others fear him as their rival. He is Trotsky to Rex's Stalin. His banishment (and eventual death) is politically motivated. For animals to be shown to be imitating humans is one thing. For animals to imitate politicians? I reckon no beast can sink any lower than that!

Dummy — with his 'bulldog face' and his speech impediment, which at one and the same time excludes him from human society and thrusts him among the animals, whose 'speech' he learns to imitate — is as close as we get to a human hero in this story. But even he is not without blemish. Banished from the animals he had been travelling with, in the dead of winter, Dummy has to fend for himself:

> On the next morning, early, camouflaging himself with dry reeds, he sat himself down among the bushes and waited there, patiently, despite the cold that penetrated to the marrow of his bones. Fortunately, his hunch paid off as, just after sunrise, a string of wild ducks appeared and began to descend to the mirror of unfrozen water. Dummy began quacking like an old mallard warning the young of some imminent danger. Some of the startled birds set off again, but the larger portion of them crawled in among the dry grasses — where he was waiting. He flailed at them with his stick and gathered so many with his hands that he could hardly bear them all away to his den.

There are only two ways to read this passage: either as indicative of man's evil treachery, luring the ducks to a cruel death by deception (something *never* to be found on God's holy mountain!), or as part of the natural way things are carried out in this world. We eat things only to be eaten ourselves.[13] The only constant is cruelty, exploitation.

....

[13]   Rafał Wojasiński once told me: 'We think we're in charge of

And then there is the case of the execution of the arsonists. In an attempt to stem this flood of animals who threaten their lives, as they both turn upon them in violence and refuse to aid them to till the soil, the desperate humans set fire to the forest in which the herds happen to find themselves. Some of the arsonists — we suppose; are they really responsible for the fire, or just handy examples of collective guilt, being humans? — are captured by the dogs and herded into the clearing to 'stand trial.'

A few dozen, powerful, brown German Shepherds were chasing before them a group of two-legged creatures who were howling in frenzy.

'People! Merciful Jesus, they're people!' exclaimed Dummy, petrified.

'The lambs and their mothers cowering in the woods from the fire — perished; the cows with their calves and the sows with their piglets — perished; the mares with their colts — perished. These are the ones that set the fire that consumed them all — and they shot their lightning at us, while we were trying to defend ourselves. A lot of us fell. We demand justice! Vengeance!' the shepherds wailed darkly.

'Why didn't you mete it out yourselves?' bayed Rex impatiently.

everything here on earth. We think we're at the top of the food chain. We're not. Mould. Mushrooms and mould. You can't destroy it; we eat it, and it lives on in us; when we die, it consumes us and lives on. Mould. The only immortality there is.'

'Our orders are to guard and herd. It's up to you to pronounce judgment, our ruler and master!'

The men, nearly naked and singed by the flames, covered in blood, half conscious, stared dully into the space in front of them, awaiting nothing more than further torment and death.

'Climb the trees! Escape that way!' Dummy spluttered, shaken with pity at the sight.

But they seemed not to understand, their eyes sweeping the crowds of animals pressing in close from all sides.

Gimpy raced up, froth on his lips. Saliva was dripping from his mouth, and his eyes sparkled with green flickers.

'Take care of them as you will,' Rex commanded.

Gimpy howled a war cry. The shepherds drew to the side, and soon the men were standing in the centre of a cleared space. They began whispering something to one another; their eyes darted all around them, ever more frequently catching onto the great linden trees that grew behind the house. But before they'd taken the decision to race there, the earth began to throb, and a frenzied pack of wolves ran up and threw themselves on them.

Piercing screams rent the air. Moments later, nothing was left but bloody remains.

Who would expect such cruelty of animals? It's not their being torn apart at the paws of the dogs and wolves that bothers us — isn't that what wild canines do when they are hungry? It's the *reserving* of the living creatures until a verdict is passed — a human trait — and the idea that a public execution serves justice — again, a human trait — that makes one shiver.

This is more than a mere flipping of roles such as we find in Alice Guy-Blanché's rather simplistic silent short *The Dangers of Feminism*. It is a reduction of all forms of life, human and animal alike, to the law of the jungle (which is, by definition, no law at all).

It's easy to see a political message behind all this. The Communist system purports to liberate the working classes from the oppression of the landowners, only to result in a different ruling class of party élite, who continue the repression of the people they purport to represent, perhaps even to a greater degree than the landowners and factory owners did. 'Master, even I, who threw myself against men, am trembling now!' says Gimpy — of all 'people!' — the wolf, cringing before his powerful domesticated cousin for help against the humans decimating the wilderness. Master, he calls Rex, the domesticated wolf in slavery to men? Meet the new boss, same as the old boss, as the song goes.

So much for the ideological thrust of *The Revolt of the Animals*. One of the things we should not overlook is the artism of the novel. Kwiatkowski is spot on when he speaks of its 'artistic consistency;' in this novel, Reymont reveals himself to be a careful and even poetic novelist. One of the aspects of his poetics that cannot be replicated in English translation is deeply rooted in Polish grammar. Not only does Polish make use of grammatical genders — male, female, and neuter — it also distinguishes (trigger warning, O ye genderphobes!) the 'masculine animate' from feminine, neuter, and even non-human masculine nouns in the plural. Polish, in short, reserves the grammatical ending 'li' in past (and some future) tense verbs for male humans, while all other nouns (including animals) use 'ły.' It is, therefore, striking to find Reymont constantly using the masculine animate endings in relation to non-humans, such as *wszyscy posnęli* ('they all fell asleep'), whereas proper Polish usage would be *wszystkie posnąły.* When he describes the wolves disappearing quietly into the underbrush, he writes *Zaszyli się w gąszcze,* where he ought to write *zaszyły się.* If this were Kipling's *Jungle Book,* with the kind bear Baloo and wise Bagheera the panther, we would assume that the author is 'ennobling' the animals by this bestowal of human grammatical tags; in *The Revolt of the Animals* — which does, on occasion, argue for the respect due to non-humans, especially domesticated breeds — the intent seems primarily to be the opposite: the animals, Reymont subtly argues, are no better than that scoundrel man.

Reymont's skills as a writer are also put on display in the structure of the plot. One of the most dramatic moments in the story occurs when the animals suddenly find themselves in an area that seems to have more in common with Dante's Hell than any portion of the Eurasian plains:

Suddenly, they butted their heads against an unexpected cliff wall, and many of the broken tumbled into an unexpected abyss. Their road was blocked by black, lazily rolling waters, from which great columns of flame continually rose into the black heavens of asphalt. Some monstrous winged creatures flickered in the bloody haze. The earth rumbled. The cliffs near the shore were constantly crumbling into piles of rubble. No one gave out as much as a peep. Even the roars of initial terror died off in their astonished throats.

What? Where on earth are we, beneath that asphalt heaven, amidst tongues of fire arising from a black stream, where strange winged creatures flit about? There are conjectures we may make: is this an operating oilfield, such as developed in the eastern reaches of Galicia in the early twentieth century? It is no easy matter to decide, but that is beside the point. The animals are confronted with a dramatic reality that they had never before experienced, and they are thrown for a loop — as are we. The location, and even the reality of the scenery, is not as important as the animals' astonishment, in which Reymont invites us to participate, by thrusting us into a fantastic landscape that we cannot understand. Whatever the reality of the nature may be, such is the reality of their stunned understanding. They *don't* understand — nor do we. It is a masterstroke of poetics.

Dramatic indeed. Yet the journey itself is masterfully handled by the author; it stretches on and on, monotonously, putting the animals' strength to the test by the meagre pastures along the way, and trying their faith by the endless plodding toward a goal that seems ever to recede before them:

The whole trek had now become one indescribable torment. The day was missing, the night was missing; there were no longer any clear demarcations to time, and this led to ever greater disorder. They slept when they felt like it, and got up when it suited them. Their rest periods became even more frequent and longer. Then, after even consuming moss and miserable lichens to fill their bellies, and slaking their thirst by licking at the frost, they moved on at the tragic pace of the condemned. Whole groups of them preferred to stay behind and just die rather than suffer on like that. Even their hopes guttered inside their breasts, while that monotonous grey, which refused to give an inch, provided the coup de grace to their prospects. On top of it all, time just kept dragging on, and the enforced blindness beat them down. They even began losing their instincts, which had been with them since the beginning of time. Few were they who sensed the falling of night or the coming of dawn. They just went on and on, endlessly, without any idea as to whether it had been days, weeks, or perhaps years that had passed by during this trek of theirs. It seemed an eternity of wandering, with an eternity still ahead of them, an eternity of wandering through this grey, endless grave, hungry, tired to the very death, blind, not quite dead yet, but given over into the power of a horrid, protracted dying. And the merciful day never arrived to shine down upon them a single, pitying ray — not a single one.

The journey goes on for *so long*. It might seem as if Reymont has run out of themes and simply begins repeating himself to fill out pages. But the opposite is true. This poetic novel presents us with an author in complete control of the reader's emotional apprehension of the story. The novel *is* interminable, and through its interminability Reymont is able to have us participate in the frustration of the animals, their yearning for it to be 'over.' To the reader interested in poetics — bold poetics, considering the fact that this ploy of the author's is based on a planned monotony, which runs the risk of losing the reader (intentional boredom as a literary strategy!) — this characteristic of the novel, which forces us to engage in the animals' suffering, is the apex of Reymont's art, passing over the fact that the interminability underscores the central political theme of the novel: Rex's human-free paradise, no less than Marx's, in which government will wither away and justice reign simply over all, will never arrive.

It is an illusion, one among many in this novel. How many mirages are there to be found here! Following Dummy's banishment for spreading mutiny among the herds, they still continue to see him, leading them, as they break away from Rex's illusion to follow a different sort of unrealisable hope, the return home. Rex, of course, has his illusion; it's flabbergasting to see how this intelligent creature could be so taken in by the songs of the cranes and embellish their poetry into a roadmap to painlessness.

Now, whether or not Reymont was an inveterate enemy of socialist revolutionism and its Leninist-Soviet proponents, who sought to spread its influence westward by a violent invasion of his homeland, it must be pointed out that he is broad-minded enough to recognise the logic of its coming to be. It may not have been the proper answer to the misery of the lower classes, but that misery really existed, indeed. The songs of the cranes soothed Rex when he had been expelled from his heretofore comfortable life by the cruelty of humans. Then, as an enemy of man, and not his ally, when he looks on 'from outside the system,' as it were, and sees how human cruelty toward animals is the rule, and not the exception, his dreams transform themselves into a programme:

> Then, right before the yard along the road he saw the old donkey, his head covered in a hempen sack, being whipped by boys harrying him towards a pit of lime.
>
> 'Don't give up! I'll help you!' he barked, carried away with wrath and compassion.
>
> He tore the sack from the animal's head. The donkey, enraged with suffering and emboldened by Rex's aid, threw himself violently at the boys, flailing with his hooves, trampling and wheezing like a rusty gate.
>
> Rex didn't wait to hear his thanks. He slipped into the yard and made his way to Blackie's kennel. The dog, shocked and frightened, didn't even think to forbid him entry. Rex laid out his plans before him. After weighting the matter a long while, the old dog growled:
>
> 'Take everyone with you. The men will be apoplectic with fury. After all, everybody's suffering the same misery, whips, and slavery. It's eating away at us all.'

How can we fail to be on the animals' side here? And yet as the trek goes on, and the reality of their situation becomes more and more apparent to the beasts, and the desire to return home begins to shake their faith in Rex, he turns to them with all the fervour that propaganda can provide:

'Persevere, and once again all the barns filled to bursting, and all the haystacks will be yours. All the fields and meadows! The sun will be yours, and warmth, and the refreshing springs. And you will enjoy cool shade in the hot weather and shelter from the wet, and soft bedding! and no enforced labour, no tax in slavery and blood, no obligation, not even the obligation of gratitude. Comrades, friends, brothers, I guarantee you with all the power of certitude that days of endless good fortune are nigh upon us. I can see them now, I feel them already — they are just beyond these mists. Can you not see the dawn there, still pale, there in the east? The breaking of the dawn has already been foretold by those holy heralds of the coming day…' he howled with the might of a lion — and was answered by roars similar to the gay thunder of springtime.

Later, they lay down to rest, hungry, it is true, but full of trusting hope.

'You lied to them like a Jewish mongrel,' Gimpy snarled, stretching himself out alongside Rex. 'That was all right for the cattle, but I demand the truth.'

However much Rex's heart may still in the right place, however much he seriously believes that he is submitting the beasts to such hardship 'for their own good,' two things become apparent at this point in the novel. First, some animals are more equal than others, as Orwell puts it. An élite has developed, with the canines at the very apex, and these — with Gimpy as their representative — demand to know the truth, whereas it's fine (from his perspective) to

keep the 'horns and hooves' moving along with a lie —
after all, the wolves are still eating their fill… Second, as
he goes on from here to state, he knows that Rex knows
the truth. Rex is in touch with the cranes who are flying
ahead, and knows quite well that it will be more than a
day until the sun breaks through, more than 'a few more
suns' until they reach paradise. Rex, suppressing the truth
for the good of his politics, is no longer a Moses; he is a
Dzierzhynsky.

From the very beginning of the story, Dummy has be-
friended Rex, comforted him, and at last he accompanies
him, the only human being on the animals' path away from
the human world. The manner in which the novel begins —
with both Dummy and Rex taking their 'stripes' from the
kitchen help — links them in our minds as oppressed beings,
who owe the 'powerful of this world' nothing, considering
their treatment at their hands. However, as with the animals
later, Dummy first comes to understand that comradeship
in oppression can only last so long. In Dummy's case, this
happens at the very outset of the trek:

> You're stupid if you imagine that people are going to
> just wave their hand at the loss of their chattel. You were
> smarter back at the manor. So the beasts have rebelled
> and now they think that they'll turn the world upside
> down. Everybody knows how to eat,' he said, with an-
> other glance at the herds, whose bellies were filled with
> grain, 'but not everyone knows how to sow!'
>
> Angry, he got up and made for the way out of the
> ruins.

'Stop! Or I'll have the wolves tear you apart, and carry your carcass back to the manor in pieces.'

Dummy stopped, horror-struck, upon perceiving the terrible anger in the dog's eyes.

'Let me go. Was I ever against you?' And tears sprang to his eyes from the terror.

'I said my piece. Someday, when we've arrived at our destined place, I'll let you go,' Rex promised graciously.

'I'll die of hunger with you here. I'm not gonna eat grass with cattle!' he mumbled in contempt.

'You won't lack for anything. The dogs'll take such good care of you, you'll even fatten up.'

'Sure! On raw meat and fresh gore! Look — I won't get far at all on foot anyway.'

'You'll ride the stallion from the manor! But now — get out of my sight!'

The command rang in such a severe tone that Dummy, not daring to say anything in reply, sought out a shady space for himself at the wall and tried to go to sleep. But the danger of the situation in which he found himself wouldn't even let him close his eyes. Sobbing yearningly, wiping his nose on his sleeve, he began to concentrate on clever means of finding a way to freedom.

The tables are turned. Now the dog is in charge, and it is the uppity man who must back down, tail between his legs as it were, out of fear of punishment from the dog, of rather a severe sort at that. As if we needed any more reminders of the fact, Reymont draws the circle closed here: those 'slaves' who have escaped have now become the new masters, and the former crown of creation grovels in the dust and seeks… escape. When he does, and reestablishes himself in power, once again the two will change positions, and who was below, will be on top, who was on top, below once again.

If such be the case, we have a situation of yin and yang here; where can good and evil be found in this ever revolving tale of oppressor and oppressed? Men are cruel, animals become cruel as soon as they free themselves from his tutelage and create a society — as primitive as it may be — that resembles man's in its being governed not by the good, the wise, or the meritorious, but the stronger. The transformation in Dummy's soul when confronted with this fact is striking, all the more so as it is set against his memories of his initial treatment in man's world:

> Everyone kicked and injured that clumsy, repellent, ugly creature with his bulldog's mug, his bandy legs, that shock of ruddy fur on a head overlarge for his body — like a balloon; with his arms hanging nearly to the earth like those of an ape; and instead of a voice, that frog-like croaking of his. There was nothing beautiful in him but the striking loveliness of those blue eyes, radiant and wise.
>
> Trampled to the very depths of misery, cast out amongst the animals of the manor yard, he had become attached to them, their brother, as if he had been born of the same flesh and blood. They gladly followed his lead, acknowledging his superiority. It was only now, during this trek, that he had begun to sense the difference between him and them, and even to consider them

foes. He had even begun to look upon Rex with different eyes — those of human cogitation. It was then that the thought of escape really dawned in his mind.

Difference? What difference? Perhaps more importantly, it is *only* a difference. He does not realise that men are better, he only realises that he is a man. When his separation from the animals finally comes about, and he finds himself totally alone, cut off from both human and canine, he begins reminiscing about the past; all the blows and swipes are forgotten, or, at the very least, they have ceased to matter as much as the society of one's own:

He thought of that house, far away, the warm kitchen, the pots bubbling on the hearth, and the aromas that arose from them on the steam. The sobbing shook him ever more painfully, and a wild sorrow squeezed his heart. He began to blame himself bitterly. Why did he join up with the animals? Even in the sties he'd had it better than here. And now he'll die a miserable death. If the wolves don't tear him apart, the cold will do him in. Is there anyone who would take pity on him? […] Tears began to pulse forth from forgotten depths. God, how happily he would snuggle once more into the dark corner behind the stove on a winter's eve, when the manor kitchen filled with people and voices! Even if he'd take a swipe across the head there for teasing the dogs. For even so, the housekeeper would give him a bone to gnaw on later, some warm milk or even bread and butter. Jesus, and how gay they all were, how they laughed and teased one another — and the fairy stories that the girl swineherd could tell! And when the house-maids sat down at the distaff and the lady of the manor would look in, there was no end to stories of the most varied sorts. It was then that they'd talk about enchanted princesses and dragons and princes — fearsome things that made your hair stand on end.

It is no coincidence that Reymont constructs the first portion of this citation from tropes that remind us of the Parable of the Prodigal Son. It is, however, an inversion of the Christian narrative, insofar as in leaving home, the Prodigal Son wronged his father, and then squandered his generous patrimony in drunkenness and whoring. He has no right to expect any kind treatment at the hands of the man he so wronged, initially, and the father's greeting of him (to his 'good' brother's chagrin) is all the more powerful therefor. The Prodigal Son rejected love for self-indulgence, only to learn that love is unconditional. And in Dummy's case? This bastard child (he has no father), committed no arbitrary treason in leaving a community that beat, mocked, indeed hated him. He has no reason to apologise to anyone. His opting for 'his own' is something like the worst American tradition of 'my country, right or wrong.'

At least in that phrase there is the acknowledgement of right and wrong. In Reymont's fable, there is only 'mine' and 'not-mine.'

Speaking of illusions, that of Dummy is his Princess — a life-size doll with a speech mechanism, due to which he believes (following the winter tales of the girls he dreams of, above) that she is an enchanted princess, and he only needs to find the proper magic word to release her from her spell, at which she will marry him, and he will become a prince (i.e. a person who outranks even his former human persecutors). Passing over the fact that this sort of fairy-tale thinking gives us to understand Dummy as a rather less than fully developed human agent, it is one more testimony to his human nature — his daydreams (one might even say his 'belief system') are fully human; animals have no part in it other than that played by the magical black steed who will appear to bear him and his princess off to her father's castle, once he discovers that magic word.

In a novel in which unbelievable things happen — a concerted rebellion of domestic animals against their human masters, leading to the destruction of the society of the latter — a novel in which animals not only communicate with one another, but make use of something that we would call human speech, Dummy's sudden ejaculatory prayer in the wilderness hits us with remarkable, because unexpected, power:

> 'Save me, little Lord Jesus! And I'll whittle you a whole shrine! I'll hang before your altar a singing blackbird in a cage! Save me, Lord!' he sobbed, making the sign of the Cross again and again.

Had Reymont brought his novel to an end here — with this appeal to the greatest of all Tertium Quids, God, Who surpasses both man and animal, *The Rebellion of the Animals* would have had the same sort of message as another work dealing with class struggle: Zygmunt Krasiński's *Undivine Comedy*, in which the only possible solution to the irreconcilable claims of Aristocrat and Revolutionary is the Second Coming of Christ. But Reymont goes further. Dummy dies banished, Rex is executed by his own revolutionary hordes as mercilessly as any Robespierre, and the animals continue on until they encounter a manlike creature, which encounter sends them into raptures of joy:

And then, after many, many days of wandering, as if they'd coursed through the world entire, those at the head of the ranks suddenly pulled up short, bellowing, falling prostrate to the earth:

'Man! Our master! Man!'

There at the edge of an impenetrable jungle, beneath the shade of a wide spreading palm tree, sat a family of apes.

The gigantic male, stunned at their sudden arrival, tore himself up to his full height.

At the sight of him, all of the herds fell down in humility and sent up a heaven-shattering roar:

'Be our master! Rule over us! We are your faithful chattel! Don't desert us!'

The novel ends with another circle closing: everything returns to normal. Despite all the promises of progress, the huge river of animality turns back on its course and returns whence it came: with the beasts' natural (though in this case mistaken) acknowledgement of their need of a two-legged master — for their own good. No matter what we think of the pessimism of this denouement, Reymont proves himself to be, if not the 'better' writer, at least the better prophet, than Orwell, who once wrote 'I am rather glad to have been hit by a bullet because I think it will happen to us all in the near future.'[14] The changes in 1989 and 1990, which Orwell did not predict (who could?!) would have made Władysław Reymont smile, for sure. Marx was proven wrong. If there is any such thing as historical determinism, it is, for better or worse, to be found in our compartmentalisation, our — for lack of a better word — natural inequality. The thing is — we cannot let this fact overcome the imperative of mutual respect.

ORWELL AND POLAND

It is rather natural to wish to compare *The Revolt of the Animals* to *Animal Farm*; we have already said a few things about this. Above all, it is important to remember that the books, as similar as they are, have different aims in mind. *Animal Farm* is a satire on the Stalinist system, a roman à clef with an easily decipherable character list, based on real-world personages. *The Revolt of the Animals* is more of a work in anthropology than politics, and a consideration

....

[14]   George Orwell, Letter of 31 July 1937, to Rayner Heppenstall. In George Orwell, *A Life in Letters*, ed. by Peter Davison (New York: WW Norton, 2013), p. 82. In a letter to Francis Westrope dated 15 January 1939, Marrakech, he writes: 'I suppose the next bit of trouble will be over the Ukraine, so perhaps we may get home just in time to go straight into the concentration camp if we haven't been sunk by a German submarine on the way.'

                                          CHARLES S. KRASZEWSKI

of the very idea of idealist utopias — none of which are realisable. Each of the books must be read and appreciated on its own.

Orwell, one of the truly great writers of the twentieth century, unquestionably a peer of Kafka and Borges, is, of course, a well-known quantity in Poland. As previously mentioned, the first Polish version of *Animal Farm*, Teresa Jeleńska's *Folwark zwierzęcy,* was published as early as 1946 by those Poles in London who chose to remain in the west, rather than return to a Communist-dominated 'utopia' such as Orwell foresaw in his two greatest works (the other being *1984*). Both of these books, obviously, along with *The Revolt of the Animals*, cut too close to the bone for the Communists to have permitted their publication in the Soviet bloc.

As Orwell was known to the Poles, so Poland was known to Orwell, and his collected letters, already cited in the edition of Peter Davison, provide us with some interesting insights into his personal take on Polish matters.

The first time that Poland is mentioned specifically is found in an extensive letter written to the *Tribune* newspaper towards the end of June, 1945, complaining of the pro-Soviet (and hence anti-Polish) bias of their reporting on the infamous show trial of 'The Sixteen' leaders of the Polish Underground State, kidnapped to Moscow and tried in political fashion, as a direct result of which a full quarter of them lost their lives. With irony, Orwell writes:

Early in the proceedings I formed the opinion that the accused were technically guilty: only, just what were they guilty of? Apparently it was merely doing what everyone thinks it right to do when his country is occupied by a foreign power — that is, of trying to keep a military force in being, of maintaining communication with the outside world, of committing acts of sabotage and occasionally killing people. In other words, they were accused of trying to preserve the independence of their country against an unelected puppet government, and of remaining obedient to a government which at that time was recognised by the whole world except the U.S.S.R. The Germans during their period of occupation could have brought exactly the same indictment against them, and they would have been equally guilty.

He goes on to accuse the *Tribune* of hypocrisy in lauding the Greek underground army, while — out of political considerations — taking the side of the Russians in the case of the Poles:

To be anti-Polish and pro-Greek is only possible if one sets up a double standard of political morality, one for the U.S.S.R. and the other for the rest of the world [...] With one side of our mouths we cry out that mass deportations, concentration camps, forced labour and suppression of freedom of speech are appalling crimes, while with the other we proclaim that these things are perfectly all right if done by the U.S.S.R.

While the context of the letter is the damage that such double-standards do to the Socialist movement, to which Orwell remained attached (although, as he admitted to Stephen

Spender in a letter dated sometime around 15 April 1938, 'I have been very hostile to the C[ommunist] P[arty] since about 1935'), it is no less true that he understood the nefarious nature of Soviet hegemony in East-Central Europe as an objectively evil manifestation that needed to be opposed. It is for this reason that, in his letter of 1 September 1945 to the Russian translator Gleb Struve, in which he mentions a Polish translation proposal of *Animal Farm* arriving on his desk at just about the same time as Struve's letter, he very generously states that 'if translations into the Slav languages were made, I shouldn't want any money out of them myself.' Such undertakings were not business proposals to him, but a manner of ensuring the inculcation of free thought in regions where its political suppression was currently ongoing. We are fortunate to live in a time when no such obstacles are put in the way of publishers, like Glagoslav, who wish to bring out works like Władysław Reymont's *The Revolt of the Animals* for English readers, and I am sure that both he and Orwell would be just as pleased as I am, to acknowledge my debt to the Polish Book Institute, an organisation in independent Poland, who generously support such publications.

Kraków, 18 August 2021

THE REVOLT
OF THE ANIMALS

PART I

1

'Now we'll settle the score, you mongrel!' she screeched triumphantly. Having driven Rex into the corner, she began to beat him with the fire poker, reproaching him furiously after each whack: 'This is for the roast! This is for the sausage yesterday! This is for the turkey chicks!'

The dog writhed, whimpering, imploring, licking her feet all the while.

'And this is for the little dachshunds, so you'll remember, you dirty beggar you, not to come near the master's little pups. Ah, let the devil take you!'

At this, she gave him such a mighty thump on the head, that the dog bellowed and threw himself at her, fangs bared. She toppled onto the floor in the middle of the kitchen, and Rex escaped through the open door. She scrambled to her feet and rushed out after him, execrating him with dreadful shrieks.

But Rex had already plunged into the nearby thicket of lilacs and acacias. Even though he was sorely wounded, hardly able to breathe, he pulled himself along the earth, crawling with the last remnants of his strength, farther on, to a safer place. It was then that a bellowing erupted again somewhere from the direction of the kitchen.

The housekeeper, firmly gripping Dummy's hair with the fingers of one hand, was thrashing him mercilessly with the other.

'You filthy bastard! You're worse than that mangy dog, you are! I'll rip out your guts I will, you disgusting thief, you! I give you food out of the goodness of my heart, and here I catch you stealing all the same!'

She was roaring so, as was the boy, screaming his head off in a vain attempt to free himself from her iron claws. It was such a furious to-do that the whole manor grounds erupted in a chaos of terror. The dogs began to yank at their chains and howl. A riot of terrified clucking shook the hen-houses. With a screech, all the guinea fowl flapped up to the roof, and the pigeons took cover in the trees near the well. The tom turkeys, wattles and tails ruffled, gobbled like mad, hopping in place from foot to foot, menacingly. The peacocks rushed near from beneath the porch, throwing a fit with their contemptuous cries. The lady of the manor herself emerged from her rooms; the young master ran up with a flintlock; the little misses too, clutching their dolls, and two ruddy dachshunds, squirming like snakes.

At last she let him go, giving way to the flood of tears and protests.

Dummy plunged into the bushes, falling at last, like a log, alongside Rex.

Both of them lay there, without the strength to move, both nearly unconscious — beaten alike and in like misery.

The sun sent down its waves of heat and a warm breeze wafted through the bushes. The rustle of leaves, the buzzing and chirping of the insects, played around them so sweetly and inebriatingly that both soon fell asleep. But even as they slept, it seemed, both continued to complain of the injustice that met them— they snuffled so, moaning quietly and mournfully. Then, without a sound, a gigantic black cat, an old friend of Rex's, slipped in through the undergrowth and, having sniffed the dog and cuddled against his side, began purring compassionately. Later, a few crows flapped down onto the lower branches of the acacias. Gradually, they hopped their way down ever lower, whetting their sharp beaks, ever more boldly.

'I'm not dead yet,' Rex growled, flashing his angry eyes in their direction. Then, turning to Dummy, he licked the boy's face clean of the blood and tears, and then, gently grabbing his smock with his teeth, he jerked it to wake him.

'Let's get away from here,' Dummy groaned, understanding the dog perfectly. 'They'll find us here.'

'I'll wait until nightfall. They want to put me out of my misery, I won't object.'

'O, you got a thorough thrashing, didn't you!' said Dummy with compassion, uprooting a thick handful of grass, with which he wiped down his friend's sides and gummy eyes.

Rex moaned in gratitude.

'Do something about those damned beaks, will you?' Rex growled to the cat. 'Those rotters are worse than people.'

'I'll take you to the byre,' said Dummy. 'I know a good place beneath the troughs.'

'It's still afternoon, and those shepherd rogues might hunt me down. And I don't have any strength left. Give me some water… I'm thirsty…'

'I'll go make sure there's nobody down by the water,' the cat said, with concern in his voice. 'Lie here, both of you. I'll bring you some water.'

And so he did, carrying it — somehow — in an eggshell, which he placed in front of his friend's snout.

'I see you had the little pigeons yourself,' Rex remarked to the cat.

'That was Jędrek from the smith's that did that! Mother Sow saw him. She'll tell you. He's a bandit, he is. He picked apart the sparrows from underneath the stork's nest. He wouldn't even let the magpies alone, and the old mother flew at me so when she saw me that I barely made it away alive. Jędrek's a thief, and now he's sniffing around for nightingale nests. The parrot's already squawked at him.'

'And don't you be going near that parrot now, you hear?' growled Rex.

'Jędrek from the smith's! You just wait, you cutthroat you,' said Dummy. Then, 'I'll drive the geese in from the fields, and maybe I'll bring you something from dinner. Wait here for me.'

And he whistled so sharply through his fingers that the terrified crows flew off to the park.

The cat got up too, carefully sliding his way, obliquely, in the direction of the kitchen.

The angelus bell had just rung, and the courtyards of the manor filled with voices animal and human, the rattle of wagons and the heavy plodding tread of herds driven in. The winch creaked at the well; the pigs in their sties squealed and grunted impatiently. The swallows chirped and whistled a bit before going quiet, and then all the voices seemed to burn to ash in the fires of the sun, falling away pulverised in the fainting silence of the sweltering afternoon.

Rex, licking his wound, was on guard, ears pricked. Sometimes he raised his head, snuffled the air with his nostrils flaring, then, moaning softly, he drowsed again.

The sun intoned its afternoon hymn. The burning air shimmered with the music of flame, and all the voices of nature — and these are infinite — flowed together into that golden symphony of light. Everything was sound, colour, and simultaneously some sort of spectral outline. The Afternoon Banshee, with a hawk on her head, hovered over the land, and wherever her golden robes brushed, everything dried and crumbled to dust; wherever her eyes, yellow as water hemlock, rested, there death reaped a rich harvest: a bird suddenly fell from a branch, trees withered, insects toppled over, dead, even streams fainted in the blistering heat. Even Rex shivered, and curling into a ball, pressed down into the damp earth and the cool grasses. She flew on, and behind her the terrified cries of all creatures spilled away, along with gloomy clods of shadow slitting the sunlight like coulters.

And the dog in his painful drowsing allowed himself to be charmed by memories, after this present wretchedness had pushed bright remembrances of days past into oblivion. Memories of those days when he lived in the manor as the ever-present companion of all. When he stretched out on couch and rug, beloved and petted. He'd kill his born brother if the Master ordered him to. He'd even tear a man apart if that's what the Master commanded. After all, he'd faced off with wolves, one on one! He used to be able to flush a boar from a slough all by himself. Everything in the courtyards trembled at his thunderous voice, everything in the parkland and in the fields. Even bulls fled before his fangs. How did it all happen, then? How did it come about that he became a homeless wretch, a miserable stray? That he's living in contempt, misery, abandonment, reduced to pilfering offal to keep himself alive? He couldn't understand it. Suddenly, such sorrow tore at his innards, like iron claws, that he suddenly leapt to his feet, tensed, and howled piteously. He was a huge dog, tawny, like a lion. Despite his sunken flanks and the wounds on his back, he was still dangerous, powerful. He rolled his bloodshot eyes, bared his fangs, and, paying no mind to the pain, set off boldly toward the manor, the tall colonnade, ready to take on anyone, anything, if only to make his way to his master and present his complaints. But it was empty all around — the door leading to the courtyard was open. He entered the building, boldly, then hesitated; snuffling the air with his flaring nostrils, he passed through the chambers, one after another, stopping in each, sniffing, looking around. He moved on at an ever slower pace, as if weighed down by the memories. Thousands of odours diffused through the air awakened in him the memory of long-dead days. Some sort of sounds, dying away, faint breaths, spectral reflections of people wandering through the huge, gloomy rooms. Every object there spoke volumes to him — once again he was perfectly oriented as to what had been going on here. Light played off a firearm hanging on the wall of one room; he rose up on his hind legs and sniffed at it; amidst the stale odours of the powder, he caught his master's scent. His memory cast ever more vivid pictures up and out of its dark caverns. He lay down and stretched out on the fluffy, white bearskin on the floor in front of the cold hearth. Again he felt the warmth of the fire and the hand of his master as it stroked him along his back… He growled with pleasure and smacked his lips, as if to lick that hand, but no one was there; only the birds twittering outside the window, the sun that beat down upon the earth, and leaves rustling on the trees. He got up and went into the next room, which was dark and empty; flies were buzzing beyond the half-closed panes. The gigantic mirrors were draped in crepe. The air was suffused with a mustiness and something that reminded him of the odours that waft outwards through the open doors of churches. As he penetrated the chamber further, suddenly he cringed with fear — there was a sort of corpsy tang to the air. He couldn't understand it. He shivered, and, casting his glance along the walls from which some large figures gazed back at him with motionless eyes, he threw himself prostrate — as they seemed to glare at him severely, and he was gripped with fear. He drew back, sidling along the walls, when suddenly he caught sight of his master. He was sitting between the windows with a large dog's head resting on his lap. Rex growled with jealousy, but, creeping near him, he began to whine and wag his tail. But his master neither moved, nor called to him.

Rex jumped backwards, as if in fear of catching a blow, but then again he crept near the feet, training his bloodshot eyes at him. Then in a low moan, broken now and then by brief howls, he laid all his misery and misfortune bare before him.

A greyish shadow seemed to tear itself loose from the portrait. The shadow fluttered formlessly; tattered and windblown, the trembling outline floated towards him, but Rex was gripped with a sudden terror. With fur bristling along his back, his teeth chattering, he withdrew backwards with a howl of unease. He remained a long while in the next room, panting, not daring to move, petrified with anxiety, and yet overwhelmed with the need to cast his eyes once more upon his master. Still, he hadn't the courage to peek into that room again. With a snuffle, his tail between his legs, he skulked quickly back to the smaller rooms drenched in sunlight. All was deserted there as well. The melodies of the parkland and the light played through the open windows. He touched the scattered toys with his nose, licking with tenderness this and that, and then, surfeited with the beloved aromas, he went out onto the grand terrace, shaded by a tent of roses and convolvulus in bloom.

The shade there was sweet, punctured here and there with tatters of sunlight. The same delightful, soothing cool could be found in the corners, and on the ancient leather armchairs.

A shaft of living water pulsed before the terrace, sparkling and glittering.

'Rex, Rex!' the parrot screeched in joy from her golden hoop.

'I was looking for you,' he growled, climbing up on a chair, as he used to do. They had been friends for a long time. She fluttered down on the armrest and, flapping her wings, began to tell him all sorts of news in her squawking voice. But before he got a chance to confide in her, the dachshunds rushed in, baying, and behind them, the lady of the house, the little master with his blunderbuss, and a whole mob in their train.

'Run, run!' gasped the parrot in terror.

It was too late. The furious woman rushed over at him and screeched:

'Out! Out! Out of my sight, you filthy thing! You bloody mutt! Out!' And right then he felt the teeth of the dachshunds sink into his legs, while painful thumps rained down on his back.

Frenzied with insult and pain, he grabbed the wretched little dogs and tore at them mercilessly, paying heed to nothing now, neither screams nor jets of water nor thrashing staves.

'Run! Run, Rex, run!' the parrot continued to screech.

At last, he tore away from the attacking mob and, with a lionlike leap, cleared the terrace and landed on the lawn. But before he made it to the thicket a shot rang out, and something like a hot handful of gravel bit into his left flank. The cruel impact was such that he was thrown headlong, but soon, gathering together what strength he had left, he leapt amongst the low firs. A second shot boomed. Tiny branches rained down upon him, like dead, green tears. He waited no longer, but, crawling through the parkland back into the yard, near the barns, he squeezed into a kennel, where he fell down, fainting with pain. Old Blackie made room for him on his pallet, but, straining against his chain, he began to howl, as if calling for aid.

'O wolves! Wolves you are, not people!' Dummy keened. Having learned what had happened from the magpies, he ran up to save his friend. He poured some water over him, and pushed a bowl of milk toward his snout.

'Drink, brother. I milked a cow for you,' he urged, carefully running his hands along the dog's sides.

'They beat me in the manor house. In the manor house!' he howled mournfully, shivering from cold and pain.

The boy swaddled him in some burlap, cradling him as you would a child, stroking him. Then he said to Blackie, 'If you do him any harm, I'll kill you like a cur!' And then he went off to his geese.

The days that followed were hard ones, and Rex hovered between life and death. His wounds bit inward at him, the sun gnawed at him mercilessly, the flies gave him no peace — but neither did the fatal sorrow he felt at his abandonment.

Only the nights brought the sacred grace of cool and relief. Dummy would run up with food and water, passing long hours weeping over their common wretchedness. For he had learned that they were on the hunt for Rex, to kill him, and he too was to be driven away from the manor.

'I'll just go off to the ponds. What do I care?' the boy decided. 'But I feel bad for you, you orphan. You've got to go off into the wide world — what'll you do?' he said in despair.

'Let me just get well again,' Rex moaned, licking the boy out of gratitude.

'We won't hand him over! We won't give him up!' Blackie growled with angry determination. He shared not only his bed with Rex, but also each and every bowl of his food, and whatever he caught while out hunting on the nights when he was let loose.

The whole barnyard vowed to keep him hidden from the eyes of people. And Dummy had told them that he'd give them what for, he would, even if it were the mighty stallions, if any one of them were to betray Rex.

And so he licked himself back into shape, slowly, but in peace and quiet, and bathed in universal kindness. Even those shepherd mutts, forgetting their old rivalry for the favours of the whippet, visited him on the sly. Every morning the herds lowed their deep greetings in his direction as they went off to pasture. Every now and then in the afternoons, some horned head or other would bend down over the kennel where he lay. The horses neighed softly, carefully snuffling the air in his direction. On the other hand, the carefree colts, such as had never yet known the rod, played with him, pulling at his ears with their soft, warm lips. The sheep, who were afraid of everything, baaed and baaed in pity at his ill fortune. When the sows sought out a place near the barns to flop on their sides and give suck to their piglets, they directed their dull, grey eyes in Rex's direction and snorted and squealed their gossip to him, grunting under the impact of the thumping heads of their greedy farrow. Sometimes, at night, he would hear his name mentioned through the walls of the barn, as the oxen, chewing their cud and smacking their wet lips, complained about their work, the beatings they received, and the food they didn't.

But the one who most pitied him was the donkey. He lived on charity in his old age; old as the world he was, and wise, scabrous, dirty, always thick with mud and ashes, beaten by one and all, chased away from wherever he happened to be. He was tormented thus by animals as well as people.

Theirs was an old acquaintance, dating from the times when he would pull the little master around in a cart. On such excursions, Rex would watch over the both of them, and thus, all three would race about the fields unbeknownst to the master.

So that hulk of a donkey ambled over daily, to stand near the kennel with his head hung low and his ears drooping, complaining himself in such a penetrating hee-haw whinny that Blackie howled in fright until Dummy put an end to it with a rod, driving the donkey away. Beaten, roughed up, still he stubbornly returned, never pausing in his lamentations.

The winged beasts concerned themselves with Rex, zealously. Every day, on every fence, they conducted quarrelsome colloquia concerning him, full of clucks and cackles, gobbles, shrieks and other such uproar. One of the moorhen, emboldened by Blackie's clemency, even took up quarters along with her little ones near Rex. She would cluck interminably to him, extolling the virtues of her children. Only the peacocks, proud as ever, kept their disdainful distance. The crows too, with their natural propensity for such things, kept careful watch from the kennel roof, patiently waiting — just in case.

They waited in vain. Rex got better. However, day by day, he also grew gloomier, more shut up inside himself. He was weighed down with ruminations of some sort, visions. He began to see the world through the prism of his deep misery and orphaned state. Earlier, he never gave a thought to whatever went on beyond the confines of the manor grounds: he felt like the lord of all, and his attitude to all creation was almost human.

Other creatures existed to be throttled, herded, teased, according to his master's command. A bottomless abyss separated his almost human existence from theirs. Then he had been roughly expelled from the manor and thrust into the depths of wretchedness. Ever more keenly, he sensed the injustice of it all. It was a festering wound, which seeped into his heart a wild desire to revenge himself upon man. At such moments, he would even have torn apart their whelps, of whom he had once been so fond, lapping up their hot blood with delight. Through the long nights of his illness, and through the even longer, sleepless days, he contemplated the means of achieving his vengeance.

So obsessed was he by hatred that everything that stank of man aroused in him a limitless repulsion, and an even greater terror. For these same contemplations uncovered to his eyes all the power that man possessed. How might one take vengeance on the hurricane? How might one fix one's fangs upon the lightning? Moments of helpless despair pierced him like knives. After all, the world entire was in the power of the two-legged creature, indivisibly so. All creation was subject to his cruel tyranny. He might do whatever he please! The creator and simultaneously the destroyer of all.

It was only now that he recognised that horrible truth, and every such minute just confirmed it the more. Confined to his pallet by illness, he became the sensitive witness of all that went on around him. No scream, no complaint, no injustice eluded his watchful heart. The nights especially were suffused with endless lamentation: the muffled bellows of the oxen as they bemoaned the labour that was wearing them down to death, their flanks, welted by stave-blows, their hunger. The tormented horses whinnied long and painfully. The cows gave voice, suddenly, to long, unassuageable lowing for the calves that had been stolen from them.

Again and again sheepfold, sty, and coop broke into a wild racket of grievance and mortal terror. The defiled earth, too, brought forth her accusations; the hacked-apart forests moaned with imprecations; the waters themselves erupted in roaring complaints at their violent channelling. Everywhere — from field and outbuilding — the whole world sent forth age-old, ever-resounding echoes of injustices suffered, violence, and death. The earth and sky were harried by the cruelty of man, whose throne was firmly fixed atop a pyramid of corpses. He could be neither vanquished nor escaped — he was like death.

Rex throbbed and seethed within like the ocean beating helplessly against granite cliffs. One morning, when the swine were squealing in despair as they were being loaded onto butchers' wagons, he growled, touched painfully to the core:

'Again they're murdering our brothers.'

'Pigs ain't no brothers of mine,' Blackie barked. 'They're meat.'

'Thieves. They'll eat them themselves.'

Rex curled into a ball, as if he had been struck by a stone. He grew quiet.

And later, when the Jew was dragging the bleating calves out of the barns, Blackie howled sadly:

'Me and Gimpy throttled one at night once, but the stableboys took it away.'

'You keep company with a bandit like that? — A wolf?!'

'Anyone who shares a meal with me's my brother.'

'You'd even do in one of your own? A child like that?'

'Hunger has no eyes. Whatever my claws can reach, my maw can eat.'

A bloodcurdling cry was then heard, and they saw the donkey run up in panic to throw himself on the dunghill.

'The master's whelp's splashed him with boiling water! It all but took off his skin.'

With a horrid, mournful bellow, the donkey rolled in the cool muck, while a pack of boys, with the young master at their head, ran up to continue their fun, pelting the beast with stones and knocking at his legs with staves. The whole manor yard was filled with the uproar, until the foreman ran up with his own stick, chased off the boys, and tried to get the donkey to rise with kicks. Mindless of the danger, Rex emerged from the kennel and growled.

'Rex!' the young master cried. 'Mama missed him with the gun! He killed my dachshunds!' he wailed, bursting into tears.

'All right then, my pigeon!' the foreman snarled at Rex, 'I'll give ye what for, on behalf o' the little lord here!' And he rushed at Rex with his stick. Rex yelped at the blow, but, filled with a sudden fury, he threw himself at his attacker and buried his fangs so deeply in the man's breast that, pulling away mightily, both fabric and flesh were torn away, as he fell to the ground.

The foreman, unconscious, fell right onto the dunghill! The little master ran away, screaming.

The dog leaped back into the kennel and buried himself in the straw, in the darkest corner of the place.

'Get out while you still can!' howled Blackie, yanking at his chain, 'They'll drag you out of here and kill you!'

There was nothing for it. Rex made his way into the empty barn, beneath the manger, where a hole in the wall gave out onto the orchard. He crawled off into the thick berry bushes, almost unable to comprehend what had just happened to him. He heard people racing to the aid of the steward, and soon thereafter, the howling of the innocent Blackie being pummelled. He decided to run off to the fields. However, the orchard was enclosed by thick hedges and a high, wire fence. At the one, closed gate there was a gardener, with whom he'd had some run-ins in the past. He squeezed his way deeper into the overgrown berries, waiting for an opportunity to escape to freedom. His dread gave him no peace. He couldn't even sleep; his unhealed wounds burned, the buzzing of the bees and quarrelsome chirping of the sparrows bothered him — these latter constantly falling in bands upon the sweet, mature fruit.

'Serve your master faithfully, and in return… you're run off!' Up above him he heard the gardener's voice. He whimpered beseechingly and crawled over to his feet.

'Don't be afraid. Look what it's come to! They're chasing you like a rabid dog! And you — you tore into my trousers once, remember? — And all I wanted to do was have a look at the parrot.'

The man crouched down beside him and stroked him kindly. Trustingly, Rex rested his head upon his knees.

'See, stupid, how they pay you back for your service? The master passes, and it's "Hit the road!" for you! You used to growl at me all the time. Wouldn't let me near the manor house. And who was it gave you that pigeon, eh? And tossed you those crow chicks under the firs?'

He continued with his complaint, but opened the gate for him.

'Now, you watch out the mistress don't catch sight of you!'

Rex ran off into the fields in search of his friend. Dummy was watching over the geese in the pasture at the wood's edge. He was sitting with his feet in the stream, piping a tune on his wooden recorder. The flock of white crested geese were wallowing about the muddy banks of the stream full of pale gudgeon and roach. The willows provided him with shade; the woods were speaking in an undertone, and the birds were singing. There was such a warmth of sun that sleepiness sank into his bones.

Dummy already knew all about what had happened from the magpies.

'So, what now? If only you were fully healed!' the boy said in honest concern.

'Eh — I'm a tough one. I handled the foreman, didn't I?'

'He was a butcher, that one — for everybody. They had to carry him to his cottage. He couldn't make it on his own.'

'He's just the first one…' Rex growled with bitter determination.

'There's a shack in the marshes. The master used it as a blind to shoot at the grouse. You could find shelter there. Even the foreman won't be making his way there. The marshes are deep, and the footbridges rotten…'

'But the flies! So many, who can bear it. I used to hunt young ducks there with the master. But the old lean-to of the charcoal burners in the forest?'

'Nobody knows about that. But Gimpy and his pack take cover there from time to time.'

'Gimpy! I'm the one gimped his shank when he threw himself at my master… He don't scare me… Now, the bitch and her litter, that's another story…'

'Hide in the marshes. There's nothing for it. And there's so much water-fowl there that you'll have plenty to eat. I even saw some young rabbits in the clover…'

'Maybe I might look for a place, somewhere? A new master?' Rex offered, unexpectedly.

'It's the hungry gap before harvest now. Nobody'll throw you a rotten potato, even. They'll chase you off, or hand you over to the knacker! The Germans in their colonies'd take you in, and sell you later in the city. Unless you're not fit for selling, in which case they'll knock your brains out and eat you. I heard as much at the manor. Swine like that don't care what they put in their mouths. Worst thing is the foreman'll never forgive you, nor the mistress… They'll hunt you down…'

'Yes…' Rex growled with resignation and, stretching out at the water's edge, fell asleep.

Undressing, Dummy waded into the water in search of crayfish.

'If I take a few to the mistress, it'll put her in a good humour,' he thought, plunging his hands beneath the sopping roots of the alders, into the deep depressions under the bank, and beneath the stones of the stream-bed. He fished with skill, never dropping his eyes from the crows, who had silently glided out of the woods to the stream, where, seeming to be drinking, they deviously sidled near the little goslings wading in the shallows.

'Hey there! Looking for a tasty bite, are you?' Dummy screeched at them, tossing a handful of mud in their direction. Foiled, they flapped off in low flight, penetrating the wheat past the nests. Then, as the sun was sinking and the cool of evening coming on, Dummy commenced driving the geese together.

'Rex,' he said, 'under the willow there is my place,' and he pointed beneath an old, forking tree that rose at the waterside, from plaited fingers, as it were. A dark cavern could be discerned between the roots, its floor laid with sweet flag. 'It's a good place to spend the night in safety,' he added, heading off homeward.

The dog remained alone now, not knowing what to do with himself. But habit won out in the end, and he set off across the fields toward the road that led to the manor. Then, as if in warning, at that very moment a cabriolet sped along the road, drawn by two greys. The mistress was riding therein with her two daughters, while the young master was whipping on the horses with a staff from the coachman's box. He accompanied them with a bitter, dogged stare, baring his fangs, and then, later, circling the park in roundabout fashion, he made his way to the farmyard, near a decrepit haystack, where he concealed himself. He felt as if he had just crawled near the barred gates of Paradise. A strong yearning was eating away at him within, and again and again he tensed his muscles for a leap into the yard. But fear held him there as if in tight loops of rope, and thus he strained at the leash within him, tussling with contrary impulses. In the end, he flopped down and lay there, motionless.

The sun was now nearly set. The world was drenched in gold and purple. An immense silence began to reign. The herds were returning, some from the pastures and some from the fields, their workday over. A thick ribbon of golden dust arose and stretched above the road, and the yearning bellows of the cattle began to be heard, as well as the deep grumbling of the exhausted oxen, the whinnying of the horses — and the whistling of staffs that thudded against quivering hide, along with the swearing of men. A sounder of swine trotted past with squeals, pushing aside everyone they met upon their path. The earth drummed with the hoofbeats of colts. Wagons creaked slowly near, crunching over the pebbles on the road. Then came a drove of sheep, shouldering one another and bleating stupidly, crowding together, driven by the dogs. Last of all the heifers came, frolicking, abandoning the path now and then to wander into the corn, for which they took some thickly falling swipes from the herdboys. Everything tumbled by; the dusk sifted its red glow over the earth like a dying ember, and all grew quiet again in the farmyard. The people went their various ways; lamps began to glow through cottage windows, and the dogs, let off their chains, went wild with joy. It was then that, unable to restrain himself any longer, Rex entered the farmyard. He passed by the barns, catching the scent of fresh milk. He rounded stable and manger and trough, giving all a wide berth, before plunging into the bushes opposite the kitchen. Such aromas wafted to him from there that his innards were twisted with hunger. Dummy was sitting at the stoop, a bowl between his knees, and a whole mob of unchained watchdogs around him.

Now and again the voice of the cook slipped through the open door.

Suddenly, the gravel crunched and the snuffling of horses was heard.

'The mistress! I've caught it now!'

He leapt into the park through a familiar passage near the chicken coops, and as he did, he knocked aside Red, who had been quietly tunnelling his way into the henhouse. The fox sped away, emitting a quick yap of warning to all the nocturnal predators. White underbellies flashed as the weasels rushed up trees; a polecat sped away along the clear-cut of the lumber stand, and a marten took a desperate leap onto a roof with a chicken in his mouth. The owls hooted and, in general, there arose such a panicky chaos that a black cat began to scold Rex bitterly.

'A fine end you've put to tonight's hunt, you have! We won't have a chance at anything, now.'

With a menacing growl and a flash of his eyes, Rex pushed himself under the low-hanging branches of the firs, as the farmyard was now quite lit up. A smudge of light flashed from the open terrace door, through which a thick braid of water twisted and sparkled, flung out and upwards.

After a while, the lamps went out again and the parkland began to resound ever more thickly with the trills of the nightingales. Like a shadow, Rex crept up onto the terrace. A little chain jangled, and the parrot fluttered down to him. Their furtive, ardent whispers were masked by the moaning of the birds and the other songs of the night. Rex lamented his hopeless situation and bade farewell to his friend forever. He was about to set out upon the paths of exile, where he would be swallowed up by a strange and hostile world. He whimpered mournfully, his heart torn in pieces by torment, terror, and despair. The parrot sobbed for him, cooling his fevered eyes with her fanning wings. Moved by his bitter fate, she suddenly recalled her distant homeland. She began to sway on the arm of the chair, fluttering her grey and pink wings from time to time, as she sang in muffled cries a litany of disordered dreams, full of longing:

My Fatherland! As far as eye can see,
  Green pampas, stretching broadly at one's feet;
The blooming garlands looping tree to tree;
  The rough-haired coconut and mango sweet!
The silver palms with fronds that flash like fire,
  Where white billows burst from the swelling sea;
The sky — immense cupola of sapphire —
  My Fatherland! Where days of gaiety
Ring out with song, and lull to fragrant rest
  Until the jungle, waking to the night
As the red sun sets in the bloody west,
  Erupts with roars of triumph, screams of fright!
O Rio Negro, sparkling in the dawn,
  When the sun rises golden from the sea,
And all creation bursts with grateful song
  And laughter sounds from underbrush and tree!
With strength renewed, from the tall palms arise
  A thousand wings, to soar above the sea,
Cutting the blue — a living cloud that flies
  And darts and dances in flight's ecstasy!
The bamboo rustles at the water clear,

While through the mud the boa glides, and soon,
Gripped by the jaguar, bellows the torn deer
Until all sleeps again in the hot noon.
O Fatherland! Forever lost to me —
Thou longed-for Paradise of liberty!

She grew quiet and hid her head beneath her wing, as if to stifle her despair. The night came on. The nightingales sang, the horned owl hooted, and the peacocks shrieked mournfully from their perches in the trees.

'Ah, wretched me!' the parrot moaned again. 'I caught sight of a mountain floating mid-river, from which arose some desiccated trees; I fluttered over casually, and it was then I was gripped by some horrid black talons! From that day on my years of shame flow on in never-ending captivity. Never-ending!' She sobbed and began to beat her wings and yank at her chain. She cried out, desperately:

'Liberate me! Tear asunder my chains! Freedom! Burst my fetters! Smash them! Smash them!'

Rex so threw himself at the hoop that it fell with a crash. He yanked ferociously at the chain, bit at it, tore at it with his claws, slamming the contraption against the ground — but all in vain.

The parrot seemed frenzied, out of her mind. She burst out, now in laughter, now in tears, now in curses, until the whole house was awakened. Soon, someone was racing through the rooms with a light; someone ran up from the kitchen, and a mongrel watchdog threw himself upon Rex. That dog received such a mighty blow from Rex's paw that he ran off with a whine, his tail between his legs. Rex, baring his fangs at the people, slowly withdrew into the park. There, at the very edge of the parkland, in the Chinese arbour that stood on a little hillock, he determined to spend the rest of the night. Still, from time to time, he crept near the manor house. The crazy screeches of his friend, beating herself against the bars of her cage, met his ears.

He dreamed of her story as he awaited the sunrise. He was enraptured with a sort of longing for such regions as those, distant and free of the tyranny of man. Growling quietly and thumping his tail against the floor, he seemed to be crawling near to that place, where the torn deer was bellowing.

The night drew in, dark, hot, and silent. Stars glowed in the depths of the heavens. The trees basked in a soporific torpor. The meadows beyond the parkland were white with a woolly mist, as if they were covered with fleece. The songs of the birds grew heated in an amorous ecstasy. The aromas of the linden trees swirled among the shadows in currents of inexpressible delight. Now and then the rustling corn sent forth its delicate incense, and sometimes resin, as thick as curls of smoke, pushed out of the coniferous forest. The earth was submerged in restful peace as the dawn was still far off. Only Rex, distrusting the mask of the night, both drowsed and watched, his head resting low upon the earth, ever ready to spring up to fight in self-defence. And although he was battered by misfortune, he was perfectly aware of what was going on around him.

There, from the wilderness of rye, resounded the spine-tingling bleats of a throttled hare.

Foxes glided about cautiously, and suddenly, from somewhere in the wheat fields, there burst forth the despairing lament of a partridge. A pheasant dam, spooked from her nest, began to scream in panic. Noiselessly, the weasels crept near the sleeping birds. Owls suddenly broke off their amorous trills and fluff sifted down of a sudden like blood-spattered perianth. Then there was a panicked splashing of water, followed by the terrified shrieks of wild ducks — the otters were collecting their wonted tribute. A snake slithered toward the mouse-holes. Then came a sharp neighing of spooked mares from the distant pastures — Gimpy must have penetrated there. Geese in the farmyard raised a wild alarm at the presence of some predator there. Dogs took up a furious barking at something unknown. The storks commenced a threatening clacking, and then were answered by the fierce scream of a crane and the echoed moaning of lapwing and peewit. The hawks, perched in the summits of the trees, patiently awaited the dawn.

And thus, on just about all hands, the implacable battle for existence was raging. Songs of satisfaction, groans of the defeated, moral spasms, cruel blows, the crunch of shattered bones, the odour of spilled blood, stifled bellows, flowed on in a hardly perceptible melody that threaded the charms and raptures of the summer night. And the trees, unfathomable in their existence, spread their canopies above it all. Their crowns bobbed among the cold glitter of the stars, while from the depths their roots took on the palpable form of spurts of water. They endured, indifferent to all the world's clamour, distant and evoking dread by their eternal silence…

At dawn, the battles of the night-time gave way to the assaults of the day as the hawks, like lightning bolts, struck amongst the birds milling about the edge of the water. Rex started violently from his slumber and leapt away into the thickets. The turkeys commenced their disputes in the farmyard and the chatter of girls filled the air. Rex was tormented with such a fierce hunger that, paying no heed to the danger, he made his way towards the henhouse with a fox's nimble tread and, grabbing the nearest turkey, ran off with it into the corn, chased by a shower of screeches, curses and stones. Having satisfied his hunger on the warm, trembling flesh, he left the remains to the crows and set off at a quick pace for the hunter's blind in the marshes.

That's where Dummy found him in the afternoon. He brought him a soup-bone and bad news.

'It's all over for you. The mistress has promised a reward to whomever does you in.'

'I'm not going to start eating grass,' growled Rex, licking the blood from his lips with pleasure.

'Everybody'll be out hunting for you. I heard the foreman spitting brimstone.'

'I know where his little geese pasture… Fat little fledgelings… They'll do nicely.'

'They've given him a gun. They're going to set traps; they might even toss about some poisoned bait. Or maybe they'll make an organised hunt of it, with beaters on the periphery. Don't trust any of the watchdogs. They'd be the first to hand you over for a scrap of the mistress' favour. The pointer bitch is looking for you… Blackie tried to mount her. She bit him, and is howling after you.'

'Blackie…' he growled menacingly. And then, 'What good are bitches to me? I've got to concentrate on staying alive.'

'You can't beat them all, poor fellow!' Dummy cooed, in pain.

'I won't come cheaply. I'll give 'em something to remember,' he growled. 'They chased me off, shot at me, made me starve, and now they want to bash my head in. And for what?' he whined in pain.

'What's more, out of spite to the administrator, Wawrzek fed the stallion some barbed wire wrapped in bread.'

'Where'd they bury him?'

'He's not quite dead yet. But he moans so, and tosses himself about, kicking with his feet — it's a terror to behold.'

'My master's steed! He was a good friend. I sometimes slept in his stable, beneath the manger.'

'And the old grey mare, who was just being tolerated now, ran off to make her way by begging.'

'She ran off… by herself… into the unknown…' Rex mused, unable to understand.

'The gardener had been using her to cart water and treated her so badly that she ran off.'

'Where'll she go? She'll be eaten by the wolves.'

'The gardener left her in the orchard overnight. In the morning when he untethered her and tried to harness her to the barrel-wagon, why, didn't she hammer him with her hooves before running off! They were hardly able to bring him back around.'

'He got what he deserved. But she won't be able to handle Gimpy like that.'

'I'll tell you something else. If only you'd left the manor fowls alone, maybe they'd spare you. And by the way, don't you even think of touching my geese! The crows picked off three of my goslings today. O, I let them know that I'll be knocking down every nest of theirs that I find in the woods, for that.'

'The bastards,' Rex growled disdainfully. 'I never laid a paw on anything living, not even a chick. But if this is how it's to be, and they refuse me food, fair is fair. War is war!'

And so it was that a real war erupted on that day. All the people of the manor, with the foreman at their head, rose up against the wretched outlaw, swearing death to Rex. The battle raged without quarter on all sides and at all times. For they hunted him by night as well as by day — hurling sticks, hurling stones, and siccing their dogs at him. He could no longer show himself in the ambit of the farmlands by daylight, for a shower of stones would break upon him as soon as he appeared, and boys armed with rods would rush at him from places of ambush. Even old folks warming their bones in the sun by the outbuildings would try and trick him to come near — since they all had their heads turned by the prospect of the reward set on his head.

At first, assaulted by sudden ambushes and threats lurking in every nook and cranny, menaced by angry bellows, shooting and pursuit, Rex lost his head and raced in terror over the fields, giving vent to his broken heart in bitter complaints against the baseness and villainy of humans. And indeed he might have fallen into their hands had it not been for Dummy's advice:

'Keep out of sight for a few days. Hide in the blind. I won't forget about you.'

2

Heeding Dummy's advice, Rex made his way back to the marsh by a roundabout route. He remained there for several days, lonely and hungry, lapping the water with burning tongue, feverish. He had neither the energy nor the desire to hunt the ducks, of whom there were so very many all around him. His days were filled with gloomy, difficult ruminations. Besides this, his wounds had not yet healed completely. He lacked strength, and, what is worse: courage. He considered himself a goner, and waited for the worst with resignation.

One morning, trailing the scent and traces left by Dummy, the pointer made her way to his hiding place. Stretching out beside the hunter's blind, she whimpered, humbly. Rex was fierce by nature: he growled angrily at the strayed arrival, gave her a rough shaking… It's a wonder he didn't thrust her into the depths of the bottomless slough. On her part, she didn't even whimper, despite the pain. She took up a post across from the blind and didn't drop her eyes from him — ever ready, at his slightest command. He turned away from her in contempt. But she was beautiful — as white as milk, with head and ears of light brown, and eyes that were big and blue. She was svelte, as limber as a serpent. Her every moment was refined, elegant; she was clean, alert, able to sniff things on the wind from afar. In the afternoon, when he was groaning from hunger in his sleep, she brought him a stout mallard, which he devoured to the very last bone. He accepted everything she hunted down for him — as if it were tribute, naturally. It never crossed his mind to share the food with her. But after a few days, when he felt the vigour return to his bones, his strength return, he deigned to cast a kindly glance upon her eyes so full of worship, and her tender courtship. She was as joyful as a spring morning, mobile, and hopelessly in love with him. She left home on account of him, after all; a home of ever-full bowls, delightful rambles over the fields with her master, and that arousal, both frightful and wonderful, when she caught sight of a hare and, pointing him out with statuesque rigidity, she heard the boom of the gun, which shook her to the core. This, all this, she gave up on behalf of that bandit with a price on his head, that homeless tramp. His lion-like physique thrilled her, as did the power of his steel-like maw and the terror he inspired in everyone. What were those mutts in the yard in comparison to this authentic monarch? — Wretched mongrels! And so she danced around him, skipping in a frenzy of love, with tender yaps. She tossed her paws over his thick nape, licked his eyes, and snuggled close, waiting, trembling, for those nut-brown eyes of his to burst into flame. He gave in, at last, permitting himself to be carried away, and together they intoned the immortal song of love. They forgot everything that was not caress, delightful game, the tempting chase of ever-hungry desire. And thus the wondrous days passed, in delight, suffused in warmth and brightness. From its rising in the east to its setting in the west, the sun poured down warmth and joy. The heavens stretched their pristine azure above the earth, at night gazing down upon them with its billions of sparkling stars. The chorus of the frogs performed almost incessantly, their croaking full of sweetness. The wetlands, exhaling at evening after days of sizzling heat, breathed forth intoxicating aromas. The birds never grew quiet — not even for a moment. A holy hymn, a song of songs lifted up by thousands of voices, pulsed in waves of unutterable charm and might.

From the most immature blade of grass, from beings hardly yet conceived, to the gigantic coniferous forest and the white clouds above the horizon, the sun resplendent, everything lifted up one immortal song of perpetual change and eternal durance. They sensed the melody of that perpetual song within them, so mightily, so densely, as if they were all alone in the universe, and the endless chain of future generations took its conception from them. They became as one individual in desire and feeling. They waded the marsh together; together they tracked and together killed. Each booty garnered only whetted their appetite for triumph all the more. The long, patient crawl, following the spoor of their quarry, the long hours of waiting in ambush, the moment of muscles tensed just before the lunge, the falling upon the prey, the battles, chases, and victories were accompanied by trembles and shivers of unutterable rapture. Then, inebriated with blood, satisfied with flesh, the moans of the torn, and the sense of their own power, they drowsed on the gory field of battle. Soon, possessed by a frenzy acquired from their commerce with men, they murdered not out of necessity, but for the sheer thrill of it — a mere demonstration of the cruel adroitness of their blows, the inerrancy of their scent, and their indomitable might. Soon, terror began to raise groans of dread above the marshland, widening its ambit over many miles unto the distant mighty river and the forests of pine and fir that darkened the far horizon. Reproaches rustled among the reeds, rushes, and dwarf alders sprinkled about the boggy wetlands. Ever more frequently were heard the laments of mothers whose nests had been ravaged. For up until that time, that world had lived at peace, under the protection of the bottomless marsh pools, the treacherous fens and impassable quagmires covered with algae and duckweed. Even in winter it was impossible for a man to penetrate these central wilds. Only the foxes — sometimes — made their way over the thin ice to the midmost hummocks, where ducks paddled gaily through water that never froze. All creatures lived there in safety, under the aegis of natural law, which no one had ever infringed.

But now that two strays had begun to wreak murder and devastation, the hearts of all were torn with anxiety. The slightest misdeed of the two dogs was noted. And they never sensed the keen, hidden eyes trained upon them from every marsh, every bush and tuft of reeds; they knew not that news of their crimes was being spread to the most distant corners of the wetlands on every puff of the breeze. Nor were the aerial sentries behindhand in their duties. The peewits, whose eggs the dogs most frequently lapped up, circled above them, endlessly emitting cries of warning at their every slightest movement. The terns dared them as well, swooping down with their short, sharp war-cries. Even the storks dived down low over their heads to get a good look at these enemies of all, because no one in this paradise of winged beings felt safe in his own nest any more. For the pointer sniffed out even the most masterfully camouflaged dwellings with her Satanic sense of smell, and Rex pitched in with the looting, fearing neither the heavy beaks of the wild ganders nor their wings that thrashed like flails. Only the fearful beaks of the cranes and storks demanded, and got, his respect. He never attacked them, even if the bitch stiffened to point in their direction. Anyway, they took such a liking to this life full of emotion and wondrous adventures that they almost forgot about men and that other world…

Only sometimes, at night, when the pointer was asleep, nestled up lovingly to his side, did Rex sense a longing arise in him, a yearning for the manor and for Dummy, who hadn't come by now for quite a long while. Also, as the days slipped by, he began to look upon his lover as something of a burden, and to feel a repugnance for the cruelty with which she preyed upon the vanquished. He'd had his surfeit of flesh, of blood, of love and of the joys of this wild way of life. He began to worry, pinched with a vague concern about the morrow. At times, he seemed to sense on the wind some danger quite near at hand. Once, catching scent of gun smoke, he shivered in terror. And one night he heard, quite clearly, the echoes of gunshots from afar. Once again, the voice of his former mistress thundered in his mind so that he ran off from his den in a panic. Taking care not to betray his torment, he would slip away at times to the edge of the fens and, with swelling nostalgia, prick his ears to catch the echoes borne on the breeze from the manor. But with them there also awoke memories of the injustices he'd suffered, and these evoked such a wild thirst for revenge that, tearing at the earth with his claws, he would howl in helpless fury. Upon returning from these secret excursions, he was more full of tenderness, somehow, for the pointer, and more full of cruelty to whomever chanced to fall into his clutches.

Then, one moonlit and unutterably songful night, he was startled awake by the fearsome cries of ganders, after which a deadly silence fell. The bitch was not at his side. She was laying in front of the blind, beating her tail against the ground and gnashing her chattering teeth. Above them floated some strange, disturbing scent. He leapt onto the roof of the blind and, snuffling the wind in all directions, caught the distinct scent — despite the sharp exhalations of the bogs and the stork nests — of wolf.

Tensed for a leap into battle, he quizzed the air with flaring nostrils and trembling ears pricked to all sides. A wolf was creeping somewhere nearby, circling; the snap of dried stalks, the rustle of parted reeds, heavy with dew, sounded ever closer. At last, in the silence, he heard a few short, bark-like growls. The bitch made a few frenzied leaps forward before, turning suddenly, she squeezed into the darkest corner of the blind. Rex lunged in the direction of the foe with some mighty leaps. The wolf ran off, and all grew peaceful once again. But the very next night, when the moon rose above the pinewoods and the fretful black waters began to sparkle with its glow, the lovelorn serenade of a wolf spurted from the clumps of alder. The song was sobbed out so passionately, shot through with such yearning and appeal, that the pointer, despite her terror, set off in its direction, deliriously.

And then the voice of the dog thundered through the silent night, like a foreboding thunderclap.

'What're you after, rat-catcher? I'm the one that broke your daddy's leg — keep that in mind!'

A terror settled over the marshes, for soon a second voice thundered in response:

'You lapper of slops! Potlicker! Listen to what a free lord has to say!'

'Filthy litter of a mangy dam!'

'Go back to your place, watching over your master's geese and crouching beneath the blows of his stave! I'll tear out your vitals! Remember that!'

'Kitchen sluts chased you away from the offal pile with brooms, and you come here, you stinking cadaver?!'

'You bag of leather! When I'm done with you, not a single bone of yours will be whole!'

'I'll drag your carcass to that offal pile for the crows to pick apart!'

'Shut your mouth, herd-boy broken free of your chain! Hold your tongue when a free being speaks!'

The pointer returned and, as if petrified in place, her head pushed forward and one paw held above the ground, full of trembling, fear, and rapture, she waited upon the conclusion of this responsorial of wrath which, like a storm, so disburdened itself through the nocturnal silence that all other creatures hid themselves, retreating to the most secret of their hiding places. Even the wind had gone still; the waters were immobile and the trees and reeds seemed to lean forward, the better to listen to this howling hurricane of hatred.

'The skinner will make a pelt of your hide for me to recline upon! Come closer, you cowardly sheep! Closer, that I might explore your ribcage with my fangs! Come on!' Rex howled in disdain.

'You punk! I'll have a nice little wedding night with that bitch of yours, and you, you dog, will sing for us!'

'I'm waiting, you rotting carrion! I'll sing you death! Death!'

And howling thus, Rex lunged mightily into the thicket where those two greenish, sinister eyes were flashing. He and the wolf rushed at each other, grappling in mortal combat. Over the ground they rolled in a swirl of yelps, splutterings, wrestling in cruel hatred. Rex was bigger and, although not as powerful or skilful in battle as the wolf, still got hold of him and, throttling him, slammed him against the ground again and again. At the very last moment, gathering the very last bit of strength that remained in him, the wolf tore himself from the jaws of imminent death and ran off with a crazed howl.

The battle was over quickly, but Rex, mortally exhausted, matted with blood, torn by the wolf's claws, collapsed to the ground. Whimpering humbly, the pointer licked his wounds and then, all the while he healed, she brought him the birds she'd hunted down. Despite the fact that shivers of an unsatisfied desire shot through her at the mere recollection of the vanquished one, she served the victor faithfully and with limitless obedience.

Everything returned to how it had been before, except that, fevered with the excitement of victory, they fell into such a murderous frenzy that the wetlands echoed with the endless moaning of those killed without pity and without need. Rex, inebriated with his conquest, his power, the terror he aroused and the bitch's adoration, began to consider himself the rightful lord of those endless marshes. He grew so brash that his thoughts began to turn to coming to grips with men… But then something quite unforeseen happened.

One afternoon, while they were drowsing in the shade of the blind, when the sun was already sinking past the pinewoods and a pleasant, cool breeze began to blow, a dance of cranes took wing and, circling in ever tighter gyres, slipped down to the earth not far from the sleepers.

Rex opened his alert eyes, and the pointer bared her fangs.

A gigantic, shimmering cloud shaded the sun for a moment, after which a mustering of storks fell soundlessly to earth next to the cranes. And then, in long skeins, the wild geese arrived. The terns landed in heavy drops, like stones falling. After them came innumerable flocks of avian small-fry. It was as if the entire winged world had assembled there in parliament. All the surrounding meadows were covered with them; the reeds and trees disappeared in feathery billows of swaying, agitated wings.

The dogs leapt to their feet and began barking, advancing at a threatening pace.

Then with a windstorm of fluttering wings, thousands of beaks, as sharp as spears, hung right above them, and a hissing like two thousands of snakes filled the air, so that the dogs howled in mortal terror, not knowing where they might escape — for all of those phalanxes rushed at them at once with a calm, grim determination that was terrible.

Huge grey cranes, strutting on legs like enamelled armour, came first, swaying heads like spiked maces.

The storks, looking as if they were clad in mournful chapel capes of black and white, pressed in from the side in a numerous crowd, threatening the dogs with the fearsome pikes of their long beaks.

The grey herons, wagging their crests in warlike fashion, moved up with stealthy tread. The wild ganders, stamping on one leg and then the other, beating their battle-ready wings, pressed on with a furious tenacity. Their dull beaks, set on their bent, supple necks, beat like hammers. They pressed in from all sides, closing ranks in a ring bristling with sharp beaks. The lapwings, criss-crossing the skies just overhead, tore the air with their incessant, plangent wails, while the remainder of the winged horde raised a deafening squall and fluster.

Suddenly, all grew quiet at the sound of one, drawn-out, whistle. Then, the largest of the cranes, who had led his clans across mountain and sea for many years now, stepped forward and, after flapping his wings, burst into a loud, solemn clangour.

'Hear me now, you scurvy four-legged pair! You stealthy belly-crawlers! A sentence has been passed on your heads, you homeless vagabonds! The wilds welcomed you, and you trampled her sacred laws underfoot! You murdered needlessly; you slaughtered for pleasure! You preyed upon helpless chicks! You have lived by violence, wrongdoing and crime. You violators of the law! You rabid reptiles! You loathsome bloodsuckers! Woe to you! Woe! Woe!'

'Death! Death! Death!' cawed an unkindness of ravens passing by overhead.

'We banish you from the wilds! Return now to your collars and your staves! You are unworthy of liberty! You creatures of the darkness, of winter, and kennel! You slaves of the human beasts! And like them — evil, mendacious and deceitful! In the name of the murdered, on behalf of the ravaged nests and throttled fledglings, on account of our trampled laws, we banish you forever! Forever!'

'Death! Death! Death!' croaked the ravens, slipping ever lower.

Then the ring broke open, revealing to them a broad path through the feathery hordes.

The dogs spurted toward the escape route. They raced on in great leaps, frenzied, in mortal fear of the death which seemed so nigh, death by those innumerable beaks. But nary a one of them struck, nary a talon tore at them, nary a single pair of wings beat against their backs, bristling in terror as they ran off.

It was dusk already when, having reached the fields, they ensconced themselves in the corn and lay down, barely alive, exhausted, and terrified. Rex, breathing hard, long scanned with bloodshot eye the waving stalks and the heavens, besprinkled now with stars, before he once again felt the sweetness of being alive. Every now and then, the memory of those beaks and wings waving overhead sent a powerful shiver all through his frame.

On her part, after having rested a while, the pointer suddenly leaped to her feet and, snuffling the wind, set out in a beeline for home.

Rex leapt up to give chase, but then remained where he was, listening to the sound of her leaps through the grain growing ever more distant. His eyes dulled in sadness; some saliva spooled from his drooping lower lip, and his proud, lofty head sank ever lower toward the earth.

3

A heavy fist of violence loomed over Rex's head. He had been banished by human ingratitude, and now he was banished once more by the winged tribes, for crimes he couldn't understand. He was abandoned by his friends and branded with the stigma of universal hatred, sentenced to the bitter existence of the homeless scatterling.

At first, he didn't comprehend the danger in which he found himself. By turns buffeted by terror and wrath, he sensed the injustice of his situation without understanding its causes. And thus, it was as if he were battering his head against an invisible wall. He prowled around the habitations of humans, deranged with horror. Now he escaped into the fields afar, crouching in ditches, now again he wandered through courtyards, returning once again, heedless of the stones flying towards him from all sides and the fierce screeches of pursuit; sometimes he hid himself in roadside thickets, intently giving ear to the echoes of the farmyards. He couldn't find Dummy anywhere. Someone else was tending the geese — an 'enemy' of his from the old days. He tried to draw near the parrot — but what was the use, since, as if to rub salt into his wounds, all the fields, woodlands, and marshes proclaimed the shame of his fall. Compassion was nowhere to be found. He lived beyond the pale of all society now, having become an object of pursuit and contempt. The stupid magpies mocked him. The crows chased after him, as if he were on his last legs — nearly carrion.

And once again, while he was sleeping amidst the bobbing, rustling corn, the hawks swooped down at him. The vile jibes of the barking foxes drove him near insane. Taking furious vengeance upon them, he tore up their breeding dens with wrathful claws. He couldn't show himself in the parklands, for if he did, those feathery canaille would raise such a commotion that men would come running up with rods and cudgels. And once, when he took refuge from pursuit by crouching among the wicker reeds at the pond's edge, the storks caught sight of him and raised a fierce alarm with their clacking, beating him so with their frightful beaks that he barely escaped death. Even his old comrades bared their teeth at the sight of him when he drew near the kennels. Blackie barked at him in alarm, for an alibi:

'Get yourself out of here! The people say you're rabid! Everybody's afraid of you! Escape!'

He became convinced of this soon enough, for, seeking somewhere to flop, he found every horn and hoof raised up to smite him. Barn and stable, enflamed with dread, barred him access, the inhabitants bellowing to the skies. And thus, exhaustion and hunger drove him to the sties, where he lapped up the scrapings left in the troughs by the pigs. But the sows gave him away, and one night, the foreman organised a hunt for him. It was only by miracle that he evaded capture, safe and whole. So, in the grip of wild fear, he escaped to the forests. With death breathing down his neck, he was forced to abandon the dwellings his kind had known from time primordial, to take shelter in the impassable wilds. Once upon a time, along with his master, he had raced about them with curiosity. But now, finding himself in the gloom, where sunlight penetrated only here and there — he stood stock still, stunned. The swaying colossi of the trees rustled and whined their mysterious fiddles above him in the anxious stillness that twined about him. Terror gazed out of his bloodshot eyes, and a drawn-out howl of despair tore forth from the depths of his heart.

He lay, curled in the thickets, for many hours, before he got up courage enough to plunge into the heart of the pinewoods. For after all, he'd always lived in a group! He was familiar with the manor, the village, and the courtyard; he knew people and animals, fields and sky; he knew nights and days, enemies as well as friends; he knew the way it all worked, laws and customs — so here, he felt himself to be thrust out, alone, into a world that he didn't understand, a strange world, unknown and somehow fearsome.

But fear of death won out over the desire to return, and so he began to wander, aimlessly, frequently faint with hunger, for — at the start — he had no success hunting. His sense of smell was dulled and his eyesight faint. He knew not how to transform his lunge into a faultless strike. He was completely ignorant of deception. He knew neither the customs nor the laws of the wilderness. He chased after everything that moved like a stupid pointer puppy. He was unable to track, and creep for hours on the trail of prey. He gave himself away by barking. He beat about the forests like a calf in an empty barn, barking at the squirrels who tossed pine cones at him. He raced after goldcrests so that the owls hooted with laughter in their tree hollows, and the whole wilderness followed his movements with anxiety — for he spooked, terrorised, and slaughtered whatever fell into his clutches. Thousands of eyes were trained upon him from their hiding places in the thickets, in the crowns of the trees, and underneath the high heavens.

'It's just a dog. A stupid, human dog! Nothing to be afraid of,' the horned owls hooted.

'Foh! He reeks of smoke and carrion,' the ravens croaked, never letting him out of their sight, and their yapping-like giggles spread in echoes afar.

'Farmyard bandit! Hooligan! Terror of the chicken coop! Ruffian!'

'He's fattening himself at our expense!' the wolves growled in umbrage, keeping track of him from a distance.

'Hit the road! Hit the road!' screeched an old magpie that had been raised by humans, suddenly calling to mind the speech of men, which she had once been taught.

He barked at her viciously and began leaping up toward the branch on which she was seated.

'Stupid! Stupid! Stupid!' she continued to shriek, beating her wings with laughter.

He pressed on ever deeper, but the screeches, threats, and wrathful howls accompanied him on his way. This difficult, lonely life was beginning to weary him. To top it all off, he was erring about deep, impenetrable forests, and continually lost his way. He feared the treacherous, overgrown bogs full of writhing nests of snakes, and the wild backwoods, from which emerged some ill-omened snuffles, deep, stertorous grunting, and the echoes of heavy stamping. He'd had enough of the endless misery and fear. For he sensed Death circling him, incessantly, just waiting for the right moment to lunge. And this is why he slept only during the day, and only in open clearings, but even then the shadows of birds passing overhead would jolt him awake in terror. Once, because it was harder and harder for him to hunt anything down, and hunger deprived him of the rest of his prudence, in broad daylight, he snatched a hefty shoat from a singular of boars. He hadn't had time to finish his feast; he had to leave the best portions behind, as he was driven off by furious sows. Later, nearly unconscious with hunger, he threw himself in delirium upon some deer drinking water. So pummelled was he then, that he was hardly able to drag himself to the charcoal-burners' shack where, for a few days, he licked at his new, and deep, wounds.

The shack stood at the edge of a clearing, thickly over-grown with raspberry, blackberry and whortleberry bush-es, among which tall young saplings shot upwards. The air was filled with an incessant racket of chatter and birdsong, and in the midst of it all shone a long lake, bordered with cane and reeds. All throughout the day you could hear the paddling and splashing of wild geese and ducks. The place was remote and unknown to men, although the wilderness knew it well. It was something of a sacred place, where the whole nation of the wilds gathered each day at the rising and setting of the sun to drink in peace and bathe at will. All around the lake, as if on guard, stood ancient forests of tow-ering oak and sublime pine trees. The air was scented with honey and vibrated with the buzzing of bees, for the hollows of the old trees were crammed with honeycombs, so that from those facing west, thick streams of the yellow liquid seeped down the bark, thickening in the air. Whole clouds of insects shimmered above them, perishing in the sweet, sticky streams, while over them, as over cobbles, swarmed countless hordes of voracious red ants.

The weather was capricious. The sun beat down mercilessly, and then violent storms erupted; the earth trembled at the thunderclaps while again and again the clouds lashed the tottering wilds with fiery bullwhips of lightning. Then the rains would pour down, booming like a sea unleashed. Then again dry summer windstorms swept in from the fields, whistling and romping like drunks tumbling about the pine forests. Then there were long rows of days, quiet, hot, and fragrant, when everything that lived sang an endless hymn of happiness and love in incomprehensible fervour.

Only Rex felt nothing of this universal joy of life. All this was stifled inside him by deeper cogitations. His infallible instinct whispered to him that to be passive in the wilds is to perish. And he did not want to perish. The will to life awakened ever greater strength within him. Once and again a current of deep, silent revolt made him spring to his feet. But then he flopped back down onto his nest, still weak and sick, but always smouldering with the desire for revenge. Vivid images of the injustice and suffering he'd experienced passed through his fevered brain, incessantly, during those long days and nights. In reliving them, he suffered anew, and so painfully that he'd howl in despair, casting blame at both man and beast. Especially as the tread of predators constantly circling his shack sounded in his ears. He felt that, at any moment now, he would have to engage in his final battle, but that moment never arrived. He couldn't understand what they were waiting for, until an old horned owl finally explained it to him:

'One doesn't kill the sick! Such is the law!' he hooted from the depths of the shack, where he'd made his nest.

And on the next day, when the sun drove him into the darkest corner of the shack, Rex began to learn from the owl the laws and customs that ruled the wilderness. He hooted monotonously, repeating it all one hundred times over. It was obscure, but Rex understood him perfectly.

Having listened his fill, he turned a haughty glare upon the glowing, yellow eyes.

'I'd rather herd sheep for men than be a king in the wilderness.'

'We have no king; we are ruled by wise, ancient laws. They don't appeal to you — but what do you know about freedom? Men taught you their freedom with sticks and starvation rations. You broke your fetters, you slave, and now you bark in bold criticism of things you know nothing about.'

'I know one thing. In the human world they're not constantly hunting one another. They don't eat each other alive, or constantly track and ambush. One sleeps there in security.'

'Because everyone's fed by the hand of man, and cringes in fear of his club. You don't eat each other, but man feeds on every one of you. What sort of image does that once grand nation of hoof, horn, and wing present to the world these days? Slaving cattle who have handed over their freedom in exchange for wretched rations and a roof overhead. For that they've paid in freedom, strength, and blood? You live, you multiply, and you die — all for the benefit of man. Your skin does not belong to you, nor your bones, nor even your fur! Shame to those who have embraced slavery! You don't even know how to revolt! All you know how to do is complain, accept your lashes humbly, and lick the feet of your oppressors.'

Rex shot to his feet, as if suddenly touched by a red-hot iron — before sinking helplessly to the ground once more.

'I used to have a nest in one of their churches, and I know what goes on there! I remember how, every day at dawn and dusk there resounded an immense moaning of complaint, pain, and despair. But can you hear the song with which the air of the wilderness is always full? That's the song of freedom — that's the song of our joyful, brave, and carefree life! That's happiness that's singing!'

Rex choked back a painful sob, torn by the claws of his memories.

'You have no idea what a joy it is, when I spread my wings and launch myself into the wind, allowing myself to be carried where I will, lord of my own strength, my own self, free!'

'Until some hobby tears you apart like a miserable wagtail!' he growled.

'If he's able, he has a right to. But there are many empty nests in the woods that once belonged to those who had a go at me. Everyone has a right to attack. Death is the payback of every blow, every death. Woe to the weak! Woe to those whose fangs or talons fail them! Life is a constant struggle! And victory is our one aim. The warm blood and quivering flesh of one's foe is the divine recompense of bravery! Praise and loot to the victorious! Death to the vanquished! Such is the slogan of the free!' the owl hooted, louder and louder.

'You win a victory over a mouse, and you begin to weave epics of heroism.'

'And what sort of battle is yours, when they sic you on some moribund cow? And still and all you tremble before her cloven hooves! Noble knight, whom even the crows pummel at will...'

'And you, consumed piecemeal by lice, for all your gallantry!' Rex snapped in reply, noticing how the owl began to pluck beneath its wings with its beak.

'Hold your tongue, slave-boy, and don't forget that you're speaking with a free being! Don't forget, you chattel, that you are nothing but a thing of man. The wilderness has given you refuge — keep that in mind! But I advise you to return to your stripes, your brimming trough and warm corner of the sty. You need to be born free in order to appreciate freedom. Out of my sight, you mangy pelt!'

Rex lunged upward at the owl but, not reaching him, he fell back to his nest with a moan.

The owl flew out of the shack, hooting with laughter so that the echoes carried far throughout the woods.

'You'll learn what a dog is yet! You'll get a taste of the fangs of a slave, you free-born bandits!' he hooted, gnashing his teeth.

He was choked by an uncontrollable fury. At that moment, he felt vilified and roughed up as never before, at anyone's hands. Those gibes of slavery scalded his innards and drove him near insane. But they were true — and that's why he couldn't digest them. He had to hear them through to the end! He tossed and turned in circles on his nest, biting his own tail and foaming at the mouth in helpless wrath.

It was only those vile slurs that showed him how tightly he was bound to that old world — with every fibre of his being. How all of that, which he had so recently cursed, was close and dear to him. And at the same time, he sensed the bottomless abyss that lay between him and the wilderness. And because he feared it, all the more passionately did he begin to hate it, cursing it with a wild howl.

This hatred, glowing to a white-hot frenzy, awoke in him hidden fighting instincts and an indomitable courage. The bloody mockery of the owl so pummelled him, like clubs, that despite his weakness and unhealed wounds he crawled his way to the lakeside and, hidden in the canes near the shore, hunted down a wild duck before it was able to get a single cry out of its throat. This gave him both strength and confidence, and so emboldened him that for days on end now he lay in ambush among the reeds, culling the water-fowl with such dexterity, that even the most watchful cranes never caught sight of him returning to the shack with his quarry. It was then that he began to disregard the laws of the wild. Quite simply, he called them out, challenged them, killing in broad daylight, in the sight of all, and raised his great, leonine head ever higher, ever more proudly.

He began to be encircled by an ill-omened silence, like the calm before a storm. He felt the thousands of eyes that marked his every step, from thicket, den, and tree-hollow as well as from the air; he was aware of the fact that a ring of danger was closing in, ever more tightly around him, and that sooner, rather than later, it would strike him. Not in vain was the horned owl inciting the wilds. His disgusting hooting, and his flight, like an eiderdown being torn, could be heard everywhere. Every now and then Rex caught the scent of young wolves flashing by, here and there. Or a fox wandering about, snuffling the air, scouting, or a lynx, hidden in the thick branches of a tree with flickering, blood-red eyes. Even the stupid squirrels seems to be keeping watch over him, incessantly hanging around the shack. And high in the sky, barely visible, the hawks were circling. It was practically impossible to hide from their devilish power of sight. Even the pinewoods and the small nation of the petty birds seemed to have joined the universal pact against him. Even the crows, who skipped around him with shrieks of delight when he generously left them copious remains, would flap off to the wolves at dusk to impart their news. The tangled brambles held him back with their sharp thorns; hanging branches whipped him painfully, and the young coppices became impassable to him. The winds interfered with his tracking, blowing away the spoor from before his nose. Yet as if with a clever insouciance and bravado Rex took ever greater risks.

At this the wilds, stunned and fearful of some sort of unforeseen ambush, began to waver in the face of such determined bravery.

One day, calling out Death, boldly, Rex was in the sacred place, lying in wait for deer. At dusk, a whole parcel of them came down to the water, and feeling safe and secure, drank long and deeply, gracefully cavorting by the shore. Rex lunged upon a slender doe, one barely grown. Tearing herself free of his fangs, she plunged into the water with a frantic leap. But Rex caught up to her in the middle of the lake. Pulling her out onto dry land, he slaughtered her, paying no attention to her tearful bleating.

He feasted long on the carcass. A large murder of crows gathered round him, waiting on their turn. Then, wolf howls began to resound from the thickets. Raising his bloody face, Rex replied with a threatening growl.

Gimpy slipped out of the birchwood and demanded a share.

'Come and get it!'

'Hand over a share, or I'll haul you in on a charge of murder in a sacred space.'

'Come and get it!' Rex growled deeply again, baring his sharp teeth to the very roots.

Inebriated with the odour of fresh blood, the wolf commenced a protracted howling, calling forth his comrades concealed nearby.

Rex didn't wait for them. He leapt to his feet, tensed for a lunge, and, narrowing his eyelids to slits, burst forth in a frightful wolf's howl.

Gimpy withdrew cautiously and slipped away along the shoreline to the other side of the lake. Rex continued to howl with such a power of pride, might, and wrath, that the teeth of all the wilds chattered, from one end of the wilderness to the other. Everything that lived scurried away to hide in den and nest and forest depths out of terror at that voice. No one arrived to challenge Rex. They all proved cowards at his call. And so, as if trumpeting his victory, he dragged the carcass off to his shed in triumph, where he threw himself down on his nest, completely knackered.

This was the very first night in the wilds that he slept through in peace, without anxiety. At dawn, he went down to the lake to drink and bathe, after which he reclined beneath the pines amid the sweet buzzing of the bees, who had just left the hive for their daily labour.

The day rose bright and beautiful. Beneath the trees the dewy gloom was suffused with the heavy, suffocating aromas of resin and mushrooms. Mists were floating out of their nocturnal lairs; covering the clearing in a bluish cloud, they lifted their clear incense toward the heavens. A warm breeze heralded the rising sun, the wakening trees trembled, and pearls of dew dropped to earth. Amidst the disturbing, soporiferous stillness the first rustlings began to weave their way through the air, the first chirpings and fluttering of wings. And when the night had paled, uncovering to sight ever more sharply the outlines of the trees, the wilderness began to throb with life. Innumerable flocks of birds began to draw to the lake. The canes waved in billows as the deer hastened to the lakeside along their well-trodden paths. The boar began to grunt, as whole singulars of them came crowding close. The wolves slid near without a sound, leaving behind no track of their passage save their scent on the breeze. Birds of prey slipped down from their perches in the trees with hardly a flap of their wings. The cries of wild geese and ducks spread abroad in the air along with their loud splashing. At the very end of it all came the cranes.

All this thick rabble of predators large and small, rooters and animals graminivorous — the whole nation of the wilds — slaked their thirst and bathed in security amidst the joyful racket, under the protection of the ancient laws that forbade, on pain of death, hunting at watering holes.

Beneath the pines lay Rex, visible to all and ominous in both physical size and the crime he committed yesterday in this place. And yet no one accosted him.

They passed him by, as if they didn't see him. Not one eye flashed in his direction. They passed him by, calmly, as if he weren't even there.

That made him anxious; he didn't trust their indifference, behind which there had to be some guile, some intrigue. The behaviour of the wolves especially enjoined the utmost degree of wariness. But when the purple dawn played upon the waters, the woodland nation dissolved as swiftly and soundlessly as the last swaths of the mist. Only the cranes remained behind. They settled about the lake in great sieges. Surrounded by thick, watchful lines, they began to teach their young. Every now and then a little herd of them, leaders at their head, would break into flight and, skimming in great circles, lifted themselves higher and higher above the pinewoods, up beneath the rose-tinged clouds, and there, forming sharp Vs, they seemed to disappear somewhere in the abysses of the sky, so that the only trace of them was the protracted clangour that marked their sky-scraping paths, after which they return to earth in the same order, only to take off once again after a rest.

Rex was still dreaming of taking revenge for his late abasement. So, as soon as night fell and mist began to enfold the clearing, he started to creep near the sieges, striving with varied means of deception to slip through the corridors of cranes standing on one leg, their heads tucked beneath their wings. But before he made it even to the picket-line, a protracted cry pierced the silence and beaks, as heavy as cudgels, began to strike him on the back.

Foaming at the mouth, his vengeance unsatisfied, he dug himself into his nest and fell quickly asleep.

It was already late at night, the moon was sailing above the forest, the waters shimmering with a bright incessant sparkle, the silver mists were curling and uncurling above the grass and smaller bushes when suddenly, from somewhere near the lake, there resounded the sobbing song of a crane.

The wilds were stunned into meditative delight. All battle and pursuit ceased as the pinewoods grew absolutely still, listening, enchanted at the song arising from the pure silence in a spellbinding, dreamy longing — like something most holy that lived deep in the souls of all, and now gave notice of itself, awakening to rapture.

Without even being aware of what he was doing, Rex crawled up to the very picket line of the cranes and, crouching in the grass, pricked his ears and listened, forgetful even of his own safety.

The cranes were settled all around the shores of the lake with their necks nestled beneath their wings. But one of them, surely both their leader and their bard, stood with his head stretched toward the moon and sang in snatches, with such a drawn-out, melodious voice that seemed to be a visible silver glimmer of fragrance and sound. From time to time he lifted his wings and, beating them, twirled about on his own axis in some sort of hieratic dance, singing all the while, ever more sublimely, solemnly, and nostalgically. He sang rhapsodies of journeys far, far into the setting sun!

He sang of lands immense, with soaring, heaven-piercing mountains and sounding seas. Then he sang the beauty of the golden desert, of blue rivers, palm groves, and of the burning sun. He sang of lands uninhabited by man, where all creatures live free, happy, immortal. He sang sagas handed down by forefathers since ancient times, collected among the desert sands, torn from yearning hearts.

Then Rex shivered, having caught scent of wolf. Beneath the pines, green eyes flashed. Foxes circled uneasily, and, beating their tails, crawled ever higher on their four legs. Lynxes hung on the tree branches. Even the squalid boars gathered in groups, their snouts raised high toward the moon. A herd of deer, the stags with mighty antlers on their heads, stood listening, completely still, as if rooted in the earth. Clouds of winged beings covered bush and sapling. Nearly the entire woodland folk pressed close from all sides. They seemed to dream, in some sort of pious, prayerful concentration, as if beholding visions of paradises lost clearly before their eyes. The consciousness of daily existence fainted away — all memories of battle, hunger, and slaughter. An immortal breath of yearning united all of these imprisoned souls and enraptured them in musings of future existences.

The leader sang on indefatigably, accompanied from time to time by the dry clacking of bills or a long, mournful cry tearing up from out of the flocks.

Right before dawn, when the moon set and a cool breeze began to blow forth from the dark depths of the night, the song grew quiet and the meadow cleared. The cranes all fell asleep, covered in thick puffs of mist; the pinewoods stood in silence. Only from time to time did a sharp cry burst forth from the pickets.

Somehow, Rex couldn't regain his balance. He couldn't find his proper place — something drove him onward so that the dawn had hardly arisen when he was racing away into the bright, broad world. He was hurrying off to his own kind. He felt such a transformation come over him that he passed by the spooked hares along his path. His heart was bursting with joyful love. He barked a friendly greeting toward the partridges he came across. He frolicked on his back among the dewy grain. He undid the ropes that bound a horse in some peasant's pasture, freeing him from a ditch into which he had blundered and wasn't able to extricate himself.

'To the rising sun! To the east!' — snatches of the song he had heard still resounded in his ears.

And indeed, the miracle of the rising sun was in the process of incarnation. It rose, great and red — a visible sign of grace, a radiant eye of mercy over the world.

It was then that some thought — still dark and flickering, but terrible in the immensity of its boldness — arose within him, and would not give him peace. A thought of journeying there — to that place, to which the cranes fly, to those blessed regions, where there is no man, and where freedom and happiness reign.

He ran through a familiar village. The dogs greeted him with distrust, one or another baring his fangs, but when he gave them a friendly growl, they accompanied him on his way to the manor lands.

Sitting down on a border mound, he whimpered mysteriously, in an excess of joy.

'I've come to lead our nation out of bondage to man. Get ready. Have someone wait for me on the hill near the woods. I'll explain everything there.

At this he leapt into the corn. Oxen were coming down the road at that moment, pulling behind them heavy, creaking wagons full of grain. Again and again staffs thumped down upon their backs.

Then, right before the yard along the road he saw the old donkey, his head covered in a hempen sack, being whipped by boys harrying him towards a pit of lime.

'Don't give up! I'll help you!' he barked, carried away with wrath and compassion.

He tore the sack from the animal's head. The donkey, enraged with suffering and emboldened by Rex's aid, threw himself violently at the boys, flailing with his hooves, trampling and wheezing like a rusty gate.

Rex didn't wait to hear his thanks. He slipped into the yard and made his way to Blackie's kennel. The dog, shocked and frightened, didn't even think to forbid him entry. Rex laid out his plans before him. After weighting the matter a long while, the old dog growled:

'Take everyone with you. The men will be apoplectic with fury. After all, everybody's suffering the same misery, whips, and slavery. It's eating away at us all.'

'All the horns, all the hooves, and all the snouts?' Rex was stunned at the perspective this presented. 'But will they understand? Will they come?' He had some deep doubts about that.

'Whoever doesn't want to, let him perish under the blows. Such a one'll have to work for the others who leave, on top of his own labour. So all this'll need to be explained to them. Is it far, this place?'

'Past mountain and sea — where the cranes winter. Far away, far…'

Blackie leapt to his feet. His chain jangled, and he growled in anger:

'They said you were rabid, and now I see you're just stupid! Get out!'

'That's what comes from trying to explain things to a sheep's head. Pour some honey before swine, and they'll still prefer slops, because that's what they've been taught to like. I hope you won't regret it,' he finished, hurt at Blackie's harsh judgement.

'Get out. They'll catch sight of you, and it's me who'll catch hell. If the others go with you, I won't stay behind.'

'You've so grown into that chain that freedom terrifies you. You don't even know how to revolt!' he complained, repeating the owl's words.

'That parrot of yours had a hankering for freedom. She escaped yesterday, and took a fine pummelling from hawks. Her wings are broken. I heard her moaning about it all!'

Rex was moved with real compassion at this news. He felt bad for his old friend. Immediately, he set out to see her, but a girl blocked his path, with a stout stick in her hand. Rex knocked her over and mauled her so that the whole farmyard rushed over to the rescue.

Rex disappeared into the corn. His ire up, he began circling the outbuildings, only not stealthily now, not at night, but in broad daylight, like a truly strong being, a leader who enjoins obedience by the force of his might. Possessed by his great dream, he gave himself over to it entirely, with all the might of a burning heart and a violent temperament. Nothing else existed for him how; nothing save this sublime goal. The dogs came to believe in him, obedient to him in all things, accepting him as their lord and leader.

A few of the most powerful always accompanied him, for defence and aid, but from a distance… they no longer recognised him — he had become so transformed by freedom. With his size, his coat, and his shape, he seemed to be a real lion. His voice was that of a lion, for when he roared in anger all of creation fell to the earth in fear. He lived at the cost of the manor, careless of what they thought. He became proud, lofty, and took a cruel revenge upon his old enemies, sparing no one.

For his permanent quarters, he chose a hill on the pastures near the woods known by people as the Castle. It was so called because of the immense ruined pile that was found upon it — the rubble of ancient broken walls and crumbling bastions, overgrown with a thicket of filberts, birch, and blackberry bramble. There, in some vaulted, half-tumble-down chamber, which despite its decay still provided protection from the wind and the rain, Rex received his helpers in audience, counselling with them and sending them forth to agitate in the surrounding regions. Usually, he sat upon an elevated pile of rubble, observing the countryside with sharp, eagle eye. Whenever he caught sight of an injustice, there he sped.

'Don't give up! Defend yourself!' was the slogan that he and his comrades bruited among the animals tyrannised by man. And everywhere it gave rise to the same consequences.

Strange things began to happen. Horses began to respond with their hooves to every blow of staff or whip; oxen tore away from their harness and, having smashed wagon or plough, walked calmly off to graze in the fields of grain. The pigs refused to leave the potato fields. The dogs, once unleashed, refused to be chained again. Even the stupid sheep began to fill the air with rebellious bleating. Only the old donkey, despite that one successful outburst, never again dared defend himself, but hee-hawed all the more mournfully at the fresh injuries with which he was plagued.

'But I'm afraid to! I'm so afraid!'

The uprising spread with extraordinary swiftness, for everywhere the dogs stood up for the oppressed and injured, leaping upon their exploiters. Continual battles arose, blood was spilled, staffs shattered upon backs, whips whistled — the curses and groans of the tortured resounded incessantly over the whole land in moans of despair. A large number of animals fell in the fierce fighting, but the earth was burning beneath the feet of men as well — as they were punctured by horn and trampled by hoof. The fighting grew sharper by the day, for now it was the season of reaping, harvest, and turning the soil anew — but the horses and oxen refused their obedience. In despair, the people attributed this stubbornness to the sweltering heat which had settled over the land, and some sort of epidemic.

Rex listened to all the news of what was happening with unruffled peace. His heart swelled with certitude of the coming victory. Lifting high his sublime head, he embraced with concern the world entire, of which he began to consider himself lord and ruler. And so, in order to hasten the advent of universal happiness, he began to circle round the villages and towns himself.

He spent more than one night in the stables and barns of the peasantry, and more than once he had to escape a thrashing. Yet he'd return again and again, stubbornly, and when the lights in the cottages went out, he'd slip in as quiet as a fox to preach the coming day of liberation. He sang of that good fortune with the ardour of an uncrushable faith. Still and all, it was hard going. Sometimes the animals listened to him in distrust, and he was answered with a deep, apathetic silence. Sometimes, heavy horned heads were lifted in his direction, and the answer came accompanied by the flash of a cloven hoof.

'Back to your kennel, dog! And let us sleep!'

'He slipped off his chain, and thinks he's found freedom!'

At last, the denizens of one barn heard him out, patiently, and after some long grumbling, constantly turning over the cud in her mouth, one of the cows replied to him with a sleepy lowing:

'Why should we need to look for a manger so far away? Who will get our warm water? Who will fork us our hay? Who'll fit our stalls out with fresh straw?'

One after another they began to sing paeans to the goodness of their human owners, and to the delights of their mangers.

'And in exchange for that, they milk you and take away your calves!' Rex growled nervously.

'The calves… the calves!' they now recalled, although with difficulty, soon enough swelling with nostalgia.

'And then they kill you and eat you!'

The huge frames of the cows shivered with the terror of death. Up through their murky memories swam images of red beards and white claws, tearing away their children, their mothers, their clans, and leading them off to destruction. And suddenly a roar of terror tore from their throats like a hurricane, sweeping from barn to barn until the whole village was awakened and men and women came running up with sticks.

'Don't give in! Defend yourselves!' Rex barked furiously, plunging into the orchard.

But the whipstocks were effective: silence fell again, interrupted only now and then by a painful groaning.

Rex foamed at the mouth in anger at their passive cowardice.

'Just let him bite through my chain, and I'll show him what I'm made of!'

'Stupid!' another cow added. 'I'm supposed to attack my master, eh? Stupid!'

'I once kicked my lady, and what did I get? I stood hungry at an empty manger for three whole days!'

But he began his agitation once again, with understanding and patience.

'They won't let us go,' one of the cows interrupted him. 'I once broke away into the beet field, and they shoved me back. Then I tried to get into the cabbages. I'd already broken the fence even, and they gave me a walloping. They won't let us go. They let dogs run about where they will, but what's a dog, after all…?'

They all fell into musing on that, chewing their cuds and lowing longingly after their pastures.

Fortunately, Rex met with a totally different reception in the barns where the bulls were kept. They understood him at once. Their eyes grew wide and fiery; they began to pull at their chains with their stocky polls, and their rough, intermittent bellows began to shake the walls.

'Lead us! Break our chains! We've had enough of barn, yoke, and man. Lead us, and the herds will follow. And whoever gets in our way will meet with horn and hoof!'

The bellows thundered ever more mightily, cloven hooves tore at the earth, and a fighting spirit blazed in their eyes, while they licked Rex with their rough tongues.

Refreshed at their eagerness, he began to course round the stables. Courageously, he crept inside the dung-filthy, narrow and humid cells where the motley groups of horse-kind had been herded by chance, and where hunger, whip and labour had levelled them all to the same misfortune.

But there he came upon some fat nags belonging to the parish priest. They didn't even want to hear what he had to say, for the reverend father gave them all a piece of bread or a cube of sugar every day. There were also some well-fed draught horses belonging to the peasants, who dreamt of nothing more than a trough of potato- and thickly milled grain-mash. The rest of them were just the rags of horses — bags of fractured bones and torn hide — rickety, mangily whipped jades, blind, with festering wounds and skeletal heads — barely breathing carrion just waiting for the knackers, in short: a splendid image of human villainy.

When Rex finished speaking, he was answered with tears dripping from pus-thick eyes, and a neighing as mournful as heart-rending sobs.

'Too late! There's no helping us now, no hope! If not to-day, then tomorrow we'll be torn apart by wolves and pecked to shreds by crows! What a cursed fate, this life of ours!'

But in the stables of the larger manors he found some elegant cast-offs. The noble blood in their veins was roused by Rex's words and swelled them with hope; memories of their old life made supple their stiff joints, and to them the taste of freedom was sweeter than oats.

'Lead us! Lead us!' they neighed hotly, and, raising aloft their haggard heads, they snuffled the breezes with flaring nostrils.

'I remember the wide world,' neighed an old, grey stallion. 'I sailed the seas! With my hooves I spurned the earth beneath me! I raced with the wind! Neither the boom of cannon affrighted me, nor the whistling of the shells, nor the flashing blades of pikes! Sound the trumpet! I'm ready for the fight! Out of my way! We'll trample flat our enemies!'

And so he spurted forward toward freedom, despite his broken wind and his advanced age.

There were others, too, who had worked long at manor, palace and city, whom fate had thrust into the very depths of misery and suffering. These were racehorses, who had been sold by their masters gone bankrupt, and had been pulled into the abyss along with them. There was also an English pureblood gone lame, with swollen joints. He had long been harnessed to a treadmill, so that now he no longer knew how to walk straight ahead, but kept turning in circles. At Rex's appeal he fell into a real frenzy of excitement.

'The pages sound the horns! Hey, hey! Cross-country! Gallop!' he neighed wildly, galloping around the tight interior of the stable and knocking against stall and wall. He lifted high his moth-eaten tail, arched his back, and, tossing his mane, kept galloping in a circle.

Rex ran from him as from one insane. At the next stable, he came across quite regular peasant horses. They were strong and healthy, grown used to labour and the whip, clever and rather lazy. When they had to, they knew how to keep body and soul together by browsing even on thatch pulled from cottage rafters. They listened to him patiently, carefully snuffling the air.

'And what's in it for us, this dog-freedom?' they asked with brutal frankness.

Rapturously, Rex painted for them wondrous images of the future happiness.

'Nobody gives you even a handful of bald chaff for free.'

'Man says: Plough, my ponies. And when we're done, you'll each get a nice feedbag of oats.'

'You gluttons! You louts! You doubters!' Rex growled, irate and disconcerted.

'Hold on! Nobody rushes about the world except for stupid colts with their tails held high! Man's a real bugger, a tyrant and a murderer. Who don't know that? Whips, pain, hard labour and skimpy troughs. but who's gonna feed us out there in that freedom of yours?'

'All the hayricks are yours! All the clover — yours! All the grain belongs to you!'

'We once thought so too. And it ended poorly. With whips and rods.'

'So, stay with man, then. When everybody else abandons him, he'll have someone to take it out on. He'll give you such oats as you'll break your teeth on!'

They were clever and careful, but they weren't stupid. So they swore to rise up at the signal.

Rex went back to his ruins. He stopped here and there to remind everyone of the hour and the place where they were to meet. But when he came across a huge passel of swine at pasture in the clover belonging to the manor, his first reaction — from long custom — was ire at the pests. But he came to soon enough, calmed down, and began to address them.

They all ran over with the sows at their head and surrounded him with uplifted snouts, gazing at him with their intelligent, grey eyes. Grunting from time to time and shifting their weight from trotter to trotter, they pressed in ever nearer. Rex was almost stifled by the stench. And those snouts, flashing with white tusks, caused him some concern as well.

'What's he want?' a huge old boar interrupted him brutally. 'You're missing some soup-bones to gnaw on, and so you come over to us to start a rebellion? It's so bad for you with man? You stuff your gob so much your belly's like a barrel; you sleep all day long and when you don't you chase after bitches, going your own way wherever you please. What more are you after?'

'The happiness and freedom of all the exploited!' he whimpered grandly.

'And that's the way a dog barks,' huffed the boar resentfully, 'who at the command of man bites, tears, and chases everything and anything! Worse than man himself, he is! He's probably in cahoots with the wolves, and wants to make of us a nice larder! O, we know all about charitable types like that! I had my tail cropped by one of you lot, and two piglets torn apart. O, but I tore up his stomach with these tusks, I did! Now, you'd better watch that paunch of yours. Go state your case to some half-wits, and steer clear of us swine! O, he's a wise one, he is. Yet he don't see that all the truth of the world, its peace and order and reasonable progress depends on pigs! And man is master, because he's the head of it all! He's the one that thinks and labours on our behalf, seeing to it that we've all got something to eat. So that we can exist! You there with that nut of yours can only lead us on to perdition. The world is ordered wisely. Everybody oughta stick to his own proper place and listen to what man commands.'

'You he only eats. But the rest suffer all their lives long in horrible torment.'

'You just shut up or it'll be you I'll make suffer! And not a word about death when sows are present. That's our secret! It's a voluntary sacrifice we offer so as to guarantee the continued existence of our kind. Clear off and give us a wide berth, you stupid dog, you!'

'Sows, shoats, squealers and you, heads of clans!' Rex suddenly howled.

But his pathetic barking was drowned out by mocking chortles.

'Stray mutt! Vagabond, thief!'

'Your freedom is worth all of a gnawed-down bone!'

'The lout! Biting the hand that feeds him!'

'He just wants to chase us from trough and sty and hand us over to the wolves!'

'Stupid! He wants to make war on man!' the enraged mob began to squeal, butting him with their snouts and pressing in on him in ever more threatening fashion. Rex understood that if he opposed them in anything they'd tear him to tatters. So, gaining control of himself, he began to feign sleepiness, letting his head droop, fanning flies away with his tail and, at last, stretching out on the ground at full length.

In the end, they let him be. And because the afternoon sun was really beating down now, the swine all scattered among the furrows and ditches, seeking cool for their fat bellies.

'Far too many pigs in the world,' Rex mused once he extricated himself from their company. 'And how hard it is for them to raise their snouts to the sun,' he concluded with a certain sadness, stealing back to his quarters. He wasn't overly worried at what he'd just gone through, for he was certain that most of them would follow him. For the idea had now penetrated to the masses and begun to spread like wildfire. Suffering from time immemorial had prepared the soil for the sowing of the faith, and for blind obedience to him who had revealed the promised land to them. What is more, to the ravishing idea there was joined that granite-like certainty that life in freedom was an endless summer filled with nothing but eating, reproducing, and rest. Word came to him that quarrels had already erupted concerning who would be grazing on what fields. He listened to these reports with forbearance and a lenient understanding.

'They're already getting nervous. We need to move out as soon as possible,' he reckoned.

From the time of that episode with the swine, two mighty shepherds never left his side for a moment.

Later, they were joined by a whole pack of feral loners and strays. To feed them all, Rex had to lead them on forays into the pinewoods, where he plundered mercilessly. At the same time he evened some old, unforgotten scores, taking vengeance for old injuries, vindictively calling out the whole woodland nation to battle. Of course, no one stood to the challenge. Even the boars wanted no part of the emboldened raiders. The predators ceded them the field, cleverly, circling about them only from afar, and imperceptibly drawing them in ever deeper. Meanwhile, the invaders pillaged the whole wilderness.

Sometimes, the wild barking echoed through the forest for days on end, giving rise to mortal fear and panic. The lawless horde murdered without mercy and without need. The bleating of torn deer and stag resounded from ever different corners of the wilds. Whoever could, hid himself, or escaped to the wildest backwoods. The wilds were petrified in dread. Even the birdsong trembled with fear, while only at night, under the cover of darkness, did the pitiful plaints and keenings begin to seethe. The owls, especially, sent up an ill-omened hooting.

'Death on all hands! Woe! Woe! Woe!'

'Freedom is perishing! The wilds are perishing! The world is perishing! Woe!' sobbed the terrified voices.

And in the impenetrable depths of the woods the wolves howled long, complaining that the dogs, possessed by a frenzy of fighting and an unslaked lust for murder, blood, and glory, were chasing them rabidly, seeking a final showdown.

'Look at them run like hares! Shame to them! Shame and death!' yelped Rex in ceaseless pursuit.

And on they chased with all the strength of their legs, furious, frothing at the mouth, in a near frenzy, into the very depths of the forest, where there were no roads, no paths, not even thick undergrowth; where there was nothing but the primaeval, soaring, thick, black forest, where sunlight never penetrated, where an eternal gloom and a dead silence reigned; where there was neither green grass nor flowers, but the ground was covered with ruddy lichen and whitish crust, and here and there in the darkness there flashed the pus-ringed eyes of ponds.

The dogs slowed their pace now, picking their way with difficulty among the fallen trunks of ancient trees, the levees of tinder and the heaps of crumbled cliff-stone. The greenish dusk gave the surroundings the appearance of being in the depths of the sea; everything in it became like a fleeting mirage. It was dread-inducing, and the dogs skulked along with their tails between their legs, snuffling the air distrustfully and stopping stock-still time and again.

The voices of the wolves vanished in the distance like tatters on the wind. Every now and then the scream of an eagle sounded high above them, or was borne away on the deep rustle of the invisible crowns of the giant trees.

Then, an unpleasant, unknown scent curled into their nostrils.

'Stop! Whose trace is that?' said Rex uneasily, his nostrils flaring in all directions.

The fur along their spines bristled. This or that dog's teeth began to chatter. More than one of them wanted to turn back.

'Forward! If it be an enemy there, death to him!' Rex decided manfully.

So on they went, in close ranks, their snouts low to the ground, their ears pricked.

The pinewoods began to open. There were more boulders; a dawn began to glimmer in the distance and daylight began to grow. At last, something like a great forest meadow was uncovered to their eyes, from which sharp white rocks protruded, like fangs pointing toward the skies. Huge beeches, as if poured of greenish bronze, stretched heavenwards. A stream splashed noisily over stones. Some kind of huge, black birds were perched on the cliffs. The sky was deep and bright and the afternoon sun warmed the earth.

With luxurious delight, the dogs lapped the water and, after rolling about on the grass, they stretched out to rest.

'We'll have a rest and then go back,' Rex decided, though he never ceased snuffling the air, distrustfully.

They all fell asleep except for one of the shepherds who, coming across a worrisome trace, flew off in pursuit of it, rushing from place to place with his nose to the ground. He growled in alarm:

'It's not wolf… I don't understand… Be on your guard! There's an enemy nearby!'

Suddenly, a deep, powerful roar shook the air.

The dogs leapt to their feet as one — ready to fight, or to escape.

Bears were crossing the little river over the stones that poked above its surface. A young boar was in front, pressing two little cubs to his breast, while the sow was bringing up the rear.

Catching sight of such monsters, never before seen by them, the dogs retreated with pitiful howls. They grouped tightly together, sharp teeth chattering, shaking in a fever of terror. Rex scratched at the earth with his claws, trembling himself, eyes fixed on the unknown enemy.

Having crossed the stream, the young male handed the cubs to the mother bear. When she began pushing the cubs with her nose, casting alarmed, backward glances as she followed them into some cliff-fissure covered with brush, the boar, raising himself up to his full height on his hind legs and roaring mightily, began to walk slowly toward the dogs…

He was gigantic — taller than a man, ruddy-coated, with a white patch at his throat. Rows of white teeth flashed in his maw.

The dogs twisted in sudden, agitated whirls. The urge to escape tugged at them, fear incapacitated them, yet anger and a hot-headed passion forced furious yelps from their throats.

In the front, Rex didn't move from where he stood, his entire body trembling with a horrid yearning for battle. He crouched in preparation to lunge, tensing his muscles, arching his back, pooling all of his strength, his head ever lower, his fevered eyes locked on the bear until, in a flash, he launched himself at his chest like a stone. The blow was so unexpected and powerful that the bear was felled like a log. But in a flash he was back on his feet. Rex didn't lunge at him again; he raced around him, attacking and tearing with his teeth whenever the occasion presented itself. Roaring, the bear spun around constantly, unable, however, to lay a paw on the dog.

Then, as if at a sign from their leader, the entire pack threw themselves at the bear. A fierce battle ensued. Every now and again the bear raised himself up on his hind legs; every now and again a dog was flying through the air to fall upon the turf, back broken and ribs crushed, while the rest just tore at the giant with even more ferocity.

Even the wounded continued fighting until they convulsed, at last, in death, so it was quite improbable that the bear would be able to defend himself much longer. In vain did he throw himself with fearsome might and terrifying roars upon the entire pack, crushing spines and dealing death with one swipe of his mighty arm; in vain he hit and squeezed, crushing them beneath his feet and his body, tearing them with his claws.

The dogs wouldn't yield. Like an oak buffeted by a strong wind, the bear swayed this way and that, torn from all sides by the fangs of the frenzied horde. He gave no thought to escape, defending himself with the valour of despair, but he could now feel the teeth sunk deep inside him. His sides were torn, as were his thighs; his ribs broken from falling to the earth again and again, yet he always spun to his feet with the last remnants of his strength, covered in wounds and tattered, the blood pumping out of him, his eyes clouding over in death — but he fought on to the bitter end. Suddenly, in a flash, when the bear had risen to his feet for the last time, Rex threw himself at his throat. Both tumbled to the earth and the rest of the pack piled on. They whirled in a tangled ball of claws, heads, horrible wounds and howling, tumbling over the turf from one side to the other, spurting blood, striking against tree, bush and stone, marking their furious progress with the bodies of the slaughtered and gravely wounded.

The ravens, floating down from cliff and tree, circled ever lower.

At last, the final, raspy roar of the expiring bear burst forth.

Rex tore his bleeding heart out of his breast and devoured it greedily, while his comrades, lapping up the hot gore, satisfied their hunger, at their leisure, upon the still trembling meat.

Rex urged them all to withdraw, worriedly glancing toward the cliff-face from time to time.

Before hastening back, the dogs howled in triumph so that the woods echoed with sobs.

On the battlefield there remained only corpses, the bodies of the expiring, and clouds of ravens, crows, and hawks, who threw themselves upon the substantial spread.

On the dogs raced, as fast as their legs could carry them — despite the exhaustion they felt after the battle — abandoning the weak and the more seriously wounded. They arrived back at their den just as the dawn was about to break.

The numbers of those returning were few. The boldest of them had fallen in battle, or lay dying, scattered through the woods along the path home.

'Too dearly bought, that victory!' Rex whined, sweeping with his eyes the pitiful remnants of his pack, who were barely able to breathe on account of exhaustion and blood loss. He especially rued the demise of the two shepherds, who had fallen in the initial attack.

Gloomily, the dogs dragged themselves to the vaulted chamber, but none of them were able to fall asleep. For some sort of evil-boding uproar was floating in from the forests. The birds sang it to the birds, the soughing trees repeated it to one another, and the breezes carried the lament far and wide, sobbing the groaning, mournful threnody:

'Our lord has been killed! Death to the bandits! Death!'

'That was a powerful king, indeed. A real king!' Rex considered, recalling the bear's terrific might and his roars. A cold shiver shook his frame and, listening to those mournful keenings of the woodland nation, he sensed their deep thirst for revenge.

'It's not likely that anyone should be able to stand toe to toe against the entire world!' he whimpered in fear, as the indignant voices flowed on in ever hotter and ever more violent waves.

The day after the battle broke windy and cloudy. At times, it seemed to Rex as if not just the wind, but the trees themselves were tearing their roots from the soil and drawing near, whistling a wild battle-song, to fall upon him. He felt so tired, unto death, that he collapsed upon his nest and fell asleep. But he was awakened again and again by each louder rush of the windstorm. For amidst its rustling, the drawn-out howls of wolves could be heard, as well as the cackling of crows, and the distant, distant roaring of bears…

'One has been killed. How many remain?' With this thought revolving in his head, he escaped into the fields to find sleep.

Later, after he had rested and calmed down somewhat, he dispatched runners in every direction to remind everyone of the day of gathering in the manor pastures near the woods.

The hour had been set for a Sunday, when the bells would call all the humans to church.

Various fears and uncertainties plagued him. All the more did he await the moment with the utmost impatience.

'To freedom! To the sun! Far, far away!' he mumbled in his sleep as well as during his waking hours.

He spent these last few days of anticipation in a trembling state of arousal. His fever tossed him from place to place. He wandered about the ruins aimlessly. He raced out into the fields, now and again creeping into the thick woods, spending hours snuffling the air and scanning the terrain, wide-eyed, with barely controlled anxiety. What was even worse, the nights brought him no rest. The owls screamed from the trees all night long the ire of the wilds — as if it were calculated to terrorise him, and indeed his heart fainted and his teeth chattered in fear. Then, during the daylight hours, it was the crows hovering above the ruins who ceaselessly cawed misfortune. And something really had to be going on in the deep and gloomy wilderness, for the emissaries he sent out to get a sense of the lie of the land returned with chilling news of some mysterious gatherings of wolves and foxes. Herds of stags were seen from time to time racing about near the ruins. The wild boars too had trampled fresh paths leading to the nearby fields. And up aloft, whole throngs of predatory birds circled high above the ruins without pause, as if on watch. Every now and then, echoes of appalling roars could be heard.

Rex was certain that some grand expedition was being readied against him.

'Just two more suns and two more nights!' he repeated to himself, to keep his spirits up, to keep hope alive… He pictured himself already at the head of innumerable hordes heading east, toward freedom.

The night before the last it was cold and rainy, so that it was difficult to catch a scent even a few steps away. It was then that the wolves sent forth a howl of peace, seeking an understanding.

Rex leapt out on top of the rubble that towered over the débris, and pierced the undergrowth with his eyes, where he caught sight of green flashes and heard heavy paws pounding the turf.

'What are you after?' he growled haughtily.

The wolves emerged, and dragged a portion of deer to his feet, while Gimpy barked, humbly:

'Praise to the victor. And spoils as tribute.'

'What is it you're after?' he growled again, stunned, seeming to smell a trap of some sort.

'We do you homage and bring you tribute,' the foxes barked, setting at his feet throttled partridges, pheasants and young hares.

'What do you want?' he howled, baring his fangs so threateningly that Gimpy fell prostrate from fear, as it were, and crawled near on his belly, whimpering beseechingly.

'Save us, unconquered one. Save the wilds!'

'Your affairs are no concern of mine! Bark on,' he grumbled, but benignly now.

'You! The victor! You who slew the bear, the lord of the wilds! Take up his sceptre therefore, and defend us!'

'What is it that threatens you? Bears, perhaps?' he said, betraying himself with tenderness.

'It's worse. Humans have organised a great hunt, penetrating from the direction of the big water. They're coming on horseback, on wheels, and on foot, and behind them come innumerable hordes of dogs. Death comes with them, too — extinction. They kill with lightning, they exterminate with fire, they trap with nets — and more than all the others it is my clan they torment!' sobbed Gimpy, scratching at the earth with his claws.

'They have no mercy upon mine either,' sobbed a fox, covering his eyes with his brush.

'A hunt? Now? At one time I used to follow hunts, but that was in the winter time, following tracks in the snow.'

'They've fallen upon us now, unexpectedly, and they're murdering everyone. Save us! Save us!'

'We're innocent! Innocent!' the foxes and wolves whimpered together. 'This is human spite. They want our hides, the bandits and thieves, living off our wounds!' they moaned, tearfully.

'O the wolves!' the owl suddenly laughed from his perch atop a bastion. 'Soon they'll be blaming it all on the sheep! And who was it throttled whole herds of colts? And who was it decimated the lambs in the sheepfolds? They've got something to avenge!' he hooted, relentlessly calling to mind all their sins.

'We live by our own laws!' snapped Gimpy with ferocity. 'Who dares deny us that?'

'Repentant wolves to church may creep; Absolved, they're back to stealing sheep!' the owl continued with his mockery. 'And who was it snatched the puppy from in front of the peasants' cottage?' he recalled viciously.

'Come a little closer and say that to our faces, you fleabag eiderdown, you rat-catcher!'

'Shut your beak, smartmouth!' Rex roared at the owl, for his part. 'All you do is spread gossip about the woods all night long. He'll teach me the laws of the wild! Get out of my sight, you feather-duster, you!'

The owl made haste to fly back to the woods. Then Gimpy set forth the matter in detail, painting a horrifying picture of the violence and fury of man.

'They'll dare anything, I know them well. But what can I do to defend you?' Rex asked, falling into deep reflection.

Then they arrived at a solution that was both simple and which stroked his ego.

'Get your kind to abandon them,' Gimpy said. 'When the dogs refuse to aid them, all their might will melt away. What can they do without horses and dogs?'

'They'll still have those lightning-sticks with them. Men are terrible in their might. They are able to saddle the wind and harness the might of the waters to their wagons. I've seen their power! And I hate them — I hate them just as much as you do…!'

'Unvanquished one, at your voice, the entire nation of field, cottage and wild shall arise. Give the command, and all horns, all hooves, fangs, and claws will fall upon the two-legged ones, trampling them underfoot and scattering them. They won't be able to withstand our impetus! We'll exterminate them to the last cub! Save the wilderness. Rescue the world from the plague of man! You'll become immortal — all future generations will hold you in honour. You shall reign in the hearts of all. Arise, say the word, stand at our head, and you will see such a victory as no eye has ever beheld. Lead us against our common enemy. We shall exterminate him! Cursed be his name for all the crimes with which he has polluted the earth,' rasped Gimpy, in the grips of a paroxysm of hatred. 'He's slaughtering everything, on all hands — everyone! He's never satisfied! He fouls the waters, murders the forests, leaving behind him desert places, death, and those loathsome fields! We have nowhere to hunt — we can no longer keep ourselves fed. The best game dies of starvation. And now he's reaching for the wilderness itself with those greedy claws of his — for our final refuge, our dens, where our clans have lived since time immemorial,' he burst out sobbing, his voice stifled by despair and fear of the morrow.

'Nothing awaits us but starvation. The elk have run away for good, no longer able to bathe and multiply here in safety. The deer search out new pastures, the does seek to save themselves by grazing in his fields. The last badgers are extinct, trapped in his irons. Even the bears are no longer safe in their lairs. Lead us, rescue the wilds! We'll fight to the last fang just so that future generations have the whispering green canopy of the wilderness above their heads — so that the dens of man should crumble into dust, and the fields once more grow over with trees. Rescue us!' And all the wolves whimpered, licking his feet and his sides.

'We won't be able to exterminate man,' Rex confessed, with deep conviction. 'You can't make the night shine with the bright light of day. But to take vengeance — that is the right of the wronged! I know the two-legged ones well. Naked things they are — wretched, with neither fang nor claw — and yet they are more terrible than all the rest! They have incomprehensible power in those heads of theirs! We can rise up against man, but conquer him? Improbable, improbable that. And whoever enters his company must, in the end, become his slave. But now I've shattered my fetters and soon, quite soon, all the folk of the fields will be inspired to revolt, and follow me!'

He raised his head proudly, and began to unroll before their mind's eye images of the near future.

They knew all about this, but only now, when he'd finished, did Gimpy whimper:

'We vow to you our faithful obedience — we will follow you!'

Rex looked at them distrustfully. But their eyes expressed such a sincere truth that he believed them.

'And now — help us! I'll lead you there by a roundabout route — I know all the shortcuts. I know where their camp is pitched. We'll attack them at night, when they've unharnessed the horses. You'll fall upon them first with yours, because the horses won't trust us — they have some old prejudices against us. By the moon, we swear our fealty and obedience to you, just save us!'

And the wolves retreated into the thickets again, to give him some time to think it over.

As a matter of fact, Rex didn't believe everything they said, but he decided to come to the rescue of the wilds, and in so doing, to satisfy his thirst for vengeance, too.

'And let mine ready themselves to strike man without fear,' he mused.

Summoning to himself a few dozen of the bravest dogs in the area, he led them off at high noon. The expedition followed Gimpy through the pinewoods along hidden paths known to him alone, the rest of the wolves racing along on their flanks. They disappeared in the deep woods without a trace, because they were proceeding in utmost silence. Only the hawks and ravens flying high overhead betrayed their progress. From time to time they rested, reviving their strength with whatever the wolves and foxes brought them. It was deep twilight before they emerged on the edge of a rocky forest meadow, well-known to Rex, where they sank once more into the thick undergrowth.

The meadow was glowing with the sparkles of campfires; the air above it was thick with smoke and voices of both humans and animals. The evening breezes wafted about the provocative odours of roasting meat. The horses were munching oats from their canvas feed-bags, and the dogs, let off their leads, were circling about the wagons, barking gaily and gnawing the bones tossed them in largesse. The hunters were sprawled about the campfires. Immense haunches of deer were sizzling above the flames, hung upon crossed rods. Glass tinkled and voices were raised in rakish song. Despite their exhaustion, everyone seemed alive with the wild joy of the hunt.

Having penetrated the camp, Rex gave a signal well-known already to the field-folk. The dogs whimpered joyfully and grew silent; the horses, tossing the feed-bags from their muzzles, began pawing the earth impatiently. The whole wilderness fell into a deep hush.

Slowly, inexorably, the moment of battle approached.

And when the humans, having stuffed themselves to satiety and drunk themselves into near stupor, lay down and covered themselves with sheepskins, when the campfires, no longer fed, began to die off in plumes of thick smoke, Rex gave the sharp command:

'Trample and disperse them! Forward! For the wilderness! For our dens! For freedom!'

The wolves sent up their battle-song, so fearful and daring that, enflamed with it, the herd rushed upon the camp ferociously. An incredible tempest of neighing and barking erupted. With wild whinnies, the horses pummelled both men and campfires with their heavy hooves, so that the air swirled with embers. The dogs, vying with the wolves in manliness, encircled the beaters and the hunters and threw themselves upon them with a rabid howl. The trampled campfires were all snuffed.

Torn from sleep, in the darkness, and in panic at the unexpected, terrifying attack, the men rushed about confused, unable to understand what was going on. They raced into the pinewoods screaming at the top of their lungs, or, frantically flailing at their attackers, they sought to escape them by climbing trees and boulders. Only rarely did gunfire resound amid the horrid chaos, for the hunters, scattered by the violent, sudden attack, decimated, couldn't get to their rifles.

And the battle raged ever more wildly, ever more cruelly. Screams of despair tore the heavens. The moans of those rent and torn in pieces alive died away in the deafening uproar of barking, howling, baying and neighing. It was only after the passage of some time that the humans shook off their terror sufficiently so as to set up some sort of resistance. Here and there individuals did battle with entire herds, defending themselves with their bare fists. The wolves attacked with fury, tearing men into rags and dragging them about the battlefield. One hunter, his clothes and face torn, covered with horrible wounds, did battle with an entire pack of wolves, wielding a firebrand. Another screamed appallingly as he was being trampled beneath horses' hooves. Still another leapt upon a stallion, who began to race about furiously, bucking, pummelling him against tree and boulder. There was one gigantic peasant who got hold of a wolf by the hind legs and, swinging him about, trumped him against those attacking him. At last, thicker gunfire began to sound from beechwood and cliff. The muzzle flashes revealed to the eye huge swarms of dogs, wolves, and men tangled together and rolling about over the ground. The frenzied horses made little distinction among those they were trampling.

Rex, with Gimpy at his side, was directing the action, at times leading the attack himself, warning his forces when he caught wind of danger, chastising the skulkers, racing about the field, his lionlike roar resounding through the darkness, firing up the beasts to do battle.

Gimpy, on the other hand, unable for long to restrain his cruel nature, threw himself again and again headfirst into the most ferocious scrums, after which, having temporarily satisfied his endless hunger for slaughter, he would return dripping with blood, and often with a hunk of meat in his maw.

'Put that down!' Rex boomed at him. 'You're not going to eat human flesh!' Rex was fired with an inexpressible horror. Something like regret was tugging at his heart. It's true that he followed the further progress of the battle with the cool and watchful discretion of a true leader, but, under the influence of a sudden revulsion he felt toward the wolves, he began to restrain his own forces more and more, beginning to use them sparingly.

'You want to conquer at the expense of our blood only?' Gimpy growled, very disturbed at this.

'You're fighting for your freedom, your existence, while we're only fighting for our honour. Remember, it is us who are helping you. And if you're not satisfied with that aid, I can pull us out altogether,' he threatened, bearing his fangs.

But Gimpy, driven wild with the aroma of the spilt blood, and the moans of the torn, threw himself once more into the fight.

Rex, on the other hand, drawing off to the side now and then, listened intently to the battle clamour with an ever growing irritation. Those despairing human voices pained him, and gave rise to some torturous self-reproach. In vain did he run from them — they pursued him, never going silent even for a moment. At a certain point he came across a man crawling toward a stream. He was nothing but remnants of meat, tattered clothes and smashed bones, covered with blood and groaning horribly. Rex was suddenly and strangely reminded of his old master, who had once been wounded by wild boars while out on the hunt. Rex had found him just like this, crawling off on all fours to the water. And so, under the influence of an odd uprush of tenderness, Rex rushed over to the wounded man and began licking his face and howling. A few wolves who had been passing came over, wishing to finish off the dying man, but Rex drove them away in fury. He could listen no more to the sounds of human despair — it was too much for him.

Now, gazing upon the vanquished, squirming helplessly in the claws of the wolves like hares, he whimpered mournfully at their shame and defilement. That age-old attachment to man shivered to life once more inside him, along with his slavish fear of man's omnipotence, and that strange solidarity with him in his misfortune. Momentarily, he felt most deeply that they were closest to him, the most dear beings to him — and that he should be fighting at their side and perishing along with them. At the same time, his hatred for the wolves and their disgusting cruelty grew and grew within him.

The battle was now becoming a disorderly, frightful shambles. The cries of those being torn apart alive grew in volume moment by moment. Possessed with a murderous frenzy, the hordes preyed upon the men, who were dropping everywhere from exhaustion and wounds. Howls of triumph resounded over the battlefield, accompanied by the crunching noise of shattered bones and the death-rattle of the slaughtered.

Only a few daredevils, who had miraculously torn themselves from the claws of the animals, made their way to the wagons and, taking up heavy axes, havelocks and pitchforks, were defending themselves like lions, though surrounded by a pack of wolves who were leaping upon them from all sides. The attackers were all the more aroused to ferocity by this unexpected resistance and the flashing of the iron, striking at them without pause. And in addition to that, there was the crack of bullets, which began to strike from the trees with ever greater precision, ever better aim.

Rex, taking advantage of the moment, howled the signal for withdrawal.

Gimpy rushed before him, cutting him off, leaping at his throat, barking with fury:

'Traitor! You're abandoning us! But we're going to fill our stomachs full to the very last shred of man-meat!'

'If you regret leaving those corpses behind, go ahead and eat them up! We have more important matters to attend to than throttling the moribund. When will you understand, you sheep's-brain you, that they're still able to defend themselves! You hear those booms? A fair number escaped to the woods, and they're going to bring up aid. And what are those dying wretches worth? It's high time to withdraw.'

'Fangs and claws forward! Kill! Tear them apart! Kill!' Gimpy howled ferociously, and, paying no mind to Rex's warnings, he threw himself at the wagons along with the others.

'They'll skin you before the night is out, you idiot!' Rex growled, not without pity, before calling to his forces to break off battle and retreat. But it was quite a while before his commands were heard, before the dogs withdrew from the fighting, and — especially — before the scattered horses were gathered together and brought in.

Meanwhile, an unearthly glow began to swell in the depths of the pinewoods. It was as if the sun were rising, but — and this was the strange thing — it seemed to be rising in all four corners of the world at once. A bloody dawn began to seep near from all directions, and, exploding from the earth, it stretched up to the very tops of the trees in flaming tongues. The sky above was black, without stars, overcast; the trees stood still, without moving, while some sort of quavering, deep rushing as of wind boomed ever louder. Rex, catching scent of the biting odour of smoke, went stock still, petrified with fear.

'Follow me! As quick as you can! This way!' he howled, when, having overcome his mortal terror, he threw himself instinctively towards the side that was still darkest. The dogs raced behind him, but the horses, catching sight of the flames, returned to the field with a squeal, trampling down everyone and everything in their path.

The dawn grew and broadened, rose and neared at a furious pace. Those still fighting could now be seen as if through a bloody mist. The nearest trees stood out blacker and loftier, and now the tops of the cliffs began to be visible in the ruddy glow.

Suddenly, all the birds cried out. A wind arose, and the fire seemed to leap at the throat of the pinewoods. Thousands of lightning bolts flashed over the black, gigantic trunks, leaping from branch to branch, exploding upwards, tearing at the darkness with bloody fangs.

A fiery ring encircled the meadow with its windblown manes. A burning brightness! The pinewoods were aflame, suddenly, with innumerable torches. A sea of flames, smoke and crashes erupted. The skies were reddened with the glow. The triumphant song of fire howled throughout the open spaces. The scorched giants began to topple and crash, sending up fountains of bloody sparks. Amid this hurricane, the despairing whimpers of the perishing animals and humans were barely audible.

4

The night was late, warm, under starry skies; roosters were crowing in the distance. Peace filled the broad spaces, and the fields and forest deeply respired the quiet. The drapes of the mist stretched out over the earth in an unbroken, cool sea of white. Not a single bird was singing, nor could the rustle of any predator heading out on his hunt be heard. Even the pinewoods were sunk in an undisturbed silence. The whole world had fallen into a deep, healing sleep, un-ruffled even by the falling dew.

Only those in the ruins at the edge of the wood were keeping watch.

Rex was sitting atop the gigantic rubble of the walls. Beside him, Dummy drowsed, answering Rex from time to time in short mumbles. They understood one another perfectly.

'The last night!' Rex growled, piercing the darkness with his eyes as if he could see tomorrow.

'Blackie barked about it to me. But I was very sick, and took little notice of anything.'

'You'll come with us,' he decided, firmly. 'You'll be of use.'

'I belong with people! But I'm not stupid. You're really going? I still can't believe it.'

Rex remained sunk in deep meditation on the coming dawn, which was almost at hand. He shivered in joyful fretting and a quiet happiness. He couldn't really imagine what it would be like. He rushed forward in thought and wandered, frightened, among impenetrable wildernesses and incomprehensible phantoms. But he was already trotting down the paths of yearning, which made his heart swell.

'We're setting out! To the east, to the sun, to freedom!' he blurted out, and, scrambling up to the very top, snuffled the air long, on all sides.

'There's wolves about somewhere, not too far away.'

'I thought they'd all been burnt to a crisp.'

'Gimpy's a clever one. He led however many remained of them out by the river. A lot of them perished, but the rest — even if their fur was singed — made it through the flames. All the humans died.'

'That's not true! I saw some of the survivors with my own eyes! They were in the courtyard, telling us all about it, until everyone burst into tears. The wolves were blamed for everything. They said that they're going to arrange such a hunt, with the help of the army, that there won't even be enough wolf left to use for seed. Even in the manor they're riled, because a few of the hands, along with the foreman, didn't make it back.'

'Don't worry about our pelts,' Gimpy whimpered, stretching out alongside them. 'We'll throttle them to the last before that happens. Better for them if they don't try to mess with us.'

'Go and bark that to their faces!' Dummy spluttered defensively.

'Their meat is foul. It turns our stomachs,' he barked, butting Dummy with his snout in disdain. 'And what's this human puppy doing here?' Gimpy snarled, baring his fangs.

'He's under our protection. Not a hair will fall from his head,' Rex warned him.

'Just let him try!' Dummy threatened, pulling out a long, flashing knife.

Gimpy knocked the weapon from his hand. Pinning it to the ground beneath a paw, he growled sarcastically:

'Nip me now, puppy!'

And Dummy, quickly grabbing hold of Gimpy's tongue, right at the root, mumbled:

'Bite me, you oily fritter! And if you're not well done yet, I'll light you another fire!'

Rex made peace between them, and soon they were lying side by side again, as if nothing had happened.

'We have no homeland any more,' the wolf moaned, manipulating his tongue with difficulty. 'Unfortunate exiles! We accept your laws, and will serve you faithfully. We'll go where you command us to go.'

'They might guard the cattle along the way,' the boy noted, despite himself.

'The wolf takes even the branded,' Rex growled.

'And you?' Gimpy shot back, 'You don't eat grass!'

'There'll be meat enough for everyone,' Dummy concluded, cleverly. 'Few they'll be, who'll fall by the wayside?'

The wolf licked Dummy in gratitude, before contentedly retreating to the thickets to sleep.

The night moved on inexorably. The stars began to pale, and the skies darkened toward dawn.

'What if the lady of the manor readmitted you to favour?'

The question was so stunning and fell so unexpectedly, that Rex shivered. A few moments passed before he could growl an answer in stifled tones:

'Too late! Have they given any thought to me at all? No, I'm done with humans forever. You can't bring the dead back to life. I've even cursed the memory of the old life. I wouldn't be able to live in captivity again, chasing after the grace of men and bearing their insults in peace. And hunger, and mistreatment. The whole nation of field and cottage is waiting on me. All their injuries demand that I avenge them; all their misfortune, that I transform it into happiness. I am their leader. They have entrusted themselves and their future generations unto me. And I shall lead them forth from their captivity, that I shall. It's too late,' he groaned, and plopping his head down upon the ground, was gripped with a sobbing-like howl.

'Man is evil, devious, disloyal. He is unable to live without lying, killing, and lording it over others. Let them try to live alone — because we can get along without them for sure. It's a long road that stretches out before us, but at the end lies freedom!'

'As long as you don't all drop dead from starvation on the way,' spluttered Dummy with disdain.

'Fields and ricks are in short supply? And there's wild game enough. The table is spread abundantly.'

'That's true,' said Dummy, scratching his mop of hair. 'But when the cold comes round? The snow and the rain…?'

'It's always green there; the warm sun is always shining. The cranes know that land of bliss. They told me all about it and promised to show me the way. They're going to catch us up later.'

'If it's such a paradise, then why do they bother coming here?'

'Who knows where the wind blows from? … Do they talk about me in the manor?'

'When word got around that you'd torn that bear apart, the mistress herself chastised the housekeeper for keeping you on starvation rations and forcing you off. She felt very sorry about that.'

Rex choked back a sob and fell deep into thought.

Dummy slid into the vaulted chamber and got a fire started. He piled a nice blaze, at which he roasted some potatoes he'd brought with him. He shared them with the dogs, and in exchange one of them dragged over to him a fat goose taken from the foxes, which cheered Dummy quite a bit.

'O, there'll be a feast,' he purred. After dressing the goose, he patted it over with clay and buried it deep in the glowing embers. He baked it like that until the clay was thoroughly fired, after which he extracted the aromatic, nicely broiled goose. All the feathers remained in the clay.

'Whoever got a prize like this once every Sunday wouldn't be chasing about the world after fortune!' Blackie confessed, digging into his portion greedily.

'It'd be more than enough for the Blackies of the world,' Rex growled, and turning his nose away from the irritating aromas, he fell once more to musing.

Dummy fell asleep at his side. What he'd said about the manor stirred Rex more painfully than he'd admit, even to himself. He swallowed it like a barbed morsel that he couldn't cough back up, even though it tore at his innards. That past, so recent and yet already so distant that he could barely make out its contours, forced some soft howls of longing fromhis bosom. But he didn't want to forget about the injuries of the suffering; on the contrary, he reminded himself of them, plaiting with determination bloody litanies of complaint and lament, while at the same time a fearsome respect for man swelled inside him. In moments of reflection like this, man grew before him in limitless might. The farther he drew away from him, the more he become simply incomprehensible, like the sun, like the mountains, the cold, and the heavens themselves.

'What are we compared to them? What? A herd chivvied on by insatiable hunger, a numberless colony of ants scrabbling along the dirt beneath their feet.'

He shivered, seeming to stand before an abyss that had suddenly yawned at his feet, from which the cold breath of extinction wafted near.

'None of us will be able to overleap it! Nobody!' The sadness of a creature injured to the death; the sadness of a frog opening his eyes to see an eagle flying near, gripped tight Rex's heart with the ice of despair. Long, long he searched out the reason for this cruel inequality. He protested against it with the voice of the whole of injured nature, the voice of the world entire. Until, at last, it seemed that he'd found the only manner of filling in that chasm.

'I've got it! I've got it!' he said, hammering the truth he'd discovered deep into his mind. 'They are not tormented by the daily struggle for existence, because thousands upon thousands of our generations labour on their behalf. The waters work for them, the air, the sun, the earth, the entire world does their bidding. This is the cornerstone of their power. But take away their slaves and their greatness is no more. Then shall they become even more wretched and helpless than us! Then perfect equality will reign!' he growled triumphantly.

'Until you take away man's reason, you won't be taking anything away from him at all. He'll always make do!' Dummy spluttered haughtily before falling back asleep.

In an instant, all the rainbows disappeared, all the castles in the clouds that Rex had been constructing with so much labour fell into heaps of rubble. Once again he felt himself a wretched, eternally wronged creature, writhing futilely in the chains of the power of man.

'To escape. As quickly and as far away as possible!' he whimpered through his teeth, chattering in pain. And then, plunging his gaze into the depths of the heavens, among the shimmering of the countless stars, he so forgot about everything that he didn't even notice the wolf who had plopped himself down at his side. And thus, in silence, they awaited the coming dawn.

At first light, when the darkness to the east began to blear and then pale somewhat, Gimpy sniffed the air and gave a quiet bark:

'They've set out! Still far off…'

Singularly and in whole murders, the crows began to leave the branches and soar, in a high, silent flight, in the direction of the dawn.

Imperceptibly, the night grew gloomy. The fields seemed to sink away, while on the other hand the trees stood out ever more distinctly, revealing against the paling sky their crowns, which looked like tangled masses of smoke.

Greenish bays of light began to smudge up from beneath the darkness, like ponds of stagnant water sprinkled with ash, and slowly began to glow with a cold shine. The sun then broke the horizon.

'The sheep are coming! And horses! I smell a lot, a lot of them!' the wolf howled, wagging his tail.

'Sounds like wagons rolling over dry clods,' confirmed Dummy, awakening.

Indeed, shortly hoofbeats deadened by the distance and thick with the dew began to be heard, and a little below that, when the dawn had completely lit up the entire eastern portion of the sky, against the background of the daybreak, low clouds — it seemed — were roiling just above the earth, growling with the thunder of drawn-out, far-distant roars.

Rex tensed himself to lunge. Trembling with impatience, he bored into the misty, far-off spaces with his burning eyes until he caught sight of the shapelessly rambling masses. At the sight, he collapsed to the earth, exhausted and overcome with unspeakable happiness. Resting his fevered head upon his paws, he could hardly breathe, so moved was he.

Gimpy turned and turned in circles of frenzy. He sent his mates off to take a look and report back, and again and again he howled in joy.

'Stop your singing, your horse of a nightingale!' chided Dummy, 'or you'll spook them all yet!'

Then, lighting a fire under the windbreak of the ruins, he began to bake potatoes and some sort of birds that Blackie, his faithful friend, brought him. He whistled while he was at it, imitating the songs of all the birds he knew.

In the bloody glow of the dawn, the roiling black masses, rumbling near from all sides, grew more and more distinct. It was as if gigantic waters somewhere had overspilled their banks, flooding the earth with wild roaring. The cacophony grew ever closer and more threatening, like the quarrelling chaos of waves tearing through dams. The resounding hubbub of roars, whinnies, and bleatings grew and grew; the thunder of the hooves was mightier by the moment. Rex could already make out thousands of horned heads, bobbing, as if fording watery depths. The air began to quiver with their hot breath, which blew near like burning breezes. It seemed as if a horrible storm were nearing, ceaselessly thundering, and shooting out lightning bolts again and again. The earth quaked, trees shook, and all the birds exploded in a shriek of terror when the countless herds fell upon the pasturelands at the wood's edge, thundering with one gigantic voice.

At the same time, the sun arose from the abyss, red and spreading its rays about the world.

In the mists hanging low over the earth, suffused now with the sunny conflagration, the innumerable herds shuffled on with ever greater grumbling, herd after herd, with ceaseless neighing, bellowing, and the barking of the dogs, who strove to preserve some sort of order. Every now and then, a thunderous uproar of voices burst forth; every now and then the roiling masses, like the splattering foam of a wild sea, scattered about the pasturelands at the edge of the woods. And before the sun had fully sopped up the darknesses hidden in the dales, thousands upon thousands more had arrived. As far as the eye could see, there was no grass, grain or bush visible — just an undulating mass of horns, polls, manes and tails. Following the path of the herds, high aloft, vast flocks of all sorts of birds were flying near. They were like heavy, leaden clouds that now and then blocked out the sunlight; at other times they seemed like black, foaming rivers rushing through the still pale fields of the sky, or smudges of wispy smoke that had neither beginning nor end. Then, in ever lower eddies, they wheeled down with wild, piercing cries. They fell upon field and wood with a deep, dull roar, like gloomy clouds of hail, until the trees began to sway violently beneath the frightening avian storm. Even the wildest backwoods felt their hackles rise — the whole nation of the wilderness, dazed by the falling hurricane, crept to ground with a moan of terror. For it seemed as if the whole world, knocked off its bases, was about to collapse with a great crash.

Only Rex sat on, immobile upon the rubble of the walls, gazing ceaselessly upon the chaos swirling all around. He was afire, in the grip of shivers of ecstasy, though as firm as a cliff amidst whirlpools and clashing waves. Whole quivers of feverish glances were directed his way, like a downpour of lightning bolts that pierced through and through. Simoons of hot breaths and the emanations of all emotions, all desires, gathered in his heart, and he accepted them all, sensing the power, the pride and certainty, that swelled within him. And the roars, the pulsing of the feet, the flapping of the wings and the desperate writhing of the pinewoods descended upon him like a golden nimbus of might.

Everyone had come, after all, in the end. Even the dying had dragged themselves there with their last ounces of strength. All that was tears, suffering, and injury gathered now before him, gazing into his eyes with love, awaiting his command, believing in him with limitless trust.

The chains had been tugged and tugged at until they burst; the ancient foe was defeated. The slaves had overcome their tyrants and now, all of their hearts, all of their souls, were trembling with one holy cry: Freedom! Freedom! Freedom!

Rex sensed it all, slowly submerging himself in deep reflections on the strange twists and turns of fate.

'What can man do now? Where is his power, his greatness? What is he now, in the face of this gigantic host? A handful of dust to be trampled beneath these hooves and then forgotten. And the animals, they shall forget that he ever existed anywhere, at any time. Just as one forgets about hunger when one's stomach is full; about snow in the heat of summer. He shall be left alone, naked and defenceless, like a puppy torn from the teat and thrown into the ditch. He won't even find a dog to lick him in pity. Man will become fodder for crows and ravens. Sentenced to starvation and measureless, unending travail,' Rex brooded vindictively. 'Let him rule now! Our roads will never cross again!'

But suddenly, as he so brooded, he was overshadowed with care — something like a sense of responsibility began to seethe in his conscience. It was even a sort of dread that flickered like a slender shadow above his soul, radiant with happiness. He scanned those innumerable masses who had shrugged off their ancient burdens at the call of his will — abandoning a difficult existence, certainly, but also one in which support could be relied upon!

'Will this crowd of innumerable liberated slaves be able to make do in freedom? A hurricane is able to tear up oak trees by the roots and toss them about over the face of the earth, but can it plant them so that they should grow again, and cover themselves once more with green?' Thoughts like this revolved in Rex's mind.

At that very moment Gimpy shifted in closer to him and whimpered softly:

'Master, even I, who threw myself against men, am trembling now!'

With astonishment, Rex looked at his eyes, flashing with frenzied fear.

'Too much of that meat on the hoof! Just let something spook them, and they'll trample us like worms!' he said, his voice catching in terror. 'My ribs are splitting already from their screeches and roars. And the stench is such I've lost my sense of smell. O, those rank mobs! They'll stifle the world entire in their manure! It's degrading even to lord it over such cattle. O, unvanquished one, take command over my clan. We vow to you our fidelity and obedience. My daughters will raise up generations of your seed. Abandon these cattle and we'll go off together in search of a new fatherland. What have you in common with them? You who slew even a bear! You, who have acquired the wisdom of man! Does your great clan derive from snouts and hooves? Do you plan on filling your stomach on grass like them, and lapping rainwater from puddles? You, the supreme fangs of the wild, can you intend to exist among a herd of rebellious slaves? With carrion for all? Truly your ancestors, who faced down elk and boar in mortal combat, will shed bitter tears over the shame of their descendant. We've still time to withdraw. I know all the hidden trails — we'll steal away unseen, and leave these herds to their fate, while we race off into the wide world, wherever our legs will carry us, led by the scent of our prey, led by our free will! We shall find new pinewoods, greater ones, where there will be food enough, where man is yet unheard of. What more do you need, master?'

'The happiness of all. Can't you comprehend that, you unsated lapper of blood?!' he growled haughtily.

'What I comprehend,' the wolf groaned in despair, 'is that we are lost. I'm sorry, master — this does not come easily. But we must part ways. We must tread the paths of our ancient fathers! We cannot serve insanity…'

'So, go!' Rex growled angrily. 'Abandon me! But remember — the wilderness will not shield you from my vengeance. You attached yourself to me, voluntarily, and now you slink away in fear! Perjured betrayer! Though you conceal yourself in a fox's den, we shall hunt you down, and the crows will carry off your tatters! Make your choice! You will be of service to me!' he thundered imperiously.

'Mercy, lord! We will be obedient unto you!' Gimpy howled, humbly licking Rex's paws.

'You'll be the rear-guard, goading on the stragglers with your howls.'

'As you wish, master. But — what falls by the wayside may be ours?' he asked, licking his chaps with his long tongue.

'All you think of is stuffing your belly. Your whole life is eating.'

'And what is it for you? And for that cattle? And for man himself?'

At a loss for an answer, Rex automatically leapt into the ruins and went up to Dummy, to have some baked potatoes and whatever leftover bones were there. After feeding him, the boy got set to leave.

'And where are you off to?'

'Home. You're about to lead your kind into the wide world, and I'm going back to mine,' he mumbled provocatively.

'But you'll be of great help to me. Stay. You know how to make fire, and you have a knife. Stay,' Rex begged him, in a heartfelt way.

'You want to lord it over cattle, then have at it. I'll only say that your reign will be a short one. People'll get tired of your antics soon enough. Look how they trampled flat the fields. I can see them running up with rods right now. A lot of blood'll be shed here — a lot of bones broken. You're stupid if you imagine that people are going to just wave their hand at the loss of their chattel. You were smarter back at the manor. So the beasts have rebelled and now they think that they'll turn the world upside down. Everybody knows how to eat,' he said, with another glance at the herds, whose bellies were filled with grain, 'but not everyone knows how to sow!'

Angry, he got up and made for the way out of the ruins.

'Stop! Or I'll have the wolves tear you apart, and carry your carcass back to the manor in pieces.'

Dummy stopped, horror-struck, upon perceiving the terrible anger in the dog's eyes.

'Let me go. Was I ever against you?' And tears sprang to his eyes from the terror.

'I said my piece. Someday, when we've arrived at our destined place, I'll let you go,' Rex promised graciously.

'I'll die of hunger with you here. I'm not gonna eat grass with cattle!' he mumbled in contempt.

'You won't lack for anything. The dogs'll take such good care of you, you'll even fatten up.'

'Sure! On raw meat and fresh gore! Look — I won't get far at all on foot anyway.'

'You'll ride the stallion from the manor! But now — get out of my sight!'

The command rang in such a severe tone that Dummy, not daring to say anything in reply, sought out a shady space for himself at the wall and tried to go to sleep. But the danger of the situation in which he found himself wouldn't even let him close his eyes. Sobbing yearningly, wiping his nose on his sleeve, he began to concentrate on clever means of finding a way to freedom. He based his hopes of escaping on his understanding of the speech of all creatures. He gazed out onto the fields, searching for the best pathway out — and grew petrified at the sight of the bellowing herds, which covered the earth, and which were continually augmented by ever new arrivals.

The sun reached mid-sky. There was no breeze; the shadows shrank, and the pale, burning sky breathed forth such a seething heat that the herds, having consumed what remained of the trampled grasses and grain, lay down to rest.

'When are we leaving?' he said on a sudden, turning to Rex, who was sitting in his accustomed place.

'When the heat lessens — near evening. When the church bells ring.'

Dummy retreated to the edge of the meadow beneath the great oaks, the heavy branches of which hung low over the earth.

'I'll wait it out in the trees,' he thought cleverly. 'They won't find me. They can kiss me you-know-where in farewell! Let the wolves or the dogs haul me down!' he mocked, looking around for the tallest tree. But suddenly, he was gripped by a paralysing fear. On all the branches there drowsed great eagles, hawks, hobbies, and flights of the most varied birds. Wherever he looked he saw the same thing. And on the ground, wolves, dogs and foxes were stretched out, resting in the shade of the trees. Every being was asleep, but alert all the same, as if with one eye open. They were aware of everything that was happening around them, and were ready to spring at a moment's notice, to the attack, or to escape.

Calming down, the boy began to ape the various voices of the birds. From the muddy wetlands nearby, some wild geese called back to him in answer; crows cawed cautiously in reply; even a wakened hawk squealed back comprehendingly. But then the owl, catching on to the trick, and angry that his sleep had been disturbed, hooted threateningly from some hollow tree:

'Gimpy — get rid of that human filth, or he'll lead all the wilds astray!'

The wolf sidled up silently, but the boy, sensing the hot breath on his nape, spun around violently and flicked alive a flame before his eyes.

'Come a little closer, my crippled friend! Closer! I'll paint your mug with fire so that your bitch will find you all the more comely!' he mocked, and setting afire a bunch of dry leaves, threw them at the wolf.

'You whelp of hell!' coughed Gimpy, hopping away from the fire and the smoke.

'And you — I'll smoke you all out like bees!' he thundered at the birds, tossing some wet spruce boughs on the fire. The choking, bitter smoke overwhelmed the oaks and lifted its black mane toward the skies.

The spooked birds fluttered off to some trees farther away, and the owl, fretting and hopping in his hollow in panic, hooted mournfully:

'Damned human puppy! I'm choking!'

'You still wanna sic wolves on me, you blind old fool?' he cursed at the owl angrily. Then, under the cover of the smoke, he climbed up the tree, where he made himself as comfortable as possible among the branches.

'Ha! I'd parade around on the stallion like a lord!' he smiled sweetly, and then began to drowse.

5

Time sifted away like fiery grains of sand. The whole earth was consumed in the conflagration of the afternoon. The swelter made it hard to breathe, and soaked one's skin with sweat. The burning breaths of air sopped up the last drops of moisture. The earth, burnt to a crust, gasped with thirst. Not a single leaf stirred, not a single voice resounded. The sky was suspended in a burnt-through yellowish film. Bluish, barely visible tongues of flame played above the fields. The air was nothing but a dry, voracious fire. A seething silence lay with unbearable weight on all and sundry. Everything seemed to melt and flow away in shimmering waves without end. The burning mirages consumed all colours. All might was shattered, as if beneath hammer blows. Even the soul fainted helplessly away. Only the sun, at the zenith of its power, wrapped in the hurricanes of its own incredible heat, rolled inexorably along its destined path.

As if congealed in fiery lava, Rex sat on high, at the summit of his crumbling bastion, which towered haughtily above the pinewoods. There the eagles rested in their beetling heights, there the owls nested.

Half the world flickered before his eyes. As far as the eye could see, the earth stretched on, as if embroidered with the whole pride of the fertile summer, advancing, rising by degrees to the east unto the whitened edges of the snow-capped mountains, stitched together by numerous rivers flashing with their glaze of molten silver. He looked upon green overspills of forest, the long tongues of lakes bent into the shape of palm fronds, their shores bedecked with paths of yellow sand, golden fields of grain upon which ricks were raised, white villages, the windows of which flashed amongst the orchards, cemeteries, where grave-crosses lifted their arms heavenward in prayer, manors spreading amidst their broad parklands, churches shooting aloft their slender spires enwreathed with green, bald, rocky hills haphazardly tossed about the landscape, towns similar to smashed mole-warrens, and here and there factories with their red chimneys stretching aloft, looking like cranes on guard. Beneath the high, pale heavens in the shimmering air of the afternoon hours, this whole, bright world trapped in the golden sheen seemed dead to his eyes, motionless, soundless, almost colourless, like a faded and dusty tapestry.

The sun was already suspended between north and west when the church bells rang out for vespers.

Slowly the bronze resounded with a celebratory, heaven-ascending hymn that arose as if from the hearts and longings of all creation. They sang sublimely, solemnly, and their prayers of praise soared ever higher, past the sun and the aether, until they reached the very footstool of the Pre-eternal One!

And simultaneously, as if in responsorial, there arose from field and wood and lowland, as if from the bowels of the earth, an explosion, fearsome in its power, of bellowing from all the animals. It shook the very trees so that torn-away leaves fell in showers, while the birds swept upwards, of a sudden, in gigantic flocks.

Hardly had these bellows died away than the wolves began their long, drawn-out, sob-like howling.

'To the east! To the east! To the east!'

The herds began their trek toward the distant mountain summits, which grew lividly blue on the eastern horizon. They pushed on in silence, straight ahead, through cultivated fields and uncleared wilds, straight through village and town and pinewood, crossing river and meadow and marsh. It was as if some invisible volcano had spewed forth a gigantic river of boiling lava, which rolled on with a gloomy thunder that didn't cease its rumbling for a second — for as it passed through, nothing was left behind in its wake but rocks, the skeletons of trees, and the naked, trampled steppe. Nothing, but death.

Every now and then — for reasons none too clear — there burst forth from the nomadic herds something like a song of unrelieved longing and power so fearsome, that houses crumbled from its tones, crushed trees were toppled, as were crossroad shrines.

The earth reverberated for many miles around from the heavy tramping. It was as if all the powers of the earth had joined together into a might such as the world had never before seen. Rex rode at the front, sitting on the back of a gigantic stallion, as black as night. Behind him sat Dummy, joyfully drumming the sides of the horse with his bare heels. Behind them, in an immeasurable horde, came mares, colts and geldings, all surrounded by stallions. The cows proceeded under the direction of the bulls; the gloomy oxen shuffled along, and under their protection came innumerable flocks of sheep with rams to both sides. Bringing up the rear crowded pigs with old sows at their head.

The dogs were everywhere that order and obedience needed to be enforced.

And finally, to the very rear, came the wolves, urging along all the stragglers with their teeth and howls.

All these were followed from afar by the most varied groups of marauders, amongst which ruddy cohorts of foxes, martens and weasels threaded.

On they walked, indefatigably, until the dark night arrived and they fell down to rest, wherever the moment found them. So exhausted and elated were they that they felt neither hunger nor thirst.

At dawn they devoured everything to be found on the fields, including the ricks, and everything in the grain bins. They drank the rivers down to mud. And then they moved on. Their pace was significantly slower, but still they pushed east, unconquerably onward, toward freedom, with the same stubbornness bordering on madness.

And thus day passed after day in difficulties and the indescribable travail of the sweltering heat.

In vain did church bells peal the alarm; in vain did people seek to hold back the tempest that was ravaging the earth. In vain did they block roads, trench fields, flood vales, setting forests aflame and piling earthworks bristling with palisades — the phalanxes rolled on with the same determined calmness, heeding neither death nor wounds inflicted by overcoming the obstacles. The only thing that grew was their fury at their former tyrants. Memories of old injuries were awakened; this, and the sense of their new freedom, made them lurch ever onward, with a bellow of anger, filling the valleys with the corpses of their dead, extinguishing fire with their own blood, paving the roads they trod with their own bones. On they flowed like a gigantic, unstoppable wave.

In despair, the people came out against them with weaponry, in an attempt to shatter this horrid tide with carbine and cannon, anything to make it halt. A war without quarter ensued. The cannon roared all through the day, tearing long deep furrows in the herds. Salvos from rifles fell upon them in thick, death-dealing hailstorms. Smoke hid earth and sun. The moans of the dying beat against the heavens. Chaos ensued. Thick smoke, the ceaseless lightning-bolts of the projectiles, thundering like storm clouds, the piercing groans and roars of those lost in the confusion, were all so terrifying that the animals began to waver, withdraw, and get into tangles, trampling one another. The earth was carpeted more and more thickly with corpses; the cannon-fire became ever more precise, and a cohort of some kind of giants was wreaking havoc with awful battle-axes.

It was then that Rex, on his black stallion, began to race over the battlefield like the wind, howling a wild song, the burden of which was Victory or Death! His words were answered by a stunning roar of zeal and hatred. Moments later, the phalanxes coalesced into a tight-packed wall and, deaf, blind, and furious — they struck!

What remained of their enemies swiftly turned and ran in disorder and panic, hiding in the trees, in the mountains, or locked up in defensive cities. All of humanity was overcome with hopeless despair.

The victorious herds, exhausted by terror and the anxieties of battle, laid themselves down on the battlefields, indifferent to the painful snorting and screams of the dying. Here and there, some loose gangs of bulls, sows, wolves and dogs tore apart the men they came across, preying upon them with cruel ferocity. For many miles in all directions, as far as the eye could see, all that met the eye were horned polls, snouts, manes and wagging tails; while through their midst stretched equally immense battlements and dykes of the dead, the perishing, and the wounded. It was a horrible shambles. The air was suffused with the stench of blood, now clotting, now flowing into rivers, ponds and lakes. The torn, bloody tatters of animal remains were strewn about everywhere, trampled into the bloody mire. Toppled, still heated cannon lay here and there like dead sharks, ringed by the torn corpses of men. From time to time, amongst these piles and valleys, thickets and ditches, grasses and ruined homesteads, the frenzied shell of an animal or man would start up, to howl with the horrid voice of torment — the voice of death.

Dummy felt something tug at his heart. But he felt shame at it, and just mumbled:

'Way too much carrion. The sun heats up, the whole world'll stink.'

'The gravediggers are on the way,' Rex said, pointing an ear toward the sky.

'That a hailstorm coming? When it starts to pour from those clouds… Jesus!' Dummy shivered in fear.

'Just listen to those hail clouds!' responded Rex, pricking his ears and tilting his head.

And indeed, from beneath the sun, from on high, that black cloud began to swoop with a whistling roar, flowing down from like a windstorm growing moment by moment. Shortly, it became ever more clear that this was a terrifying screeching of birds they heard. The cloud of birds of prey wheeled above the herds, blotting out the sun with their beating wings and whirling like leaves spun by a hurricane. The cloud began to split and light poured through the cracks, revealing wind-tossed streams of eagles, vultures, ravens, crows and hawks. A moment later the entire battle-field was covered with a tangled feathery roof, thundering with enraged screeches. There was a ceaseless beating of innumerable wings, and innumerable talons and predatory beaks began to hammer everywhere, and yank, and tear, and devour.

Horror seized the herds and terrified bellows began to rise above the whooshing of the wings and the sinister choruses of caws. The sheep especially bleated an inconsolable plaint, drawing thickly together in tightly-knotted groups. A universal panic was in the offing, which might erupt at any moment, as those never-sated beaks plunged blindly, drawing no distinction between living and dead in the tumult, so that more than one living back was bathed in blood and more than one snout had to fight off rapacious talons.

With no little effort, the wolves spooked away the attackers — for a moment, and Rex, taking advantage of this, led the turbulent herds a few miles farther away, to an area as yet untrampled, full of food, rich villages, green meadows and silver streams, at the foothills of the mountains which, though still distant, were already lifting their snow-capped summits more mightily into the blue sky.

'We'll wait here for the cranes. They promised to guide us through the mountains and farther on, eastward.'

'They'll be here any day now. The time for migration is coming,' Dummy mumbled. Then, taking possession of an abandoned house, he built a huge fire and cooked some food for himself, Rex, and his ever-faithful friend Blackie, who stretched himself out on a bed beneath a gigantic eiderdown.

'Well, who's on top now?' Rex growled, stretching himself out, like in the old times, in front of the hearth. 'We can handle people!' he boasted, warming his sides.

'Any old cow is mightier than a man, but they shredded your ranks something fearsome!'

'Let's not reckon up those who fell for freedom's sake!' he barked back haughtily.

'Our destiny is to be victorious, or to perish!' Gimpy howled, appearing at the threshold.

'You've got as fat as a pig on those battles,' said Dummy, lightly kicking the wolf in his round tummy.

'Every government is nourished by the governed,' he barked, licking clean his wet maw.

'Everyone has a right to happiness,' yapped Blackie, poking his nose out from beneath the eiderdown. 'Everyone is equal!' he said, casting a challenging glance about the room.

'You're saying a sheep is my equal?' Gimpy growled. 'Just let one of them come by here and try and eat me, and I'll show you equality. It was some learned jackass that started braying like that about equality, and then other donkeys believed in those fairy stories — like that one about happiness. Your happiness used to be when they'd toss you some offal from the kitchen. A horse's happiness was a bunch of clover or a trough full of oats, while even a whole crowd of colts couldn't satisfy me. Where do you see equality here, you booby? Your master taught you to bark, and so you do. You don't understand that they live according to their laws too; that the only thing that matters to them, too, is life.'

'Whoever is born must die,' Rex growled in disdain. 'The rest is just the sound of the rushing wind.' And he took himself to the bowl of meat and potatoes that Dummy had set before him.

'Stinks too much of man in here,' said Gimpy, giving himself a shake and going back outside.

'Arrogant,' mumbled the boy, eating from the pot. 'All he believes in are his fangs and his claws.'

Blackie humbly waited for leftovers, and when they had all eaten, they were overcome with a deep slumber.

The night fell, but they didn't sleep long, for soon they were startled awake by bellows and screeches of terror.

Rex leapt to his feet. In front of the animals, the entire sky was blood red with an inferno of flame. The spooked herds scattered to all sides in panic. The gigantic pinewoods were aflame; billows of smoke curled above them in thick black tangles. The trees were blazing like torches, the air was shivering with loud cracks and snapping.

Whole flocks of sheep pushed toward the flames with a stupid, fearful bleating. The horses were whimpering in panic.

'They want to burn us to a crisp,' Dummy opined, rubbing his eyes. 'People are bastards, they way they fight, whether attacking or in defence. They'll be spilling boiling lard on us before long,' he said, turning to Rex, but the dog had already leapt upon his stallion and raced off to calm the panic.

The woods burned deep into the night and the ever thicker smoke covered the earth in a stifling cloud.

They had just returned, near dawn, to the tumbledown cottage when once again the alarm sounded.

A few dozen, powerful, brown German Shepherds were chasing before them a group of two-legged creatures who were howling in frenzy.

'People! Merciful Jesus, they're people!' exclaimed Dummy, petrified.

'The lambs and their mothers cowering in the woods from the fire — perished; the cows with their calves and the sows with their piglets — perished; the mares with their colts — perished. These are the ones that set the fire that consumed them all — and they shot their lightning at us, while we were trying to defend ourselves. A lot of us fell. We demand justice! Vengeance!' the shepherds wailed darkly.

'Why didn't you mete it out yourselves?' bayed Rex impatiently.

'Our orders are to guard and herd. It's up to you to pronounce judgment, our ruler and master!'

The men, nearly naked and singed by the flames, covered in blood, half conscious, stared dully into the space in front of them, awaiting nothing more than further torment and death.

'Climb the trees! Escape that way!' Dummy spluttered, shaken with pity at the sight.

But they seemed not to understand, their eyes sweeping the crowds of animals pressing in close from all sides.

Gimpy raced up, froth on his lips. Saliva was dripping from his mouth, and his eyes sparkled with green flickers.

'Take care of them as you will,' Rex commanded.

Gimpy howled a war cry. The shepherds drew to the side, and soon the men were standing in the centre of a cleared space. They began whispering something to one another; their eyes darted all around them, ever more frequently catching onto the great linden trees that grew behind the house. But before they'd taken the decision to race there, the earth began to throb, and a frenzied pack of wolves ran up and threw themselves on them.

Piercing screams rent the air. Moments later, nothing was left but bloody remains.

'You told them to escape up the trees!' Rex growled menacingly, when he and Dummy were alone.

The boy trained his fearless, blue eyes upon him, pulling out at the same time his long, sharp knife.

'You're with us, and you want to aid our enemies?'

'Why did you order the wolves to tear them apart?' His voice was heavy with lament.

'You heard why! And they could have defended themselves! Don't look at me like that!' Rex tensed to spring.

'You're just the same sort of rabid beast as Gimpy!' burst from the boy's lips, after which he ran into the room and dove under the eiderdown. Blackie tried to comfort him with a friendly lick of his tongue, but Dummy just kicked out with his foot, sending the dog flying to the floor.

Digging himself deep into the bedclothes, Dummy exploded into spasmatic sobbing. He wept for the people. His soul had awakened inside him, and human misfortune tore at his heart. And even though he meant less to them than his friend Blackie, still he began to look upon his old human tormenters as born brothers. Up until now, he had felt nothing in common with them. His conception had been nothing more than a drunken mistake, and wickedness had abandoned him at the stoop of the manor kitchen, where he had been nursed by misery, neglect and disdain.

Everyone kicked and injured that clumsy, repellent, ugly creature with his bulldog's mug, his bandy legs, that shock of ruddy fur on a head overlarge for his body — like a balloon; with his arms hanging nearly to the earth like those of an ape; and instead of a voice, that frog-like croaking of his. There was nothing beautiful in him but the striking loveliness of those blue eyes, radiant and wise.

Trampled to the very depths of misery, cast out amongst the animals of the manor yard, he had become attached to them, their brother, as if he had been born of the same flesh and blood. They gladly followed his lead, acknowledging his superiority. It was only now, during this trek, that he had begun to sense the difference between him and them, and even to consider them foes. He had even begun to look upon Rex with different eyes — those of human cogitation. It was then that the thought of escape really dawned in his mind.

'You must understand,' said Rex, poking his head into the room, 'that people stand in our way. So we must exterminate them.'

'You'll live to see the day when you'll be whimpering for a crust of bread from beggars in the street, you king of dogs, you!'

'Why didn't you stay at home with the donkey? You'd have made a fine pair.'

'You got that right. He who piddles about in the mash trough will be devoured by the swine,' he replied tearfully.

'Clamber up a tree and see if they're firing the woods in front of us. Birds have been flying in from that direction, escaping, and the stench of burning wafts in with them.'

'Why don't you send the crows to find out?' Dummy complained, but he got out of the bed nonetheless.

'Get a move on, you human whelp, while I'm still in a good mood!' Rex growled impatiently.

As quick and deftly as a squirrel, the boy scrambled up a towering tree. And because his sight was as sharp as a hawk's, he was able to see for miles. He began to call down what he beheld.

'The forest is burning; the flames are coming this way. But the fire won't reach us — it'll be cut off by broad mudfields.'

'We'll have to go around. What's beyond the forest?'

'Something yellow. Sand? Corn? And a lot of mountains, but small ones.'

'Don't bark about the fire to anyone. The herds'll get spooked at the slightest thing, and we've still got a long road ahead of us.

'When do we set out?' Dummy asked, shimmying down to the ground.

'The cranes are supposed to guide us through the mountains. They can arrive at any moment.'

'A few more days and everything will be eaten down to the roots. From up there, all you can see are trampled fields, and nothing but mud in riverbed and pond. We can get to the mountains without the cranes.'

'I'm off to have a look at the pastures,' Rex said, and left, accompanied by the giant shepherds.

Dummy whistled to Blackie and the two set off to wander around the town in which they were quartered. The white houses, standing amidst their gardens — some with a second floor, overgrown with flowers — were empty. No windows or doors. Here and there, even walls had been knocked down. Inside one could see all the furniture smashed and horridly befouled by wolf, dog, and swine. Whatever could be plundered, had been. Nothing remained in the orchards but broken trunks, and the vegetable gardens had been uprooted, with nothing left behind but trampled soil. Flocks of terrified doves fluttered here and there over the red tiles of the roofs and onto the great trees that lined the streets.

Arming himself with an axe he happened to find, Dummy began to hack his way into locked pantries, cupboards and cellars, where he found all sorts of food. There was more than enough for the whole pack summoned by Blackie. They devoured bread and fatback with especial relish.

'Tired of raw sheep and warm blood, are we?' Dummy mocked them, trying on some pairs of shoes. He found some that fit — they were his first. Delighted, he stroked them, kissed them, and, his heart beating in joy, pulled them back on his feet. Then he found a suit of a ruddy colour. It, too, was as if tailor made for his figure, so he pulled off his coarse shirt and trousers, pulled the new togs on, and gave a whistle.

'You look just like some lord's whelp,' Blackie barked, sniffing him all over.

'Why not? Am I any worse?' he squawked haughtily, gazing at his reflection in a mirror. 'That you, Bastard? Maybe it's the little lord, Foundling? Maybe one of their lordships, Retard?' he said, calling to mind all the hurtful nicknames that had been spat at him, while prancing coyly in front of the looking glass, unable to recognise himself in this splendid red costume and new shoes. 'Maybe it's yourself, Dummy?' And he waved his arms and gestured, marking the reflections that gave back every one of his movements.

'Ha, ha, ha! It's a monkey, that's what it is! Ha, ha, ha!' someone laughed, as if from the depths of the mirror.

Dummy gave the glass a kick and it shattered. But the laughter continued. Then he saw a starling sitting atop an armoire. Dummy lunged in his direction, but the bird flew out through the window, settled on a high tree, and continued to trill his challenging, sarcastic laughter.

'What does a beast like that understand!' Dummy whistled in a starling's voice, but the bird couldn't be provoked to come near.

So he flung a stone in his direction before going off to search through the other houses. He nearly squealed with delight, finding in them such things as before he'd only seen through windows, or in his dreams.

He took it all in with eyes lit up by unutterable happiness. He sprawled on couches, rolled on beds and carpets, gazed into looking glasses, tried on garments — even women's dresses — lounged in deep armchairs, banged on pianos with his fists and trampled in delight over piles of pillows, satin fabric and linen. Surfeited at last, he took for himself a cutlass in a leather belted sheath, a revolver, a snaffle for his stallion, a warm saddlecloth, and — the most prized item of all — a splendid crop of just the sort that he would sometimes be struck across the back with by the little lord.

Laden with his treasures, he was on his way back to his quarters when, through the smashed pane of some store, he caught sight of a rocking horse. It was as large as a calf, grey, in red harness, upholstered in real horsehair. He gaped at it breathlessly, his heart stopped still in wonder and profound joy. At last, he leapt up onto it, smacking his lips, slapping its neck, drumming its sides with his heels, whipping it with the crop, rocking for all he was worth. He screamed, wept, and laughed in turn, as if he were insane. He rested his head against the hobby's neck and closed his eyes; it seemed to him as if he were racing along at breakneck speed, until the horse was frenzied and the wind was whistling in his ears. And so he flew on, madly, into the wide world, ever faster, with blazing speed.

Tiring at last of such a jaunt, Dummy leapt to the ground, gave the hobbyhorse a pat, and then it occurred to him: 'Good grief! How stupid a person can be! I've got a real horse!' And taking out his anger at his own stupidity on the toy, he busted it and threw it through the window. Then he returned, dissatisfied with himself, and ranging around the store with his eyes, he suddenly shivered in holy fear — as if he'd stumbled in front of an altar. There was a large wardrobe set with reflective glass panes, and on its shelves there were dolls of different sizes and costumes. There were bears, ruddy ones and white ones, horses, jumping-jacks and, besides these, piles of swords, guns, drums, horns, and thousands of other wondrous things that he was seeing for the first time. He blessed himself and rubbed his eyes, unable to believe this great good fortune. He devoured all these miracles with feverish eyes, breathless and afraid lest it all dissolve like the mist. He stood there gaping, moved to the core, astonished, tears flowing down his cheeks.

'O dear Jesus, how pretty!' he sobbed out in a voice thick with ineffable joy.

In one corner of the store sat a doll in her own cabinet. She was about the size of a five-year-old child, with brown hair and eyes of sapphire; matte white her complexion was, and her lips blood-red. Her hair was smoothly parted above her forehead. Her face was long, almost severe — and absolutely gorgeous. She was wearing a fancy dress of yellow and red, and had green slippers on her feet. He could have sworn that she was real and, drawing in close to her, he mumbled something… at which she smiled! A hot flash coursed through him and a holy terror constricted his throat. He was stunned — it was numinous. He withdrew a step — and her eyes followed him. The hair on his head began to bristle. He was afraid to move or to breathe; his soul lay prostrate in the dust, in prayerful humility. Then he fell to his knees, folded his hands, and prayed to her with whimpers of delight and adoration — in a mumbled stream of ecstasy unexpressed in words.

And then Blackie rushed in, barking and lunging up at the doll, trying to grab her by the hem of her dress.

'Who are you barking at, beast?' the boy snarled, grabbing the dog by the scruff of his neck, 'Who?' And he gave him such a thwack with his riding crop that the dog sprang away with a yelp of pain as if he had been scalded.

'He's nothing but a stupid dog!' Dummy said to the doll, apologising for his friend, 'he wasn't angry…' Drawing closer, he grasped her hand, almost without thinking.

'Mama! Mama!' she babbled in a childish voice, and stretched out her arms toward him…

Dummy didn't know when or how he got back to his quarters, but when he came to, Rex was taking counsel of Gimpy and the shepherds. Squeezing into his nest on the bed, Dummy hid his head beneath the eiderdown and only slowly regained control over his nerves, shaking off the mortal terror which had chased him back home.

At dusk he told Rex all about his adventure:

'She must be real. Live. She spoke to me, reached out her arms to me, looked at me,' he assured him, solemnly.

'I bit the leg of something like that back at the manor once. Sawdust spilled out.'

'You just try and touch her, and I'll rip your guts!' he threatened, flashing his cutlass in front of the dog's eyes.

'Put that fang away, and stop your squawking. The cranes are already awing. The eagles screamed down the news.' Rex sniffed at Dummy. 'You've got new skin,' he said. 'She's not alive, I tell you. I bit one of them — sawdust, and besides that, she stank.'

'What can you know of the affairs of men?' Dummy mumbled with haughty disdain. He went back to his nest but he couldn't fall asleep. He kept thinking about the doll, and about the dangers that might threaten her from the dogs and the wolves — especially from Blackie, who might throttle her out of jealousy.

He leapt out of bed, but didn't know what to do. He ran outside, looked up at the moon, listened, and at last, when the herds had all settled down so that only sleepy bellows or the barking of guard dogs could be heard, he unsheathed his cutlass and ran off.

It was a bright, calm, moonlit night. The doll was sitting there just as he had left her: immobile, with eyes wide open, submerged in the silvery gleam of the moon. He hesitated long, before, overcoming his emotions, he seized her by the hand and clasped her to his heart. Then a thing happened that made his blood run cold: she put her arms around his neck in an embrace, and some quiet, enchanted words passed through her lips.

He sat down in front of the store and, despite his dire dread, did not release her from his embrace. Listening to her more attentively, he calmed down somewhat. She spoke to him with some sort of apian-like buzzing.

'I don't understand your speech!' he moaned in despair, pressing his fevered head against her breast. And once more there spurted an awesome, inebriating melody. It was like the aroma of jasmine on a steamy late spring night, the sound of the moonlight or the distant echo of the soul fluttering in the heavy shackles of the flesh. And it set his heart rocking like a forgotten bell until it groaned with the yearning of suddenly awakened dreams.

'Mummy!'

The word escaped from the depths of his bosom like a bloodied cry, imbrued with deep sorrow, while bitter, burning tears welled in his eyes. Injuries, emerging suddenly from unconsciousness, howled inside him, and with unrelenting blows pain began to hammer his soul into a human shape. He had no idea where all this was coming from, and why it was tormenting him so. And what it left behind in his heart was an immeasurable tenderness and a desire to cleave unto the weak, to bring assistance to those in need, and to scatter this excess of feeling like largesse.

The music ceased and the doll lay there with her eyes shut, and a light, pale smile on her lips.

'Sleep, sleep, little missy!' he whispered tenderly, lifting her up carefully, as one would a little child.

He laid her down on his bed, covered her with the eiderdown, and watched over her, cutlass at the ready. Sometimes, straining his ears to catch her breathing, he was gripped with worry, lest that calm of hers as she lay there be the calm and cold of death. And this awoke in him an ever greater dread and superstitious, worshipful awe. He took her for a living thing. The only thing he could not understand was: why was she so different, so unlike those girls he'd see from time to time back at the manor? Until it suddenly flashed upon him.

'She's bewitched, for sure!' he thought, calling to mind all those fairy stories he'd given ear to in the manor kitchen on a winter night, tales of spellbound princesses, of knights, of people transformed into trees and animals.

'She's bewitched! If only I could light upon the magic word, and say it, and she'd wake up!' he dreamed feverishly, imagining how he would break the spell that bound her and lead her to the king, her father, who would then give her to him for his wife, and he'd go about dressed in silver and gold — and be a grander lord than the master of the manor himself. With such dreams weaving through his head, he fell asleep.

It was something of a fitful slumber, as he called out in his sleep, and kicked off his shoes, for his feet felt as if they were on fire. At dawn he sprang up from bed.

'Spellbound! O, if only to find the magic word!' he flailed about in concern, gazing at the sleeper.

Then a cry arose above the herds, thundering ever louder and mightier.

'The cranes! The cranes!' It was as if the entire world were crying out the words.

And indeed, growing minute by minute, a drawn-out clangour sounded from the western sky, after which gigantic dances of cranes began circling ever lower. They swept in wide rings above the herds for some while before, steering the great wedges of their columns toward the east, they rose into the blue and flowed onward, marking their heavenly path with plangent voices.

All the herds set off after them with a sort of solemn determination.

The living tide, miles wide, rolled on with a wild rumour through fields and forest, city and village, leaving only a trampled vacuum in its wake, and silence, and death.

The land began to rise toward the mountains and grow dry; then, the sublime, still-distant summits, the snow of which sparkled in the sun, disappeared, hidden behind ranges of foothills covered with forests, full of deep valleys and gorges. Only the clamour of the cranes, like an interminable song of the clouds, led them on through those labyrinths of dark wildernesses and blinding heights.

Dummy, having draped his shoes over the neck of his stallion, stuck his 'enchanted princess' into one of the uppers, so that from a distance it looked as if she were standing on the horse. The dogs joyfully barked at the sight of her smiling face, and the birds fluttered, chirping, onto her outstretched little hands. He shooed them all away, jealously, from this apple of his eye. He held green branches over her head to shade her from the swelter of the afternoon sun. Then, at night, when they were all resting, no one saw him kneel at her side and whisper something secret into her ear, waiting for her to answer, all atremble.

'If only to find that word!' he tormented himself, continually.

'If only to break the spell — we'd leave all this cattle behind us! I'm a man, after all,' he assured himself, gazing around at the innumerable polls of his companions. He felt ever more foreign among them — completely different. He was filled with sharp umbrage at their uprising against people, for he did not recognise their reasons for so doing, and felt that what they aimed at was lunacy.

'Whether yoked or free, a beast is still a beast,' he thought, censoriously, but still he began to take note of the sufferings they bore with a compassion he'd never before felt. For the road was now becoming ever more difficult and torturous. Days of blistering heat had arrived; the sun beat down mercilessly from its rise to its setting. No cooling breeze ever blew. The air was a terrible liquid flame, which seared the earth. Mountain streams sparkled here and there only with the tiniest threads of water. The valleys were choked in a venomously scorching boil. There was no cool to be found in the forests on the charred mosses and grasses, nor did the trees offer any shade. They came across fewer and fewer fields under cultivation; there were fewer and fewer villages, and feed was ever more sparse. There were days when there was not enough to go round. Tens of thousands of them collapsed on the ground to rest with empty stomachs, exhausted unto death. The nights brought no less trial and torment, suffused as they were with the unslakable swelter. The starry skies hung above them like some heavenly gardens blooming with silvery flowers, but the earth had become a Hell, which offered neither comfort nor sleep. Desiccated, thirsty thrapples wheezed in torment. Their stomachs were twisted with hunger. Some quiet complaints, grumblings and groans began to swarm through the darkness. But their faith in the future was stronger than the wretchedness of their present life, stronger even than death. Dawn had hardly broken when the wolves were already howling the daily reveille, and the cries of the cranes once more sang out from beneath the clouds. And so they set off on the trek, onward, onward, indefatigably persevering, never casting a backward glance to those who ever more thickly marked the wake of their passage with their bones — those innumerable ones torn away by hunger, exhaustion, illness, and some fierce, unknown enemies. They rolled on, covered by a cloud of dust like some heavy, grey weather tumbling just above the surface of the earth, and the sounds of their bellows, neighs and trampling hooves and paws was like the rumour of a gathering storm.

After many, many days of incessant wandering, they found themselves on an immense plateau. The always-distant, snow-covered mountain summits appeared once more in all their titanic majesty, soaring into the sky like the altar of some fearsome might hidden in the clouds.

They greeted the sight with roars of universal ravishment. They dreamed now of an end to all suffering, as their fevered eyes seemed already to behold freedom and happiness, just beyond these sky-scraping summits. Joy uplifted their flagging hearts with trust. All grumbling now ceased. Their hearts were filled with a warm uprush of hope. And what was more, cooler winds were blowing here, bringing with them cooler days. A gigantic river, flowing along between deep banks, was filled to the brim with ice-cold water. The only frightening thing was the steppe, which spread wide on all hands like an immense, unconquerable mesa, here and there dotted with rubble piles of weather-beaten rocks, little clumps of trees, and thorny brush. The rusty, cracked earth was covered with grasses similar to grey, tangled lichens and low, blood-red mosses. Some animals, never seen before, scattered before them, spooked. During the cool nights they were awakened from sweet, longed-for slumber by deep, horrid roars that sounded like underground thunder. Even the wolves were frightened by them, and the dogs hid away from them by squeezing in amongst the horned herds. But no one among them had seen a man for quite a while — not even the birds circling high above the earth. There were no traces of any human dwellings, or roads, or even the scent of smoke on the wind. They were engulfed in a completely new world — one that was fearsome because of its foreignness.

Famine came, as the supplies stored up by men were no more to be had. They were forced to nourish themselves on grass that was as tough as bristle and thorny growth as bitter as wormwood.

'No meadows! No potatoes! No grain! No clover!' wailed the herds.

Their limitless wonder gave rise in their souls to a disturbing fear.

They couldn't understand it.

They had been certain that, everywhere, inexhaustible stores had been stockpiled especially for them — and of these, the nefarious hand of man had somehow deprived them.

Where had all the full barns gone? Where are the potato fields? The corn? The fat pasturelands? What had become of it all?

But it wasn't people depriving them of anything, because there were no more people. And no supplies, either! Those deep, wrenching sentiments festered inside and among them, as they could get no sight of anything beyond these horrible facts.

Rex was torn and buffeted too, unable to comprehend it. On the other hand, Dummy mumbled venomously:

'You've got your freedom, what do you want food for? If there are no men to sow the fields, there will be nothing for you to eat. And as for men, they'll get along fine without you. Nobody here admits it yet, but all of them would like nothing better than to return to their full troughs. The wolves have nice fat bellies, and yet even they have had enough of a good thing already!'

'Even if we must all perish from hunger — all of us! — no one will return to the yoke voluntarily.'

'O, you'll perish all right — all of you — and that before too much longer. And I will too, along with you,' he added sadly.

'The wild animals get along fine without any help from man, and so shall we. And you keep your mouth shut about going back, or I'll have them trample the life out of you. Anyway, we haven't much further to go.'

'You well know, because you're the king of all this cattle, and the storks have told me…'

But Rex didn't want to listen to him any longer. Snarling at his stallion, he raced down to the river, along which the herds were stretched out at rest, grazing on the wretched, thorny grass. He was in the grips of an ever greater anxiety at the trek, which seemed to keep drawing out longer and longer. Day after day passed and that damned, empty steppe seemed to have no end. Sometimes, he'd race out far ahead, and, clambering up some pile of stone, strive to make out the end of the plains. But in vain — as far as the eye could see, the wasteland stretched on, like a rust-coloured shroud marked with wretched vegetation and rocks. Above it hung the empty, greyish, cloudless sky. Only the gigantic range of snowy summits closed the horizon, lying athwart their road like huge piles strewn in disorder — the remnants of crashed planets and suns glinting with phantasmic light off the eternal glaciers. He drew back from this sight with an incomprehensible horror.

One night, he came upon the cranes, who always preceded the herds in the journey by several hours.

'Far! Far! Far away!' they sang to him in response to his question.

He sped away, to wander amongst his groups. They were resting along the sheer banks of the river. The moon was at its full. They lay there, calm and sleepy; only here and there could some muted groans be heard. They were quiet and sunk deep within themselves, indefatigably chewing the cud of their wretched browsing, but as soon as they caught sight of him, they woke from their corpse-like numbness and their heavy, dull gaze followed his progress with boundless love. They were quiet, and still bore all of their misery with calm. They suffered with the resignation of slavish habit, without groan or grumble.

But Rex sensed that they were on their last legs, and wouldn't be able to bear much more.

After he had returned to his den, Dummy picked up the thread of the interrupted conversation.

'The storks told me that there's a whole week yet until we get to the mountains, and then come the mountains themselves, and then another steppe, and after three days of that, the sea. But at the foot of the mountains there are large fields, water, and forests.

At the break of dawn, Rex ordered the wolves to start chivvying the herds with all they've got.

'To the east! To the east! Smartly, now!' he wailed rushing about on his stallion, 'It's not far now!'

And so they rumbled on, like a cloud of hail pressed on by the wind. They were driven on by an intensified hope, and by hunger, and by death, which seemed to whistle over their heads like a horrid whip, from the lashes of which thousands fell. But no one gave them a second thought; the living thundered on, blinded by the promised propinquity of happiness, and by fear too, since, at Rex's command, the wolves were right at their heels, and tore to ribbons any of those who straggled behind. To cap it all off, they had now entered a zone of constant storm and hurricane. Such winds blew up as hid the sun behind dust clouds; the very rocks were torn asunder, and the heftiest oxen were knocked over like toys. The winds tossed the sheep about and gnarled into frenzied twists and funnels that tore and pulled at them from all sides, in all directions. Horrid downpours fell, turning the steppe into a turbulent, raging lake. Thousands of rushing streams tore the cracked earth into deep clefts and ruts. Even when the weather was at its most beautiful, a sudden calm could seize upon the air, and the sky fall upon the earth in black, drunken clouds. Wild whistles and thunders, like the earth set drumming by the feet of immense hordes, would ensue, followed by thick salvos of hail falling amidst lightning bolts and the roaring of thunder.

The bravest among them were seized with a panicked terror. Gimpy and his mates took cover in the thick underbrush; the foxes dug themselves dens; the dogs took shelter beneath rock piles, and even Rex crouched under the steep overhanging banks of the river. Only the herds, exposed to all the atrocities of the storm, stampeded in all directions in lunatic commotion, unable to cope, and in this way thousands perished.

Dummy, along with his princess, his stallion and Blackie, was always able to shield himself from the violence of the tempests. And when they had passed, he was the first to call together the scattered, before the rightful leaders reappeared. And because he possessed a drop of human reason, later, upon sensing a storm in the offing, he was able to find fairly effective means of staving off, somewhat, utter catastrophe from the herds. They began to trust him blindly, and before they had quite emerged from that horrid zone, he had become the de facto master and leader of the immeasurable groups. It was to him that their frightened eyes were turned; only him did they seek out in moments of danger. He governed them like a born leader and enforced discipline with the help of his revolver.

Rex began to fear him. Dummy's angry, flashing glances especially made him tremble.

'Man!' he snarled in helpless wrath, unable to bear those imperious eyes for long, before having to avert his own.

'That human puppy's plotting against us, the traitor,' seethed Gimpy, inching toward the boy.

'One more step, you bag of mange, and it'll be your last!' mumbled Dummy, raising his weapon.

They parted in seeming peace, but from then on, lupine eyes followed his every move. And the thing is, rule and leadership had never even crossed his mind. He'd had his fill of this wandering and had determined to return to the world of men. He'd already talked his stallion and Blackie over to his plans and it was nagging him to convince as many of the cattle as possible to rebel and return to men along with him.

'They'll just die in vain — and now it's the fall and there's so much work in the fields. They'll be happy for the work, and the full stomach, and the roof over their head,' he confided to the 'enchanted princess.' 'They'll invite me into the sitting rooms, they will, after I bring them so much cattle!' he mused, dissolving in a sweet longing for his old mistress, the lady of the manor.

So when they'd arrived again in a peaceful region, and the herds had settled down for a few day's rest, Dummy began to wander about the camps. He kept his ears pricked to all voices grumbling in complaint — and there were more and more of those. He engaged in long conversations, and complained along with them, lamenting their common misfortune, and sowing the seeds of a return to man. Sometimes he was greeted with anger and growls, sometimes with astonishment, but most often with drawn-out, sorrowful sighs. What was awaiting them? Misery, famine, and death. Even now they looked like little more than skeletons covered with skin, torn and hanging from them in limp folds. They could hardly remain upright. Thousands had been flung upon the earth by mortal exhaustion and apathy — these preferred to die of hunger rather than to set off yet again in search of wretched fodder. The protracted moans of the dying were heard all through these days and nights. The hordes of animals thinned out with terrifying speed. All the young animals were perishing. The wolves might say why the sheep were going extinct so fast. Nor were there many pigs left. And whatever of the hoofed and horned were lost — that no one reckoned. Their numbers grew less in direct correlation to their fading hopes. Almost daily, when the sun rose gigantic and shining above the snowy summits, a great roar arose and beat against the heavens.

'We'll never get there! Never! Never!' seethed the chorus of gloomy despair and complaints.

In vain Rex tried to calm them, and buck them up, wailing those hymns of his about the happiness awaiting them there. They listened to him in meet silence, but as soon as he moved on, the complaints and lamenting erupted, heavier than before.

'Let'm yoke me up, let'm beat me even!' the oxen moaned, chewing the cud of the bitter, wounding thistle, 'as long as they let me eat my fill! Oh, to eat, to eat!'

'I knew they'd fill the fodder trough full,' said a horse with a dreamy, faraway look in his eyes. 'And then they'd lead me out to work.'

'And then they'd wale away at you with their rods, until your thick hide split!' his neighbour, a haughty stallion, mocked.

'But then in the afternoon there was more fodder, and rest.'

'And a few leftover swinges!' neighed the other, pounding the earth with his hooves.

'But then in the evening there was the warm stable, half a manger of oats, and a little clover behind the ladder,' he sighed mournfully.

This reminiscing of days past ended in a fierce brawl: hooves splitting, bones smashed, and fraternal blood spilled. And there were ever more such altercations, rows, and bloody settling of accounts. Some sort of vengeful, chippy irritation began to spread like rabies. Everyone was more than happy to take out his misery and frustration on others. Now, whole days and nights passed in sharp quarrels without pardon or quarter, of which Dummy took good advantage, doubling his efforts to encourage a return. His words festered in their souls with images of lost happiness. Many of them, in the throes of the frenzy of a past suddenly recalled, wanted to return immediately. They roared on all sides:

'Rescue us! Lead us! We want people! We want masters! We want food! Lead us!'

And yet there were just as many who, after giving ear to his urgings, cast them aside with contempt.

'We're not going back to beatings. We prefer hunger to full-bellied slavery. We aren't able to slave anymore. We want to live for ourselves. We're not going to be meat for man's table anymore. Go on back if you want, but stop trying to incite us to treason.'

This mutineering ended badly for Dummy. One morning, Blackie growled to him:

'Rex and Gimpy are with the elders, talking something over, by the rocks. They're barking about you. I heard them.'

'Don't be afraid. I'm able to defend myself.' And he pointed to his revolver and that razor-sharp cutlass.

'You'll kill a few of them. And then the rest will tear you apart. Let's get out of here now!' he whimpered in frightened alarm.

'Go tell the others. Have them gather in groups and lag behind, but without giving themselves away,' he commanded.

But there was no time for that, because a cohort of wolves suddenly rumbled up, surrounding him. Gimpy barked:

'We're banishing you from the pack! On account of your old friendship, Rex grants you your life. Don't threaten us with those lightning bolts of yours, or he'll have you torn apart! We took you in out of pity, and you've paid us back with treachery and mutiny. Off with you!'

The boy looked around for support, but when he saw all the bared fangs and eyes aflame, he leapt upon his stallion, whom they'd herded near. With his princess pressed close to his bosom and his revolver in his other hand, he rode off at a trot, surrounded by the wolves. Blackie remained with him as well. He huddled close to him, his teeth chattering. The wolves harried them on like this for two days, hardly pausing to rest. At last, when they arrived at the predestined place, they howled at him to dismount. Then they threw themselves on the horse and Blackie, devouring them both in the wink of an eye.

'You just try to lead men on us, and you'll die,' one of the wolves warned him before they thundered off.

Dummy stood there in shock, gazing around him with heavy eyes. Only now did he understand the horrid severity of the blow that had fallen upon him. He was completely alone in the deep desert wastes — weeks away from the nearest human dwellings, without food, without help, without a horse. His hackles rose, but he didn't despair; he didn't even weep. He gathered his things together, slung his boots over his shoulder, stuck the princess into one of the uppers, grabbed himself a thick, knotty staff from among the bushes, and set off boldly, westward. He kept to the river, wandering back over a path thickly strewn with skeletons, bones, and carrion, on which gigantic vultures feasted, screeching. From time to time, hunger emboldened him to take from the birds a portion for himself. He went on, armed in the certitude that, if not today, then tomorrow he'd find the magic word that would break the spell that held his princess enchanted.

'And you all can go straight to Hell!' he shouted in the direction of the east. 'You'll all croak before I do!'

And on he went, fearlessly. He nourished himself on whatever came to hand, and because he was extraordinarily clever, and the river was full of fish, and he had flint and tinder with him, he wasn't much troubled by hunger. Whenever he chanced upon a bigger fish, he baked it on the hot stones, washed clean the princess, sat her down across from him at the campfire, and had a real feast. He would offer her some of the fish, and he spoke to her as if she were alive. He kissed her hands and feet, pressed his head to her bosom and listened to that heavenly music, which was the voice by which she spoke to him. He worshipped her in inexpressible happiness. When heart and stomach had been fully satisfied, he would set off on his road again.

He was like a grain of sand rolling blindly across those unfathomable, wide-stretching plains. Against the backdrop of the giants all around him, he was so small, wretched, and weak, that even the wild animals left him alone. He went on, never spending a thought on danger; it never crossed his mind. He slept beside the great bonfires he lit, and when he caught sight of the wedges of birds flying off to their winter quarters, he sang to them in their speech. A great swarm of them fluttered to the earth all around him — and before they'd caught on to the deception, he'd supplied himself with comestibles for a good few days. He used the most beautiful of their feathers to garnish his princess' thick locks.

After two weeks of this almost carefree, joyful life, he began to get anxious, for at night it got really cold, and a frightening wind began to blow just before dawn. The icy breath was blowing in from the east. And when the dawn broke, a pale, frozen sun sparkled upon the frost. Dummy stood lost in deep cogitations, ranging his frightened eyes over the whitened land. For he had given no thought to winter, and had completely forgotten its fearsome fangs. His heart began to flutter with profound concern. Distractedly, he scratched at his tousled head, and after a short spell of meditation, he pulled his boots on over his bare feet, wrapped the saddlecloth around him, and, belting it with some string, set off on his further travels, with the princess pressed to his bosom. He was being hurried on his way by fear, by ever colder days, and by those winds blowing in from the east. What was more, now hunger began to torment him. The birds had hidden themselves away somewhere, and the river was beginning to freeze over near its banks, making fishing all the more difficult. But although he was partially frozen himself, wretched and barely able to set one foot in front of another, still he plodded on doggedly, constantly whispering into the princess' ear some fantastic words he'd invented.

'Don't be afraid! I'll find it yet and break the spell!' he mumbled. 'You'll come back to life; a raven-black horse will magically appear, and we'll gallop off! But goodness gracious, sooner rather than later!' he sighed desperately, for the days now arriving were cold, windswept, and so sad that he would sometimes wait them out, hiding in dark caves. But what was that worth, when the nights were even worse — dark, icy, stormy, full of groans and roars as if whole herds were running rampant in the darkness. His hair stood up on his head and he couldn't sleep on account of terror and cold. But when dawn came, and it was somewhat calmer, he'd set off again, overcoming hunger, cold, and exhaustion, led on by the still flickering hope that, maybe today, maybe right away, he'd catch sight of the smoke of human dwellings — or at least pinewoods, in which he might find shelter. And yet, it was all in vain. As far as his eyes could see, there was nothing but an immense, horrible wasteland; a steppe marked here and there by stains of bushes, split through the middle by the ribbon of the twisting river. And thus it appeared unto the very horizon, where the grey sky met the earth with greenish piles of cloud that looked like shattered blocks of ice. The terror of those empty spaces, the deathly silence, and his loneliness, gripped him suddenly by the throat, with such an uprush of fright that he snapped inside himself at last, like some dry, wretched twig. Breaking out into a despairing wail, he sobbed and howled beseechingly:

'Save me, little Lord Jesus! And I'll whittle you a whole shrine! I'll hang before your altar a singing blackbird in a cage! Save me, Lord!' he sobbed, making the sign of the Cross again and again.

The next day, the cold was so intense that the earth itself sounded like a drum beneath his feet, the river froze over, and it was painful for him to draw his breath into his lungs. The winds died down, to be replaced by an ominous stillness, broken only by the dull pops of the cracking earth.

There was no question of going any farther on that day. He went only so far as to find a spot where the river bit deeply into the bank, forming a sort of a marshy bay overgrown with reeds and bushes.

'An unfreezing bog, and water without ice. Birds just have to stop by here!' he thought, and then, with his knife and his nails, he dug out a spacious den under the steep bank, for cover. He faced it with branches, spread leaves about the floor, and, having set the princess in the deepest recess, he dug himself in beneath the litter. He began to sense a blissful warmth under the leaves, and, in a sleepy voice, he mumbled, addressing the cold as he drowsed:

'You can kiss me you know where...' And then he fell asleep, despite the biting cold.

On the next morning, early, camouflaging himself with dry reeds, he sat himself down among the bushes and waited there, patiently, despite the cold that penetrated to the marrow of his bones. Fortunately, his hunch paid off as, just after sunrise, a string of wild ducks appeared and began to descend to the mirror of unfrozen water. Dummy began quacking like an old mallard warning the young of some imminent danger. Some of the startled birds set off again, but the larger portion of them crawled in among the dry grasses — where he was waiting. He flailed at them with his stick and gathered so many with his hands that he could hardly bear them all away to his den.

'O, there'll be a feast!' he boasted to the princess, 'and the rest'll be taken care of by the cold!'

He ate his fill and slept soundly, recovering his spent strength, but thoughts of the road stretching before him worried him more and more, because the frigid cold was growing with each passing day, and frost as thick as the thickest hailstones covered the steppe with its woolly fleece, into which his feet kept sinking, making progress difficult. The marshes too began to freeze over by degrees; the warmer eyes of living water were blinded under cataracts of ice; fewer and fewer birds happened by. The days began like open graves shedding the gloomy glow of tapers about the horrid silence of that frozen earth. Bloody flares of sun seeped through the thick tangles of fog like the tormented flashes of the eyes of the dying. Dusk descended of a sudden, like the fall of impenetrable black crepe. The nights, on the other hand, were like a fairy-land. The nearly black heavens were sprinkled with the silvery sand of the stars, sparkling with billions of twinkles, winks, and icy lightning flashes, which stunned the eye. Everything became a sea of shimmering light. On one such night, he heard some ominous howling, from not too far away.

'Wolves, maybe?' Dummy thought. 'Maybe Gimpy and his pack? The trip back would go more gaily with company,' he thought, quite cheered. Then, pricking his ears toward the approaching echoes, he clambered up onto the high bank, despite the terrible cold, to have a look around the steppe. And indeed, he caught sight of some strings of shadows slipping towards the river. At the very front raced a gigantic stag who, pinning back his antlers, flew on with the last of his strength, stumbling more and more until, having reached the steep bank, he paused there and bellowed in despair. The wolves then caught him up and now wild howls of triumph tore the air. But then the stag tumbled down the bank, and with giant leaps reached the marsh, through which he tore with all his might, sinking here and there. He extracted himself again and again and hurled himself with all the might of despair until, at last, he plunged breast-deep through the thin skin of the ice. Before he could clamber out of that, the entire frenzied pack fell upon him. A furious battle ensued. The stag pulled himself out of the mire, defending himself with his antlers, pummelling the wolves with his hooves, and then escaping anew. Falling into the marsh, he fought to the bitter end until at last he fell, torn apart by the fangs.

'Oh, you scoundrels you, you just wait!' mumbled Dummy, moved to the core. Then he shot his revolver in the direction of the furious tangle. The flash of light and the report of the bullet shook the air like a thunderbolt. He let off a few more rounds, and then ran up to the stag, gun in hand. It lay there dead, its sides torn and its throat bit through, but a few wolves were still writhing in mortal agony, tangled in their own torn innards.

'Some of that belongs to me,' the boy declared and, paying no mind to the whimpers and howls of the dying, cut away a large hunk of meat from the stag. He'd only dragged it back to his den when he caught sight of the returning pack. They were driven close again by hunger and the scent of fresh blood. They devoured the remains of the stag, and their wounded and dead comrades too, until the air was filled with the sound of bones crunching in their mighty jaws. They even licked at the bloody stains in the snow and then, having finished their feast, they began snuffling the wind for traces of Dummy. In order to scare them off, he sent up a howl of terror for all he was worth. They halted, pricking their ears in all directions. But soon enough it became apparent that he hadn't tricked them, for once more they began a tentative upward climb toward him. They came ever closer; a fearful swarming began to be heard in the bushes.

Now the boy started to feel the heat; his heart began to pound.

'None of Gimpy's friends? They'll tear me apart like a rabbit!'

He looked around for some sort of succour, and soon began making a huge pile of all the branches and reeds and dried grasses that he'd stocked up. When the wolves had crept so close that he could smell their loathsome odour, and he caught sight of their eyes flashing in the bushes like fireflies, he struck the tinderbox and set the pile aflame.

The pack, spooked at the flames, which climbed ever higher, ran off into the steppe.

'They'll be back tomorrow for sure,' he confessed to the princess, feeding the bonfire constantly. 'Now that they've taken measure of me, it'll be hard to keep them away,' he said with deep concern. 'We have to stay here — there's no escape.' He wiped the sweat from his face. 'We'll have to defend ourselves with fire every night, all night long. If we leave, they'll throttle us like lambs, if we don't freeze to death. What's to do?'

Terror stared into his eyes. Fearless up until now, he felt his strength ebb away. He seemed as helpless as a child, prey to any chance evil. He began to sob, loudly, just as he had once after the housekeeper had given him a beating without any reason. He thought of that house, far away, the warm kitchen, the pots bubbling on the hearth, and the aromas that arose from them on the steam. The sobbing shook him ever more painfully, and a wild sorrow squeezed his heart. He began to blame himself bitterly. Why did he join up with the animals? Even in the sties he'd had it better than here. And now he'll die a miserable death. If the wolves don't tear him apart, the cold will do him in. Is there anyone who would take pity on him? In such sorrow and pain, just before dawn, he dug himself into his cot of leaves and wept himself into a deep slumber.

The high sun of late morning, and a bitter cold, such as he'd not yet experienced, awakened him. His eyelids were frozen, his body numb. He was barely able to breathe. It took all the effort he had to make a fire. Then, after eating somewhat, he betook himself to collecting fuel for the coming night. It was a real struggle for him to accomplish this; he kept stumbling and falling, his head was aswim with dizziness. He was covered all over with sweat. Now he was gripped with fever, and now he was shaking with such cold shivers as even the fire couldn't dispel. Until at last, as the dusk fell, he felt so mortally exhausted and sleepy, that, despite his consciousness of the danger lurking nearby, he spread his bed with the plumage of the birds he'd killed and, curling into a ball, he fell asleep.

Dummy was awakened late at night by howling and barking. The wolves were fighting amongst themselves over what remained of the stag and then, after all that had been devoured, they began to creep towards his den. He chased them off with fire, but they kept circling till dawn, howling with hunger and wrath. He kept up his watch, feeding the fire, although that took much effort, as weak and weary as he was. At times, as if blacking out, he didn't know where he was, or what was going on with him. Then again, he was overcome with indifference. At such times, even the howls of the wolves and their suspicious racing about couldn't hold his attention. Even the fresh roast of venison tasted foul in his mouth, and he flung it away in disgust. It was with no little relief that he greeted the day. He nestled back into his den, but he couldn't fall asleep. He was tortured with an unslakable thirst. He drank water, swallowed icy rime, but nothing helped him. He wandered about aimlessly all day long, knowing not what to do with himself. He was tormented with boredom. He gathered up stores of reeds and branches like an automaton, and later plucked the birds he'd trapped. His sighs were even more deep as he ran out onto the steppe, searching for a sign of some human being through his quickly freezing tears. Loneliness and longing would fall upon him heavily of a sudden, and twist him horridly inside — like a serpent squeezing his heart. Tears began to pulse forth from forgotten depths. God, how happily he would snuggle once more into the dark corner behind the stove on a winter's eve, when the manor kitchen filled with people and voices! Even if he'd take a swipe across the head there for teasing the dogs. For even so, the housekeeper would give him a bone to gnaw on later, some warm milk or even bread and butter. Jesus, and how gay they all were, how they laughed and teased one another — and the fairy stories that the girl swineherd could tell! And when the housemaids sat down at the distaff and the lady of the manor would look in, there was no end to stories of the most varied sorts. It was then that they'd talk about enchanted princesses and dragons and princes — fearsome things that made your hair stand on end.

He shook his head and cleared away these daydreams — and once more he felt ill, lonely, and helpless.

'Am I going to die, or what?' he thought, and curling up into a ball, shifted himself right up next to the fire. He felt himself sinking into an inexpressible bliss, by degrees, as if in a mother's embrace. Burning flames seemed to pierce him through and through. His head was buzzing, and a sweet drowsiness, rocking him tenderly, shut his eyes with warm kisses.

The stars were already looking down upon his pale face, sparkling off the frosty crystals that gripped his hair, when detonations of ice cracking in the severe cold yanked him out of the blissful depths of slumber. Catching sight of shadows slipping along in the brush near the riverbank, he fanned the bonfire to life, picked up the princess and set her down next to him. He gazed deep into her eyes.

She sat there smiling, rosy-cheeked from the dancing flames, wonderful, gazing at him with those inscrutable eyes. Dummy tossed some handfuls of underbrush and branches on the fire, and the flames shot higher yet with a gay crackling and roar. He felt warmer, brighter, more positive. Suddenly, his own eyes blazed, his face blushed red, and his heart trumped inside his breast: The word! He'd found the word!

'I'll say it now!' he mumbled. 'I'll pronounce it and everything will change!' he said, casting about his triumphant

　　　　WŁADYSŁAW STANISŁAW REYMONT

eyes. 'It came to me by itself! Who cares about wolves, cold, and poverty now! O Jesus how it shook me! At last!'

And at last, he whispered something into her ear, and leapt away, petrified.

'Jesus and Mary! Jesus and Mary!' he repeated, signing himself instinctively with the Cross.

For she grew in his eyes and stood before him in golden crown and red cape, and behind her, a black stallion pounded the earth with his hooves, jangling his golden bit and stirrups.

His heart froze in wonder at the miracle, in a sublime elevation, and a sort of holy terror.

She spoke to him with that same voice of music that he could never understand.

'To horse, my prince, to horse!' Each word sounded in his soul like a bell of Resurrection.

He leapt onto the saddle, took the reins in hand, thumped the stallion's flanks with his heels, and off they went, racing with the wind. She sat before him, and he held her tightly, never ceasing to urge on the horse.

Nothing but the winds that whistled in his ears and smote him on the face; nothing but his breath, catching in excitement, and the horse in his element, his juices flowing; nothing but the scenes that passed in quick succession before his eyes — lands, pinewoods, rivers, and that song of superhuman happiness that rang in his soul. And on and on they race, speeding through the world entire, racing to her father the king, racing toward their wedding feast...

PART II

6

The gigantic clouds, similar to rust-coloured cliffs vaulting the heavens, began suddenly to crack, crumbling to pieces and tumbling into shattered piles of rubble. The wide-spreading blue was now completely lost beneath this flood; the far distances over-glooming ominously. The flashing eyes of day were covered with murky cataracts. The unstoppable wind moaned with a piercing rush. Some birds lifted up a horrid shrieking. The invisible pinewoods boomed like the sea torn by hurricanes. Bloody tongues of silent lightning flashed in the dismal grey. Some sort of frenzied, wild roar burst again and again from the earth. Twisters bloomed on the steppe one after another and, twirling like giant, sky scraping spindles, they shuttled together the weft of the dying day. A torturous silence suddenly fell. The mirages of those monstrous spindles whirled their drunken twirling even faster. They looked like a forest of naked trunks bearing only ruddy, tangled crowns at their very summits. Then all at once, a frightful chorus of thunderbolts resounded. They fell so thickly as to become one, terrifying thunder-strike, from the force of which the clouds themselves were toppled, spilling onto the earth their heavy, stifling mist, like tonnes of sand. All was lost in the impenetrable greyness, and the earth, beneath these hurricanes of unending thunder, seemed to be hurtling into a depthless abyss. All of creation was paralysed in mortal horror. Incomprehensible powers were trampling the shivering earth. The lighting-bolts sang a hymn of destruction. Destruction howled the winds that rose in the darkness so that the universe seemed one huge bank of sand blown through limitless spaces.

'Don't move! Crouch in place!' howled the commands when the herds began to bolt. Rex, along with the shepherds and the whole pack of wolves, ran about the herds, using their teeth to impose order where barking went unheeded. He shouted his throat so raw that he could barely whimper; only a bloody froth was spraying now from his chaps. He was nearly worn out with the labour, but, finally, having calmed the general panic, he fell prone on a hillock, his lungs striving for air, his tongue lolling at full length from between his jaws. But the herds had all crouched down now, surrounding the hillock on all sides, in a ring that the eye couldn't compass. This incomprehensible thing that had overcome both sky and earth tormented them with frenzied terror. The air was trembling with drawn-out, mournful lowing and moans! The horses beat against the earth with their hooves, whinnying in frenzy. Amidst the moiling grey, the sapphire eyes of the sheep flashed all the more brightly as they sent up their tremulous lament. The wolves themselves began a frightened, quavering howling that burst forth here and there. The dogs, in a frenzy, their noses pressed to the ground, scurried about here and there on the trail of… something. They knew not what. The yearning bellows of cows and oxen boomed forth a gloomy basso continuo. Even the pigs, usually so wisely indifferent, were squealing now in anxiety.

For they were all suffering equally. And to make matters worse, these dry mists stuck to their hides in icy sheets, piercing them to the marrow with cold. Every now and then, those heavy polls were lifted heavenward, and tearful eyes strove to penetrate the darkness. But there was no sign of any change in the offing. The day did not return, and the mists just grew thicker. Only Rex remained calm and in control of himself. He'd lived through more than one storm. At the moment, he was recalling the fierce blizzard that once blew him back and forth across the fields for three days on end. At last, he waited it out, starving beneath some rock.

'They always had it nice and warm and peaceful in their barns,' he growled, out of patience with their moaning.

'Even the wolves have had enough of this weather,' one of the shepherds grumbled in reply, pricking his ears.

'So let'm find us better!' Rex was getting angry at the constant complaining.

'What if this darkness never passes?' one of the dogs sighed, scratching himself furiously.

'Then you'll croak right here along with your fleas! Enough wising-off! Sleep!'

And he stretched himself out as comfortably as he could and tried to fall asleep himself.

The hurricane passed on to other places; the shattering of the lightning bolts grew more and more distant. The voices of the herds fell silent too. The winds flew off, beating their fainting wings. Slowly, a cold, numbing silence fell. All were soon atrophied into a stony calm. Their hearts beat ever more softly, their terror passed, and finally, that gracious brother Sleep arrived to overcome all with miraculous forgetfulness, so that all fevered eyelids drooped, weary polls fell to the earth as if a switch had been turned off, and all the exhausted were submerged in a luxurious sweetness. Finally, Rex drowsed as well, checking only first to make sure that night had indeed fallen. Still, he did wake up from time to time, pricking his ears and stretching out his neck, snuffling the air. But, as all he smelt was the sharp frost coming on, he hid his snout between his paws and went back to sleep.

There was not the slightest rustle to be heard in the deathly silence. The piles of mist lay about dead, like extinct boulders left as prey to time. The rhythm of life, deadened, concealed itself in the disorder.

It might have been after midnight, at the hour when roosters begin to crow about the villages, that Rex suddenly sprang to his feet with bristling fur and ears on alert.

He had caught the sound — clearly — of a familiar voice: that of the Foundling. The only thing he couldn't discern was where it was coming from. He leapt from where he had been lying and began, with wild leaps, to make wide circles. The mumbling of Dummy resounded long — somewhere before him, or above him, but he couldn't catch up to him and, at last, he returned to his cot, out of breath.

'There's not a shred of him left by now!' With that rough comment, he doused the sudden yearning that had sprung up in him. 'But maybe he made it back to his own, and was recalling me?' Instead of an answer, his memory spread wide the doors of its wondrous granary and buried him beneath a heap of living fragments of ancient experience. With eyes open wide, he gazed into the magic mirror. It was as if he had leapt into the past, and were experiencing it anew. He barked gaily at the sight of the old manor, beating his long tail from side to side as he coursed through the rooms. He tensed to spring at the sight of the dachshunds, and raced over the stubble after young rabbits. Catching sight of his old master, he bounded up to cuddle at his feet, growling happily; then he drowsed, stretched out in full on the lion pelt, his sleepy eyes fixed on the dying embers of the hearth. And at last, he threw himself in sleep so violently upon some enemy or other that he fell upon the backs of the shepherds sleeping nearby. The dream vanished leaving behind nothing but the gloomy night, the silence, and the sleeping herds. But he longed no more for the past. Now, it was becoming simply hateful to him.

'To the east! To the sun!' All his faith and hopes sang out in him again. His concern for the herds was aroused once more, absorbing all his attention, all his strength. He tensed inside himself for his next deed of redemption.

'Spring will come, and back there — not a single horse, a single ox, not even a dog! They'll all croak of starvation. Who'll do the work for them?' Sweet feelings of revenge upon people flowed through his frame like the stream of hot blood pulsing out of a vanquished enemy. Then, suddenly, he shivered, turning his snout in a different direction, as a billow of frightful stench wafted over from the direction of the herds.

'Foh! We'll be stifled! Make sure they don't lie in so close to us.'

'Didn't stink for people. Didn't they shovel up whole piles of it to cart away?' one of them growled.

'People will eat anything. Even such things as our brothers won't even sniff at.'

'When will the day come? It's time already!' He cast his anxious eyes around the deep darknesses, but there wasn't even a sliver of a sign of the coming dawn. And his unerring instincts told him that the sun ought to be on the rise already. The shepherds knew it too. They circled about anxiously, howling at the gates of that never-ending night, but the master wouldn't spread them wide to let out the sun.

'Maybe it's got lost somewhere in those blue fields?'

'Or the lord of the manor's overslept… That happens. We used to bark at his door until he woke up.'

'You'd come back from the night watch and go straight to the fireplace… There'd be potatoes bubbling in a pot, fatback sizzling, and the fire would warm you through and through when it was cold and snowy outside… Heaven that was, Paradise!' they reminisced softly.

Rex put a quick end to their blissful musing with his thunderous voice:

'To the east! Hop it!' Thus sounded the order, passed on and on over the thousandfold hordes, until it reached the very ends of the great camp. The herds arose lazily. They were sluggish, chilled to the bone, and starving. And yet from sheer passive custom they began to move out again in fairly disciplined ranks, straight across the foggy, empty spaces. The howls and teeth of the wolves urged them on into something like a trot.

'Where's the sun? Where's the day? Where?' resounded the sad lamentations.

The cranes were no longer signing their usual morning song.

They dragged on with bowed heads, halting for the slightest of reasons, browsing on the bitter leaves of some sort of bushes. The thick frosts snapped and cracked beneath their feet; here and there they cut themselves on icy shells that wounded their legs like knives. And all the while they kept moving on blindly, completely sunk in a pea-souper so thick that they could hardly see a foot in front of themselves. Every now and then they tumbled against one another or tripped on some stones, tree roots, or each other's limbs. This caused cursing and fights to break out here and there.

'We're gonna shatter our legs! Where are they herding us? And the plains were so even before!' they moaned.

All the urging from the rear was for naught, now. They moved on ever more unwillingly, fearfully, and apathetically. Whole groups of them broke ranks and, remaining to the rear, threw themselves down upon the ground like felled trunks. Others suddenly stopped stock-still, paralysed, afraid to move at all, and bellowed for all they were worth. And yet the wolf's teeth and claws were at least so effective as to regroup the herds, even if with difficulty, and push them onward. But now all bonds between them had been severed. It was a hard thing to enforce any sort of obedience. For the whole trek had now become one indescribable torment. The day was missing, the night was missing; there were no longer any clear demarcations to time, and this led to ever greater disorder. They slept when they felt like it, and got up when it suited them. Their rest periods became even more frequent and longer. Then, after even consuming moss and miserable lichens to fill their bellies, and slaking their thirst by licking at the frost, they moved on at the tragic pace of the condemned. Whole groups of them preferred to stay behind and just die rather than suffer on like that. Even their hopes guttered inside their breasts, while that monotonous grey, which refused to give an inch, provided the coup de grace to their prospects. On top of it all, time just kept dragging on, and the enforced blindness beat them down. They even began losing their instincts, which had been with them since the beginning of time. Few were they who sensed the falling of night or the coming of dawn. They just went on and on, endlessly, without any idea as to whether it had been days, weeks, or perhaps years that had passed by during this trek of theirs. It seemed an eternity of wandering, with an eternity still ahead of them, an eternity of wandering through this grey, endless grave, hungry, tired to the very death, blind, not quite dead yet, but given over into the power of a horrid, protracted dying. And the merciful day never arrived to shine down upon them a single, pitying ray — not a single one.

Their sufferings grew day by day, as did such a hopelessness that even the grumbling went silent; their complaints died off — they no longer had strength enough to protest. They dragged on like an immeasurable procession of somnambulistic mirages, from which now and then some lonely, shattering roar of despair would burst forth.

At last, Gimpy went out scouting. He was gone for quite a long time; when he returned, it was with downcast eyes.

'I could find the sun nowhere. Nowhere, nowhere, nowhere!' he whimpered grievously. 'I ran to the east, I searched in the west. I pierced the fogs to the south. Everywhere, the same, horrid, impenetrable Night. Not a ray of sunlight anywhere!' he despaired.

Later, Rex galloped off himself on his black stallion, laying low everything in his path as he went on, like the wind. He also returned with nothing. A bloody froth dripped from his fangs and his eyes had a gloomy glow to them. He threw himself down onto the ground next to the shepherds, and, for a while, breathed with difficulty. The news of his expedition spread, and before long he was surrounded by an impatient rabble, thirsting for hope.

'The night will be with us for many marches yet,' he said, unwilling, afraid, to reveal the whole truth. 'I came across the cranes… They sang that it'll get brighter in a few days' time… They've seen the sun… It shall return to the earth… Fear not… We just need to hold on a few days more! Patience… Courage…!' he spluttered solemnly.

'Sure, wait and wait till it's too late! But the wolves'll have something to eat!' someone growled, less than satisfied at Rex's words.

'Only a man can lead us out of this mess!' another declared with a bold roar.

'Silence! The next one who mentions that name will die on the spot!' Rex bristled, baring his fangs.

'Sure,' agreed Gimpy. 'And meanwhile, we're perishing. The herds are mere skin and bones…'

'That's where it hurts you!' came a mocking bark. 'You need some nice fatty flesh!'

'Dried bones, no marrow, like wood-chips!'

'The wolves're dragging their bellies on the ground, and still they're complaining!' the dogs barked.

'And you — are you herbivores? You're dreaming of the offal tossed you from the cottages, of the refuse piles…'

'May your tongue go palsied! We have to eat carrion and whatever else we come across. But we don't murder.'

'And no one stops you from eating what's left over… You can dig right in…'

'You disgusting bag of filth! We'd rather die of hunger than eat your leftovers! They reek of you a half-day's march away. Maybe it's all right for foxes and vultures!'

'Neither dogs nor wolves are in much of a hurry to see the end of the road.'

'Because they live off us! At our cost!' Here and there, such voices were raised.

'Where is the sun?'

Some threatening roars broke out, suddenly.

'Lead us there! We've had enough of this wandering! We're cold, it's dark, and horrid! We're hungry! Rescue us or we'll perish! Return the day to us!'

Fearing lest even worse consequences should erupt, Rex leapt upon his stallion and, ringed with a triple defensive cordon of canine and lupine teeth, pressed through the restive crowds, trying to calm them.

'The time is not far off now,' he barked loudly, 'the sun is waiting just beyond the fogs! Before we've had a few more rests, it will shine down upon our faces, warm us up, and once again uncover to our eyes the wonders of the earth!'

'Before that sun rises, our eyes will be eaten through by the damp…'

'This night will devour us, hooves and all! Where is that Paradise of yours?! You promised us! Lead us there already!'

'It's just in front of us… We'll get there soon… It's the prize awaiting those who persevere, the brave… Only those who doubt, the mean-spirited, will perish. Those of you who patiently hold out will be found worthy of that happiness…'

'Give us food! Give us drink! Give us shelter! We're dying!'

'Hold out!' he howled with all his might. 'Our struggles and misfortunes will soon be at an end! And remember this well: whatever sort of misfortune falls upon us arises from the villainy of men. It is they who have submerged us in this fog; it is they who have blocked the sun from us. They are the ones starving us and scalding us with this cold. They are taking out their vengeance upon us. They want to break us and force us to return. They want to enslave us by tormenting us with hunger and night, so that we should return to their rods and their yokes. At any time, they might even suddenly appear amongst us to tempt the weak and the doubting. Death to the sly tyrants! They're going to tempt you with troughs and pretty words. Don't believe those filthy snakes for a moment, because if you do, they'll drink your blood again, just as they used to do. For a bit of wretched fodder they'll turn you back into slaves. Don't let them! Their reign has ended. Lift up your hearts! Don't sell your freedom, which has been bought at the cost of your blood!

Persevere, and once again all the barns filled to bursting, and all the haystacks will be yours. All the fields and meadows! The sun will be yours, and warmth, and the refreshing springs. And you will enjoy cool shade in the hot weather and shelter from the wet, and soft bedding! and no enforced labour, no tax in slavery and blood, no obligation, not even the obligation of gratitude. Comrades, friends, brothers, I guarantee you with all the power of certitude that days of endless good fortune are nigh upon us. I can see them now, I feel them already — they are just beyond these mists. Can you not see the dawn there, still pale, there in the east? The breaking of the dawn has already been foretold by those holy heralds of the coming day…' he howled with the might of a lion — and was answered by roars similar to the gay thunder of springtime.

Later, they lay down to rest, hungry, it is true, but full of trusting hope.

'You lied to them like a Jewish mongrel,' Gimpy snarled, stretching himself out alongside Rex. 'That was all right for the cattle, but I demand the truth. I need to know! I confess that, up till now, we've been well fed. Some of my mates have gotten a little chubby even. But something's beginning to stink here… I've got to think of myself. This uprising of yours might end badly for us. I wouldn't bet a chewed-over bone against your going back tomorrow. You aren't capable of living in freedom. The people will set out the best fodder for your return — but us they'll welcome with bullets! And if that stupid cattle, driven raving mad with hunger, decides to turn hoof and horn on their leaders? I'm not looking for such embraces!

Too great a disgrace it'd be for the son of my father, to be ripped apart by pig-snouts. There's a chasm that stretches between us. We've been living free since time immemorial, and free we shall remain. And you — it's hard for you without those whips and troughs and chains, and filled bowls. You agitated the cattle to revolt, but in the name of what? That they're going to be eating and lazing and multiplying and living without care, to die the death of fattened layabouts. Those aren't ideals fit for wolves. Our element is battle, deception, victory and the free unfettered game of life! We don't even give ourselves up to death without a fight,' Gimpy confessed with surprising candidness. 'Is it true that the daylight will return soon?' he asked unexpectedly.

'It'll return,' Rex replied, gnashing his teeth, moved strongly by the wolf's sincerity. 'The cranes flew up with that news.'

'That's news to me, that you met with them.'

'Are you following me about, you bag of fleas?!' Rex flared in anger.

'The guards are out and about as usual. You didn't forbid that,' Gimpy said, sidling away from him a bit.

'I don't need you watching over me. I'm in no danger among friends.'

'Of course. And yet, some fraternal hoof, some friendly horn, some faithful tusk might just catch you in the side — by accident, you know. Things like that happen, even among friends,' he said, with gentle courtesy.

'They're all devoted to me. I led them forth from the house of bondage. I'm their leader and their brother.'

'And that's why it's safer to keep a certain distance between yourself and them! And they shouldn't suspect it!'

'You don't understand our society. You understand nothing but killing and destruction! And your bandit customs…'

'I don't like barking that mimics speech. You think you're the wisest of all? You took your swipes from people, but not their reason. You've poisoned yourself with pride. You've never been free and you'll never understand freedom. What've you ever had in common with that herd? A common hatred of a common master. Instead of leaping at their throats and lapping their blood, taking your vengeance upon them with your fangs, you incited that rabble of slaves to revolt against them, and now you've become the servant of those stupid cattle! You've gone bad, dog. And unless you've got some hidden motives, if you're only after their happiness and well-being, then you're all the more stupid, a hundred times over, for thinking that you can make them into a free nation. Or maybe you've taken a liking to being in charge? I don't know what the attraction of being the leader of sheep might be. Let's get right down to basics: Why do all those horns, hooves and snouts and all the rest of them exist? So that we'd have something to eat. We, the truly free ones, the rulers of forest and field! The only one stronger than us is man, but you've even stopped understanding that…'

'Why did you come along with us?' Rex asked with reproach.

'Because I love you, my dog-brother. And I wanted a change of scenery, some camaraderie, to air my fur a bit. But I'm tired of this company already. Incurable boorishness, and on top of it all, such stupidity as doesn't even arouse one's compassion. Fresh meat and nothing more. In the face of it all, all intellectual interest just falls away,' he said, intentionally provoking him.

'You swore obedience,' Rex reminded him sternly. 'I have need of you.'

'To urge on the lazy and arouse a humble fear of power. And we serve you faithfully.'

'The sheep might bear witness to that…'

'Can you imagine a sheep eating a wolf?' His belly began to quiver with laughter. 'I like to reflect upon the order in nature. After all, it'd be against all the rules of logic if, for example, sheep were to die of old age!'

Rex remained silent. The two of them fell asleep simultaneously. They were awakened later by the penetrating cold.

'And just as there was no daylight yesterday, so is there none today!' whimpered Gimpy, shaking the icy frost from his fur.

'It will come! So I have said!' Rex retorted proudly before giving the order to set out. The herds moved off in a disciplined order such as had not been seen for a long time, with joyously renewed energy.

'Three more rests,' the dogs explained, 'Just one, and one, and one!'

They completed the first stage in haste, the second in a fever, and the third — possessed by a frenzy of expectation. But the day grew no brighter. The thick drapes of fog were not parted even a crack. The grey, impenetrable walls of brume enclosed them on all sides, shutting out the light of the sun.

Their newly stirred hopes were overturned in ferment, and their souls buried under the darkness of despair. Suddenly, all their strength and will to journey onward evaporated. They threw themselves down upon the earth by the tens of thousands — as if flinging themselves into the arms of merciful Death, but Death did not rescue them, nor did Sleep deign to soothe the forespent. Even rest renewed not their strength, nor helped them to forget their woe. And so, prodded into a frenzy of misfortune, they stampeded in any and all directions until they were breathless, in the grip of hunger and terror.

How many such terrible nights and days passed for them in this way — who knew? The only thing that was obvious to all was that the day was nowhere to be seen; the sun was nowhere to be found; there was no end, anywhere, to this endless night.

'Only man can save us!' was the verdict passed by the pigs during one period of rest.

'Dummy wanted to save us, and they chased him off!' his old conspirators reminisced.

'What he wanted to do was herd us back over into the clutches of people! As prey to man again!' one of the steadfast reasoned in reply.

'Even so! What's this freedom of ours worth! We're going to perish! Night and starvation will devour is! They deceived us, they did.'

'We want to go home! Back to people!' they sobbed in the darknesses, with a still incomprehensible yearning and unrest.

No one fell asleep at the time customarily set aside for rest. The deep rumbling spread wider and wider through the masses. A sense of having been treated poorly, of being wronged, began to be hammered into shape under the thick skulls. At last, they began to think things through and, suddenly, it all became clear: they had merely handed themselves over to the arbitrary will of Rex.

'O, wretched us! What misfortune! After all, he's nothing but a dog — a homeless stray, an ungrateful rebel! O cursed hour of our frenzy, in choosing to follow him!'

And where was he leading them anyway? Into the very depths of misfortune! And how had he been able to seduce them and tear them way from their time-honoured nests and dens, from their life as they had lived it since time immemorial? With a stupid fairy story of happiness! A wretched mirage! All the hunger, cold and illness they'd suffered through were nothing compared to this never-ending night, this torture of erring through blinding cloud-banks of fog, these grey, empty eternities of space. Nothing remained for them now but death, to which they looked as if to their final saviour, the only one left them. For just a few more stages like this and they'd all fall away.

'We need to escape. To escape, and go back!' The thought arose like a brilliant flash. Night, everywhere! How to get away from it? Escape — where? The herds began to be torn and pecked at by the vulture beaks of doubt. 'Man will lead us out!' And again something flashed behind their eyes like lightning. 'Man will save us!' The prayer-like whisper descended over the camp like a soothing dew. 'Man! Humans!' In those words there resounded humility, fear, and a moaning appeal. 'Human beings!' Their breaths fell into a joyful rhythm: 'Man, man, man!' An anchor had fallen, catching in the very depths of their hearts. Let the lightning bolts fall, let the hurricanes rage; now they had entered a safe harbour; now a sweet wave was bearing that life-boat of theirs, rocking it, swaying it, crooning to them a wondrous song of lost happiness.

The world was a cold one. The animals' breath froze in the air. They all huddled together for warmth. The vicious misfortune suffered by all united even old enemies. Hope, suddenly awakened, burst forth in flames of friendship and compassion. Everyone wanted to be his fellow's brother. The sheep welcomed among them the pigs, shivering with cold. Mares sought warmth among the dogs. Powerful colts nestled up close to shaggy wolves with a childish trust. Even the shepherds keeping watch at the edges of the immense camps lay down next to the cows. Everyone sought encouragement and warmth from the others. All were submerged in a limp silence and exhaustion. But fantastic mirages floated through their brains; elusive whispers swarmed among them, and every now and then some voice was lifted, to die away again, without an echo, so eerily, that ears trembled and heavy polls were lifted in concern. Every now and then it seemed as if the aromas of clover and young wheat wafted near; the flaring nostrils snuffled at it long and hungrily before it was transformed into the sharp odour of the manure piles among which they were lying. With groans they bade farewell to such pleasant deceptions. Try as they might to beat them back, unclear, freakish visions slid through their daydreaming heads, wonders of misty recollections and things which seemed never to have existed. Until at last, when sleep flew off, their eyes, half-open behind their heavy lids, began to see things — old and far off things — and that's when the yearning fell upon them. It arose from their torments, their terrors and their misery like a poisonous exhalation from boggy marshlands. It took possession of them like a mighty wave falling with fury from on high, plunging down onto the icy wastelands unlit by sun or stars, hurling them down into an abyss, into the deepest depths of dismay, dread, and paralysing fear. And before they'd caught their breath, it would lift them up and carry them onto the broad, flat shores of silent, sleepy bays, over which their eyes wandered of their own volition, off into the farthest sunlit distances unto fields fragrant with the smoke of human settlements. And again, like an eagle a defenceless lamb, it sank its cruel predatory talons of regret into their hearts, tearing at them with torment and despair, before plunging them beneath its unutterable weight into the muck, trampling them mercilessly, confronting them with the entire horror of an existence without sunlight, with no tomorrow, with no sliver of hope. They would start up of a sudden, flailing this side and that, racing around in a circle, tearing at the earth with their hooves and running off —anywhere.

For they had not burst their chains. Homesickness wound itself around their souls like the folds of a snake that throttled them ever more tightly. Rasping moans escaped their throats; their heavy polls sank to the earth and that strange, inexpressible pain so tore at them, that they fell prone before it, in mortal exhaustion, entirely at its mercy. They gushed burning tears, and torment became the harbinger of a perverse delight and inebriation. 'O, Death our redeemer!' sobbed all of creation.

The spectres of memory kept creeping out of their dark dungeons. O most sacred grace! Days dead and gone were resurrected. Before their feverish, stunned eyes there played visions of fields where spring reigned in all its glory, and fulsome summer, and long calm nights in which something like a song heard long ago resounded, 'O blessed wonder!' What was it telling them? What? The mists vanished, the scales fell from their eyes. 'How was that? When was it? Where?' They wallowed in delight, with trembling and disbelief submersed in the flickering images. Their old masters threaded among them, their terrible eyes flashing in the darkness, their voices, which awakened shivers of fear, sounded above their heads pressed prone to the ground. But, strange as it was, none of them was afraid anymore. Their hearts were overcome with a sweet fainting humility. Their tongues wanted to feel the contact of their benevolent hands, their very backs and necks arched toward their merciful caress. What a peace it was that enveloped their soul! Just as once upon a time, just as before, just as it always had been.

And in such a sweet mist of coalsmoke their memories sifted down to them the smells of barn, field, and cratch. They sensed some sort of warm dusks to the west, sprinkled with the golden powder of the roads, ringing with bellows and trampling hooves. They're returning in droves, returning with full bellies, sated. The human whelps are squealing all around them — now and then even whacking rods against their sides! A mother's tongue against one's hide felt no sweeter. The winches at the wells are creaking, and cool water splashes into their troughs, refreshing, sweet. Their belaboured bones were aching; what bliss it is to lay oneself down on the dry straw in the darkness, in the warmth, amidst the drowsy buzzing of the flies. Without a care in the world. 'Let the master worry about it; it's up to him to make sure that we're wanting nothing. That's how it's always been, after all, for thousands of generations. And that's how it always should be, always…' So their memories, evoked by passionate longing, swarmed about them.

'Only idiots rebel against ancient laws.'

'It's a high tribute you pay for trampling them underfoot.'

'Should've listened to me! I knew all along how it had to end!' mumbled Shrike, bitterly, chewing his wet cud. He was an old ox with one horn knocked away.

'That mangy dog's stolen it all from us. What do I care for all the wool I've kept?' bleated a ram.

'He's stolen our happiness, our life. He's led us out on a wild chase and given us over into the hands of misfortune.'

'Should've listened to me!' the ox repeated, trying to make himself heard above the rest and pressing out to the front.

'It's Rex's fault! And Gimpy's! Let's trample them down! Tear them apart with our hooves!' grumbled the rams.

These words were answered by a general bellowing and by long strings of laments, sobbing, complaint and anger.

'Enough of this chasing after nothing! Let's go back!'

'They've gotten fat on our misery! Their swollen bellies are brushing along the ground.'

'And so sweetly did he speak. So tenderly and sublimely!' an old sow lamented.

'A web of promises, to entangle fools!' Shrike stated sententiously.

'Where's Dummy? He was always with us. He remembers the way back, and he'd intercede for us.'

'Let him lead us back! Dummy! Dummy!' ever more voices cried.

They began to seek him among the crowds, amidst the darknesses. Someone had seen him not long ago. Someone recalled his rebellious urgings to return, with emotion. Someone else began to speak of his wisdom and goodness, and everyone could still see him as he rode at their head upon his giant stallion. The companies of animals were aroused. The hope of rescue again flamed to life within them, of a sudden. All eyes waded about the fogs in search of his slim figure. Every now and then, voices called out to him from different quarters. A fever ignited their imagination, and they sought him with ever greater impatience. Eyes were peeled to catch sight of him, voices called out for him, sighs billowed in his direction. The blood rushed to their heads and their eyes flashed with madness. Dummy became their one and only saviour, appointed by despair, and their last, unique hope.

And then at last, some yearning eyes caught sight of him and pointed him out to the others:

'There he is! In front of us! You see? He's pointing out the road that we're to take!'

They all saw him at once: a gigantic mirage took shape in the fog, appearing just as their hearts longed to see him.

'After him! Let him lead us! Lead us! Rescue us! Save us! After him!'

An immense roaring like thunder was raised, and all the companies rumbled after that mirage.

Only Rex and those closest to him remained, clueless as to what had just happened.

'They'll be back,' Gimpy assured him. 'They've gone off in search of the sun. You think those thick skulls even know what they're doing?'

'They'll drop like flies. Again.'

'There'll still be enough of them for us.'

'Stop talking rubbish. I feel sorry for them. Truly. And we're so close now to happiness.'

'Pity is a slave's virtue. Through pity kings and kingdoms perish.'

'A wolf's principles! You can win power over the whole world with your fangs, but you won't sustain it.'

'Listen here, you king of slaves! I don't want to rule over anyone. I only want to live, for myself… to live free…!'

They carried on with their quarrel. Meanwhile, the frenzied groups raced with all their strength after Dummy. They seemed to see him, right in front of them. Against the grey backdrop of the night, his gigantic shape flickered — he was racing ahead on his horse; his blanket fluttered from his shoulders on the wind like a red cloud; his curly, hempen hair shone in the gleam of the moon. He pressed the princess to his breast, and with his right hand extended, he pointed forward, somewhere.

They pressed on in closed ranks, never letting their eyes drop from him. They sounded like an unstoppable wave crashing though all the barriers in its path. They understood one thing only: that they were on their way back to their homes, back to people, back to the happiness they had lost. Every now and then some joyful, triumphant roars split the air. They seemed to be soaring forward, on wings. They could already scent the green fleece of the fields in their nostrils; larks sang in their souls; the wind, sweet with fresh young greenery, cooled their fevered eyes. 'Faster! Faster! Faster!' They grew more and more impatient. No one knew how long they had been racing behind that chimera. But no one complained of the difficulty and pain of the road back. Thousands, weakened, remained to the rear; thousands perished beneath the hooves of their own brethren, but the rest kept rushing on, without pausing to rest. Just another leap forward and the day would reappear — there would be villages, and a flashing sun! 'Faster! Forward! Faster!'

Suddenly, they butted their heads against an unexpected cliff wall, and many of the broken tumbled into an unexpected abyss. Their road was blocked by black, lazily rolling waters, from which great columns of flame continually rose into the black heavens of asphalt. Some monstrous winged creatures flickered in the bloody haze. The earth rumbled. The cliffs near the shore were constantly crumbling into piles of rubble. No one gave out as much as a peep. Even the roars of initial terror died off in their astonished throats. A deathly silence ruled, unbroken. In those charnel, empty spaces, the spectre of Dummy vanished. The bloody waves began to slowly swell, to rise, and with their red tongues to lick at the hooves of those standing closest. They drew back in horror at the new danger. The waters seemed to rear up behind them, billow upon billow, swelling ever deeper, spilling in along the sides and with a sudden, predatory rush, to grab at them with rapacious coils.

A mortal fear hurled them backwards. Far away they ran, driven off in their wild, frenzied rush to escape…

On they flew, mindless and aimless, until they struck up against some thorny, impassable thickets. They turned back again, and after a long run fell into stagnant swamps yawning with deadly exhalations, where greenish will o' the wisps flickered about like the eyes of wolves. They turned aside once more, seeking an exit on another side with the stubbornness of despair. But they were just spinning in a vicious circle, from which they were unable to break free no matter how much effort they spent, how much pain they underwent. They longed for the day, or at least the light of stars, at least the palest sliver of dawn, and yet the fogs still wrapped the world in thick drapes. Everywhere, and always, those woolly, impenetrable clouds hung, and that eternal night dragged on, without end. There was no way out anywhere; nowhere was there any help. In vain did their eyes, bloody with torment, seek out Dummy. In vain they howled all their longing toward him, and so great was that howling that the night itself reverberated with the moaning of their mournful lament, the orphaned weeping of the moribund. They seemed like a sea imprisoned for all ages between those tight, rocky shores, eternally and futilely beating against destiny.

7

It had to be somewhere near dawn when Rex, sleeping on a hill beneath the shelter of some branches, suddenly shook the dew from his fur, which had been dripping thickly upon him from the branches above. He snuffled at the air, nostrils flaring; it was a damp, warm wind that was blowing. The mists were strangely troubled. The warm air foretold a change in the weather. He gave himself another shake and, sweeping his eyes around the turbulent darkness, froze in wonder: here and there, stars were prinking through. He fell to the earth, held his breath, and only after a long, tormenting pause did he once more lift high his head. Aloft, high above the quickly disintegrating mists, a thousand stars were sparkling. Still, he didn't leap forth from where he was, he didn't bark — he didn't even move. Just — calming down his racing heart — he drank deeply of that silver sparkling before his eyes. Waves of heat flashed through his frame, shaking him like burning shivers, so that he had to cool himself down again and again by licking the wet leaves and branches.

The mists continued to grow thin, and sag lower, so that on the navy blue fields of the skies, more and more thickly there bloomed the radiant blossoms of the stars.

'They're shining again!' he whimpered softly to himself, afraid of spooking the vision. He thought, perhaps, that he was just dreaming it all. So as not to dispel it and send those stars scattering away, he closed his eyes, tightly, and then, after a moment, opened them once more, slowly, carefully, in quiet anticipation. But the miracle endured.

He contemplated it all in the humility of speechless thanksgiving, shaken by shivers of happiness. The mists fell to the earth in thick white tangles, so low that here and there the bald summits of the hills began to appear, as did the black crowns of the trees.

'The day is breaking!' A joyful, mad shout swelled inside him. All at once, he felt like leaping into the midst of the sleeping herds and waking them, barking the glad tidings — the horrid night was over! The sun would soon be up! But he couldn't move; he hadn't even strength enough to set his huge tail thumping. He just clung to the earth ever more tightly, shivering, rattling his teeth in a fever.

And the day arose as it always had done before: the sky paled, the stars went out, and in the east the first rosy smudges of the dawn began to smoulder. On the earth, from beneath the troubled fogs, the usual chorale of sighs and sleepy moaning could be heard — the animals were fast asleep.

This strangely deep sleep of theirs — so it seemed to him — was troubling.

'Many of them won't rise to greet the sun,' he thought, having decided to wake no one. He tensed of a sudden, and turned his bold eyes toward the spreading gates of the east. Once more he knew to where he was to lead the companies.

Suddenly, from the summit of the heavens, where no eye could reach, came the whooshing of thousands of wings and the clangour of the cranes in flight. Their tiny black wedges could just barely be made out against the pale dawn. Their cry flowed down lower, and lower, and ever more loudly until, having awakened the herds, they soared up again into the skies and flew onward in the direction of the still distant sun.

The wolves howled, and the rest of the animals began sluggishly to arise.

Gimpy ran up to Rex, strongly shaken with the wonder.

'Cranes. And so the dawn will break soon.'

'What did I say? They'll go mad with joy at the sight of the sun!' Rex growled, giving the marching order.

But, somehow, no one was in a hurry to leave. They all gazed around the sky and the earth with flummoxed, terrified stares, not completely understanding the miraculous transformation. Their bones were aching, hunger twisted at their stomachs, and a deadly fatigue so exhausted all their strength, that they couldn't sense their own salvation. But when the rest of the mist hung in white tatters from the bushes and the grey daylight struck their eyes, they looked about themselves in wonder, as if seeing themselves for the first time. They drew away from one another, as if from incomprehensible visions. And to top it all off, they looked horrible: their skin hung from them like torn rags. They were filthy with mire from their hooves to their spines. They were covered in wounds, sores, and muck — the very picture of repugnant, barely breathing carrion. The whole campground looked like one huge sea of muddy stench, punctured everywhere by the thousands of hooves. They got to their feet unwillingly, with a moan of deep despair, as if all the more unfortunate in the first light of the dawn. A sort of inexplicable hatred and revulsion pushed them away from one another. There was none of that paroxysm of joy that Rex had predicted — just the opposite. The bright, wise eye of the day uncovered inevitably to their sight the whole reality of their situation, and this gave rise in turn to bitter lamentation and anxiety. The purple eyes of the dawn envenomed their own; the celadon flushes blushing in the sky brought them nothing but pain. The very brightness terrified them, in which everything appeared in its usual, and yet horrid, shape. They saw themselves in that reality as wretched things, small and dispossessed, and at the same time they felt themselves to be one unfortunate herd of be-ings at the prey of ever new suffering. Desperate roars rent the air and rolled above the camp like a long, prolonged thunderstorm. Despite the wolves' teeth and the barking of the dogs, the herds could not be budged.

An inexplicable terror tore at them as if with claws. They were frightened by the coming day. In those long, merciless nights, they'd forgotten about themselves — they'd even for-gotten about life, as they tumbled into the ditches of death with a calm resignation. So pleasant it had been to just yearn, curse, and perish! So good it had been for one to forget all about oneself and feel oneself to be nothing more than a blind particle of a great mass, with no will of one's own. And now this horrid day had to rouse them from their mori-bund drowsing, force them to live and become conscious of themselves. Who among them had strength enough to lift such burdens? And where are they off to, now? And why? The old faith and hope had completely died off inside them. They looked upon the pale expanses of the sky above them, and the ragged mountain ranges and distant empty spaces of the world around them, as if seeing them for the first time. Those immense vistas seemed so crushing to them that a monstrous fear overcame the last bits of their consciousness. Their irritation swelled greater with each passing moment, leading them closer and closer to madness. Here and there voices of rage began to bellow, hooves pawed at the earth, pounding it rabidly, and a sudden, irrepressible fury hurled them upon one another. They trampled and smashed one another senselessly. Old pretensions and grudges awoke once more. Everyone felt himself to be the wronged party and took it out on others. A wild, contentious chaos erupted all over the campground, and to make things worse, innumerable flocks of predatory birds were now hovering over their heads. Whole clouds of ravens, vultures and eagles flew in from the north and, circling lower and lower, cawed and screeched in anticipation of carrion. Sometimes they would even swoop down in numbers upon an animal laying apart, and rip it to shreds in the wink of an eye. They feared neither hoof nor horn. Finally, the wolves succeeded in chasing them off, but they just perched thickly on all the trees, bushes and hillsides, to patiently await their next opportunity.

Suddenly, the sun arose above the mountains, huge, red, like an eye plucked from its socket and dripping with blood. The whole world stood still in the flood of its light.

The sheep began to sob out in an incessant bleating, but the rest just stood there in dumb wonder.

'Stupid sheep,' was the verdict of the impatient cows, who turned their backs upon the sunrise.

'I only just warmed up and here, it's "get a move on" again!' complained Shrike, the old ox. 'They give you a glimpse of the day and then they hide it away again. Who hasn't seen the sun before? Who cares?'

'Their arses ain't felt the sun in a month's time,' snarled some old sow.

'They give us the sun, but where's the fodder? Where's the fresh water? The barns?'

'No, they'll keep us here, up to our joints in muck, under the open sky!'

'Where've we gotta go now? Chasing the wind over the fields!'

'And the wind blows straight into the eyes of the wretched! Dogs go barefoot everywhere!' resounded the complaints.

Rex, driven to exasperation, repeated the order to march.

'They just turn away from us, muttering. They don't even want to hear of moving on!' the shepherds reported.

'Why? They sobbed at night — now it's day! They yearned for the sun — it's shining! They complained of the cold — it's warm enough; they're hungry— well, there'll be enough to eat there. And yet they don't want to move!'

'It's right now that they're up in arms? Who will ever figure out that mob!' Gimpy growled in reply.

'They fooled us with darkness, now they'll fool us with day. Don't believe anything a dog says — don't listen to them. We don't need no government of dogs. They want to wear us all down to death!' The drawn-out lowing of the oxen resounded here and there.

'It's time to teach those cattle a lesson!' Gimpy howled through clenched fangs.

'Go and teach them, then. It's high time. I don't know what else to do,' Rex barked, staring at the restive herds.

Rex was shaken with despair, the despair of helplessness, as it looked an improbable thing to bring anyone around to their senses. The campground had become one Babel of agitation — the cattle all inflamed and frenzied. The whole confusion of voices seethed chaotically from one end of the camp to another.

The sun was now high, warm and bright. The sky stretched out its marvellous blue canvas above them. The air was scented, the snow on the distant mountains sparkled, and the whole world was suffused with the brisk, intoxicating gusts of spring. But the beasts were insensitive to it all, blind even to the greenery of the fields. So enraged were they, that they knew not even what was going on with them. Every now and then someone new pushed himself out in front of them to give expression to the universal ire, anxiety, and helplessness, only to be shoved aside without any rhyme or reason, battered, trampled, cast shamelessly beyond the pale to perish beneath the beaks of the lurking birds of prey. Shrike, the old manor ox, harangued the longest, being immense and of incredibly powerful voice. He strove to save his comrades, but just didn't know how. At last, he was made to cede his place to some breeding bull or other, who demanded to be heard, using those horns of his to emphasise the point. He lifted his mighty poll and flapped his gums a long while, striking the earth with his cloven hooves and bellowing so loud as to be heard far, far away. But only heifer and quey, gazing at him with burning eyes, gave ear to him, ready to do his bidding.

'What does he know?' protested the horses, shunting him aside, finally. 'They've only kept him around to keep them in calves, and now he's going to be imparting wisdom?'

Then it was the pigs' turn to put forward some wise suggestions. They squealed one after another, bobbing their snouts, ready to devour the world entire and dare anything — but still they were in no position to offer any salvific advice. Nothing came of all this speechifying but even greater confusion, irritation, brawls, and stupefaction. And the upshot of it all was that they didn't want to march off with Rex, they didn't want to return to people, and they didn't want to stay where they were.

The sun had already passed its zenith and still the air reverberated with thousands of roars, bellows, bleats, whinnies, and stamping hooves. Finally, the soft, warm dusk was able to deal with them, and hungry and quarrelsome as they were, quaking with agitation, they flopped down right where they stood and fell into a deep, dreamless sleep.

Rex, informed of it all by the shepherds, finally turned to Gimpy:

'What are we going to do?'

He gazed up at the moon, which had just risen in the sky.

'I know what to do,' the wolf barked sneeringly in reply, withdrawing somewhat to the side.

Then a huge she-wolf leapt in from the bushes and lay down near Rex.

'I'll fix you,' she growled and, licking his muzzle, stretched out at length beside him.

Rex wasn't taken with her tenderness, but he was even more surprised at her being there at all.

'Lead us, master. Who cares about all that pestilent meat? They'll fall in behind us anyway. Their fear will drive them. What can they do by themselves?'

'Keep your stupid advice to yourself,' said Gimpy, angrily. 'What are you after here?'

'Boys! To me!' she called, taking note of his arched back and blood-red eyes. 'I've got some accounts to settle with you. And you keep running away from me like a rabbit!'

'You scurvy bitch! I can't seem to keep your flea-ridden hide away from my den. I'll have you cast out of the pack. Out of my sight!' he snarled, lunging at her with fury. Yet before he could snap her in his jaws, she was ringed about by the fangs of young wolves, like a sharp palisade. He barely had time to leap aside.

'Mutiny!' he seethed. So irate was he, the words seemed to be boiling in his throat. His anger, hatred, and wounded pride nearly stifled him.

'Your fangs are rotting away, the moths are laying their eggs on you like some old mangy blanket, you can no longer see at night, and still you want to rule?' she mocked him acidly. 'The calves kicked at you yesterday, and you ran away! Not long ago, the swine were snuffling about your belly with their snouts, and you didn't even dare to growl!'

Her words lashed him like whips and smarted so, that he tore at the ground with his claws and howled hoarsely, awaiting an opportune moment to attack.

'Get up and stand to!' she cried. 'You can't avoid death forever! We've had enough of your rule and your deceit!' she howled, preparing herself for a mortal grappling. She was immense — the largest in the pack, a true pack-mother. As dry and nimble as a sharp blade; springy, with legs like iron, flames seemed to play along the sparkling, razor-sharp fangs of her maw. The scars of old wounds could be seen white against her dark hide. Beneath her knitted brows her angry eyes flashed like lightning. Bloodthirsty she was, atremble with the will to fight. She barked short and hoarsely:

'Stand to! Stand to!'

But suddenly she herself was surrounded by a wall of some hundred shepherds, and Rex barked threateningly:

'That's enough! Now's not the time for settling scores. Gimpy will remain with the herds.'

The order was sharp and threatening. The she-wolf grovelled close to Rex, and whimpered:

'As you wish. I'll stay by your side, master. I'll watch over you.'

'Stay. We'll leave tomorrow at dawn, if only we two.'

Rex threw himself under the bushes, but sleep did not come quickly, for the she-wolf returned with a hunk of meat of some sort, which she placed before him, and while he sated himself, she filled his ears with an unending stream of complaints against Gimpy.

At dawn, when they arose to set out again, the whole camp was already afoot and awaiting his commands.

'And once more they've changed!' Rex exclaimed in wonder. 'As docile as sheep.'

'Do you think it might be a trick?' the she-wolf said, uneasily.

But Rex, leaping on his stallion, rode out in front of the columns. The she-wolf trotted at his side, and all the herds, as far as the eye could see, waited in readiness.

'To the east! To the sun! To the east!' the shepherds howled.

And the herds began to roll on like a huge flood: calmly, evenly, and quietly rolling toward the mountains flashing in the distance with the silver summits of their glaciers.

8

The days rolled on evenly, like a blue-grey wheel: calm, monotonous, and so similar to one another that it was impossible to tell whether today might not in fact be tomorrow, or yesterday once again. Time flowed on slowly, lazily, like deep, great waters that covered the whole earth. Pale dawns arose without any fanfares of light; grey, and like eternal, tireless pilgrims, on they trudged over their endless road, passing through gloomy noon-times, treading through mournful dusks, and laying down for heavy sleeps in the dark nights — nights without stars or moon, nights like coffins of eternal silence. And that's how it was every morning, always.

And so, every morning, that same sky unbuttoned its grey shroud above the world.

And so, every morning, that same doused, dead light sifted into their eyes like powdery sand invading each nook and cranny.

And so, every morning, that same painful, incomprehensible yearning awoke in their hearts, driving them on and on like a bullwhip.

But the mountains, flashing with their silvery mirages of snow and ice, were always beyond their reach — always as distant as they'd ever been. The earth kept stretching out endlessly at their feet. The herds went on, indefatigably, in one broad flow, so that it might seem as if everything were flowing along with them — as if they were being borne onward through the deserts of the universe aboard a ship of titanic dimensions. For no eyes could get their bearings in this monotony of identical hills, identical trees, identical rivers and identical days of greyness: the grey sky, the grey earth, which they were passing through. No winds blew, no rains fell; the sun was not intolerable, nor did the cold gnaw at their bones. Day after day passed by, one as alike to another as the beads of a rosary. At times it seemed as if they were treading in place despite their incessant march forward. And at last, the monotony transformed them all into its image and likeness of perfect greyness, silence, and deathly peace. The quarrels grew still; all altercations and opposition came to an end. There was no more jostling, roaring, or woeful bleating. Even natural distinctions among them were blurred. The self-same lot that made them so like to one another on the inside, led them to cease recognising their outward differences as well. Colts wandered on amidst wolves, sows sought out warmth in the cool nights beneath the bellies of cows, calves progressed alongside stallions, and old oxen dragged on with their heads hanging low along with the pigs. They had become one gigantic being with one shared emotional state, prodded onward by one and the same instinct. Even memory was unable to knock any of them off this iron balance. Whatever had been before — their old lives, people, ancient sadnesses or joys — faded from their consciousness like the stalks of yesteryear on fallow fields, and crumbled into dust.

They wandered on now without any of those nagging questions, in humble obedience.

The very poorest fodder tasted good to them; the bare and rocky earth received their tired bones like a luxurious couch when they sank down to rest, and sleep brought for-getfulness of everything.

The shrill cries of the cranes awakened them each day at dawn. The howling of the dogs and the wolves drove them on and on, farther and farther.

'Over there! Beyond the mountains! It's not far now!' Rex would often bay, to encourage them.

And so they pushed on to those mountains with ever greater strength, determination, and the madness of an unshakable faith that soon they would reach the prom-ised land. Their eyes, shining as it were with a petitionary prayer and the dumb bellow of yearning, were lifted again and again in the direction of the mountains so longed for, and so terribly far away.

At last, after many such days, they unexpectedly reached at dusk a point where the land, so even heretofore, broke off suddenly, falling away in jagged cliffs toward some depres-sion that looked to them like a depthless chasm. The distant prattle of streams, echoing in the thousands, resounded like frenzied thunderstorms, lightning bolts, and the roars of wild creatures wafted upwards from the dark abysses, which smelt of dampness and rot.

The startled crowds stood before these seeming gates to unknown worlds, straining their ears with curiosity, snuf-fling the air.

'No one moves! Hold your place!' the shepherds warned, feverishly.

Then fell the night — a very contentious and cold one, windy and full of anxiety. Only the dawn would uncover the mystery to their eyes. Meanwhile, they stood there, pressing close to one another, too frightened to move an inch, for all around them lay black, treacherous fissures, and the earth so trembled at their feet as if it were to break away at any moment and disappear into the abyss. The ghastliness was heightened by the thunder and lightning, bursting forth every now and then from somewhere in the very depths of the darknesses below. Their backs and legs went numb and a drowsiness overcame them; hunger and thirst twisted their innards, yet they stood there patiently, awaiting the still distant dawn and already dreaming, as they drowsed, of what that dawn would bring. From somewhere came a whisper of hope that this would be the last night of their torture and torment.

'Tomorrow! Tomorrow!' the hushed voices floated about. And here and there, short cries: 'Tomorrow!'

As if painted images, all that they desired presented itself to their gaze, and fed that firm faith in the coming morrow. Slowly, all the herds, shifting their weight from one leg to another, lolled their fever-consumed tongues around that terrific desire for the blessed, long-awaited dawn. Then, their swelling hearts could no longer contain their violent emotions. They burst forth in a sudden, real hurricane of cries. The horned crowds began it with a mighty, sublime roaring, which was soon accompanied by the rest of the mixed voices. The chorale continued on until daybreak with such a solemnity and fervour, as if they were standing before the gates of Paradise.

Rain began to fall after midnight. Shortly thereafter it became a downpour, falling mercilessly until the misty outlines of the world began to emerge from beneath the trembling glaze of the water and take shape. Then the roars died down, and after a momentary silence, the song of the cranes resounded in the softened, grey air and the flapping of innumerable wings sifted down.

Rex appeared, along with the she-wolf who now never left his side.

'Onward! Onward! Let's go!' he howled in a commanding voice.

There was no need to repeat the command. They all rushed forward into the black throat of the gorge like a river bursting through dams, and, with a frightful jostling and roaring, they flowed on in an unstoppable, ever-swelling stormy current. Some of them still cast glances behind them; some of them even wanted to hold back, to go back, but the ranks had now gathered momentum and — carried away by the general impetus and the steep declivity, they all spilled into the lowlands in ever greater numbers, ever more precipitously. In the shadows of the sublime, wild cliffs, the thousandfold tattoo of their hooves thundered like a storm, which set the forests on the summits to sway. Avalanches of stone spilled down the slopes and the bird-life, startled, sped away in flight, shrieking.

In places, the gorge was cluttered with rubble fields of weathered stone and heaps of broken, rotting trees cut through by streams. Here and there deep crevasses lay athwart their path; now and again they had to swim through deep valleys flooded with water, which had the appearance of green bowls scooped out of the cliff-faces. Then again the gorge would narrow into a tight, dark throat where they would tear and bloody their sides by scraping them up against the rock wall in their passage; horns would be cracked and split. It is impossible to describe all the obstacles they fought their way through in gloomy and obstinate silence. But they were borne along on their madness, which prevented them from even sensing the horrors of their march. They were as numb as stone to all suffering. Crushed by falling rocks, drowned by treacherous waters, swallowed by crevasses, they were persecuted continually by hunger, slaughtered by the immense travail of the journey. Whoever fell was trampled to pieces by the hooves of thousands. Whoever gave in to weakness, even for a moment, or fainted — perished. Whoever remained behind was also lost forever. From all sides, death stretched out her pitiless claws toward them.

There was neither mercy nor pity for the weak. Everything seemed to conspire their death. Each day preyed on them more cruelly. For as soon as they had paid their bloody tribute to emerge from the mountain passes, they suddenly found themselves fallen into a region of ice, snow, and persistent storms. At night, the mournful moans of those freezing to death would pierce the icy winds from beneath the snow-banks. Nor were the days any more merciful: the frozen sun gazed down with its icy, greenish eye on those moribund lines struggling through the raging maelstroms of snow.

And when these had been conquered, their road was blocked by soaring, dead pinewoods. The trees stood thickly together. Ancient they were, prehistoric. Beneath their vault a reddish darkness reigned — like the marriage of day and night. They stood ramrod straight, scraping the heavens, like

　　　　WŁADYSŁAW STANISŁAW REYMONT

columns of copper. They were all rotten, sifting into dust, held together in their accustomed form by eternal immobility and the timeless stillness of death. The earth beneath them was dead too — covered with cadaverous lichens.

But the most horrendous thing of all was that the merest more pronounced bellow, the slightest contact, and even the heavier footfall would send the forest crashing down, the gigantic columns crumbling into punk. And thus began a desperate, silent battle with this powdery, corpsy sand, which sifted down all around them. It feel silently in innumerable rusty cascades, covering the herds in thick coatings. They waded through it knee-deep; then it reached their bellies, until at last only their polls thrashed about wildly above the surface of the ruddy storms of dust. Thousands of them were buried alive in it, while the rest, holding their breaths, pushed on, one leg in front of another, passing by each tree, one by one, carefully, in mortal terror.

They were led on by instinct only; that and the clangour of the cranes, singing with each new dawn somewhere high above the forests. Then, at last, before the deathly exhausted herds, there appeared immense green foothills, bathed in the bright, joyous light of day, spreading wide. The sun was shining, intoxicating breezes were blowing, the lush grasses, thickly sprinkled with wildflowers, were swaying. Innumerable brooks were babbling sweetly, immense cedars spread about a mercifully silky shade, and the stillness of the warm afternoon rang with the incessant buzzing and chirping of insects.

The foothills gently sloped downwards into a valley that the eye could barely encompass, from which those giant mountains, which had been drawing them on for so long now, seemed to spring. The ice-covered summits sparkled in the sunlight like silver torches. Their slopes, clad in the green raiments of forests, crisscrossed by the white smudges of waterfalls and frayed here and there by the wild courses of naked cliffs, were the very image of majesty and grandeur. And there, from the left side, sparkled the ungraspable broad, blue surface of the sea. The air trembled with the rhythmic beat of the waves.

For a long time yet, they remained blind to all these wonders, and for a long time still, filled with the terror they carried out with them from that mortal struggle, they lay on the ground, their polls resting heavily on the earth, completely exhausted, no longer paying any heed even to hunger, or their still bleeding wounds.

'I can't go on any farther. I'd rather just die here,' bellowed one of the breeding bulls, as if echoing the thoughts of all.

And thus whole days passed before they betook themselves to grazing and slaking their thirst, at which time, having regained some of their strength, they began to look about them.

Rex, having made his rounds among all those who had got through, returned to the she-wolf greatly perturbed.

'Is this everyone?'

A horror constricted his throat; he could barely catch his breath

'Gimpy's gone. So are the other wolves,' the shepherds explained.

'I knew they'd turn traitor,' snarled the she-wolf. 'They ran off before we even got to the gorge.'

'But the herds — is this everyone?' he fretted, unable to believe his eyes.

'The rest of them left their bones along the declivities and in those cursed pinewoods.'

'It would have been better had no one survived.'

'Don't worry, we'll soon join the majority,' the bolder shepherds bit back with rancour.

'It's not far now,' Rex promised firmly. 'Not far at all.'

'Sure! Wait and wait till it's too late! But the wolves'll —'

But before the wisecracking dog could finish with his mockery, his blood was dripping from the fangs of the she-wolf, who taught him some respect.

'Where did the cranes alight at nightfall?' Rex asked, pricking his ears and snuffling the air.

'I'll take you to them. My ears are sore from their shrieking.'

'They're afraid of you. Stay here and keep watch.'

'I can't even remember what they taste like,' she huffed with contempt, and after pointing out their direction to him, she went off to have a look around the resting herds.

From the immeasurable legions who had rebelled against the yoke of man and set off in search of freedom, only a few thousand survivors now remained.

As a matter of fact, her wolfish heart was rent by pity for the first time in her life as she swept her eyes over those wretched skeletons lying about helplessly.

'Bones, nothing but ragged skin and bones!' she whimpered in compassion.

She was also deeply moved at the sight of the sheep stretched beneath the cedars.

'You made it,' she said gently, creeping a little closer. 'How is it with you?'

'We don't know! We don't know!' they bleated in panic, hastening off to the safety of the rams' horns.

It seemed as if all the pigs had gotten through. They were lolling about the sandy banks of a stream. At the sight of the she-wolf, they began to lift their snouts threateningly, perking their floppy ears in alarm, training their round, intelligent eyes upon her in fear…

'I didn't think I'd be seeing you again. And almost all of you made it through!'

'Because we were picking up the rear, as usual. We don't have the legs of a stallion, you know.'

'And when the pinewoods started to crash and sift down, we went along on the sides — carefully and slowly.'

'We only rush to the trough. We're in no hurry to die.'

'You're lucky,' she growled with respect.

'We're smart enough not to push our way in there, where others are perishing.'

She crept up closer to the horses, but one of them kicked out with his hooves and neighed brutally.

'Take yourself off, bitch! You slink around here, I'll give you what for!'

The horned nations greeted her just as inhospitably. One of the breeding bulls even swung his horns in her direction.

'You looking to sink your teeth into some tripe? Go fill your belly back there in the pinewoods!'

'How few of you remain — how few!' she lamented sincerely, until her long, drawn-out howls, like threnodies, resounded on all hands.

　　　　WŁADYSŁAW STANISŁAW REYMONT

The breeding bull raised his heavy poll and bellowed mightily in contempt.

'Lightning never strikes the weeds! Mangy hides like yours even escape the flood! Off with you! We can't bear your stench.'

She howled in reply, and all the mares started rearing and flailing their hooves.

'Stupid meat. You're lucky I'm not peckish,' she snarled high-mindedly.

It was getting dark when she returned to Rex's den, bringing with her a piece of meat she'd hunted down. It was still dripping with fresh blood. They set themselves to devour it. Nothing could be heard for a long while but the crunching of bones and gluttonous slurps. Finally, sated and licking his lips with relish, Rex began to speak of the cranes.

'They'll rest at the water until the moon turns and the storks arrive. Meanwhile, our groups can rest too, and batten on the grazing. They'll get their strength back — there's thick grass everywhere. And I've seen some heavy, fat birds around the fields. They almost fly into your mouth themselves. So we've got to be careful not to be too greedy. They're thinning out,' he added, as if casually.

'I don't like birds. Too much trouble plucking feathers. And traces remain.'

'We haven't far to go. Just beyond these mountains,' he said, gazing at the summits growing ethereal in the deepening night.

'We can get over them. But how are the hooves and horns to pass through?'

'We'll follow the valleys. The cranes will lead us through.'

'What do they care about mountains or seas? They fly on over everything with ease. But will the herds want to move on at all?'

'You think they won't? So close already to paradise?' he mused.

She curled herself into a ball and seemed to drowse.

The moon rolled out onto the dark heavens. The icy summits were as if doused; silver mists began to unravel over the earth. The world was flooded with silence. The only sound to be heard was the distant, ceaseless beat of the waves, which thumped and thumped like the rhythmic pulse of a mighty heart.

Rex couldn't fall asleep. A dread of sorts had awakened inside him.

'I'm not sure you can really trust those aerial vagabonds,' the she-wolf snarled so suddenly that it startled him.

'Those winged things have it good wherever they are. What can they know about the things of earth?'

He had just been turning over in his mind the cranes' directions, and their tales.

'What can they know about our life?' she said with a yawn, as if bored.

'Their wings bear them away from all bad weather. They have no idea of the hazards of battle or the sweetness of victory. A stupid beak like that swallows a frog, and that's fuel enough for a whole week's flying. And they're never lacking in muddy puddles. And they're all swelled up with pride, because men don't choose to hunt them. What sort of paradise are they leading us to? Bogs, probably. Bogs and water.'

'At least our exploiters and murderers won't be there. Not a single man.'

'But will we have anything to eat there? And I'm not thinking about myself now.'

'They sang some beautiful songs to me about that place, and I believe them. They never lie.'

'Every fox lauds his own brush. The only thing I wonder about is, if it's so heavenly there, why do they fly in to our lands to breed? We don't have our nurseries on the other side of the world.'

'It's a mystery,' he snarled back, none too happy with the turn the conversation was taking, 'Impossible to understand.'

'That's what the owls hoot from their hollows in the trees. "Mystery! Mystery!" Blind in the sunlight, so they think no one can see anything!'

And she gave such a howl that the sheep began to bleat in terror.

'Quiet! Or I'll run you off!' he growled threateningly, made anxious by the doubts her words sowed inside him. He simply couldn't allow himself not to trust the winged ones. All his faith and hope, the whole future of all four-legged nations, was born of those wizardly songs. Wasn't it the clangour of the cranes, and only that, which had led them through the wild spaces of this horrid world? The road behind them, paved with the bones of their fallen, was testimony to that. They had cast everything aside to push on ahead through every Hell that stood in their way, to reach that dreamed-of land of happiness. And it wasn't far now, not at all… Once again they sang to him of its wonders! Feeding his soul with new faith. Anger was speaking through her, the she-wolf, a creature of the dark, blinded by the light.

He couldn't fall asleep. The moon shone directly into his eyes, and from the valleys below, sunk deep in fog, now and again sounded the echoes of such bellows as set his skin to crawl.

'It's a rough road ahead of us!' he said, listening and shivering…

'We'll push the herds on in front, to test it out.'

'What could that be, bellowing so horridly?' he said, alarmed.

'We'll find out when it falls upon us. Go to sleep now. It's nearly dawn.'

The new day dawned, but the bright sun did not dispel those doubts, which resurfaced along with some strange, incomprehensible dread. He avoided the she-wolf and visited the herds, concerned. He raced about their ranks, checking in on nearly every individual animal. He engaged them in friendly conversation, speaking to them with fiery conviction of the goal of their long trek so near at hand. He pointed to the mountains beyond which all their sufferings would end. He strove to infuse them with the whole of his faith in that fortunate tomorrow, repeating in his thunderous leonine voice what he had heard from the cranes. The more he felt their growing reluctance, the greater was his zeal. But it seemed to him as if he were haranguing the deaf and dumb. They lifted their polls and fixed their heavy eyes upon him, but his speeches were answered only by an ominous silence. He strove harder and harder — to no effect. He sought out better pasture lands, clearer springs, cooler resting places for their break at noon — to no avail. The distrust grew stronger by the day. Some sort of invisible, ever deeper chasm grew between him and them, and yet they'd fed well; their sunken flanks had filled out once more; their hides had taken on a healthy glow; their spines had straightened again. Even the words they spoke grew sonorous and mighty. Yet, simultaneously, there was more and more griping. He caught wind of it one night as he slipped in among them under the cover of the mist.

The swine, making good use of the nuts spread beneath the cedars, grunted lazily:

'What sort of fodder is this? Bitter as wormwood, rotten… Oh, those potatoes and grain… potatoes!'

'Or these grasses,' neighed some other troublemaker. 'It's like chewing nettles! My mouth is on fire!'

'What I'd give for a quart of oats or a twist of hay!'

The cows, who could hardly be seen among the lush, tall grasses, were also moaning:

'Such fodder. You eat all day long and still your udders are empty and you haven't any strength. Oh! Beet leaves! Oil cakes! A tuft of dry hay! Those were banquets, those were…'

The oxen, gone lazy, with bellies as round as barrels, moaned sobbingly:

'Bent down all day long, pulling up blade after blade of grass, and at night: an empty stomach, a sore back, and to top it all off, go and find some sweet water! This freedom's not worth a stray mutt to me. We're not made for such happiness. Oh, how we used to march in to a ready meal! The manger smelled of fodder from afar!'

Even those stupid sheep kept up their endless bleating about there being no one to fleece them.

Old Shrike, who had emerged fairly battered from the pinewoods, and kind of off in the head, wandered about, unable to find a place for himself, bellowing constantly:

'I said it'd end badly! I told you! Let's go look for a master. Let's go look for a man! Ooo! Ooo!'

Rex returned to his den torn and embittered.

'Despicable meat!' the she-wolf whimpered after listening to his report. 'They'll be filling their troughs for them right away!'

'They stuff themselves to the gills, do nothing, and — what more do they want?' he whined.

'They have it too good. Misery'll bring them back to their senses. We've got to move on.'

'But now I'm worried. Will they come? I felt hatred among them. And why? Why? It's true that the pastures here are trampled and worn, and the water is fouled. But how to get them moving?'

'With promises. Promise them whatever comes to mind. They'll believe you and follow.'

'What?!' he snarled, scandalised.

'Promises are made to be broken, and fed to fools like bread. And you won't really be lying, after all. Happiness lies in hope. What's been keeping them going up till now? They also say "hope is the mother of fools." But I'd howl to the ends of the earth that hope is everyone's mother. Let the shepherds go round as if they had a secret — that the journey will come to an end in a valley just beneath these mountains, that that's it, the end of the long hard road. Freedom and happiness. You've got to get them moving with something. Because if they develop a taste for this blissful lazing about, they won't budge another inch. And anyway, is their lot so terribly hard? They eat until they're fit to burst, there're no men slaughtering them, no crop or whip or lash whistling above their heads. Let's just hope that they won't be worse off there, where you're leading them.'

'No foot of tyrant's ever touched the soil there,' he growled passionately. 'Your advice is good. But what next, when we make it to the mountains?'

'By then they'll have forgotten what you promised them, and they'll fall prey to new promises and again allow you to lead them on. They've got to be deceived. For their own good.'

'You've got a head full of tricks.' The she-wolf had aroused a respect in him bordering on dread.

'Everyone who's free has to rely on his wits. Our kind doesn't live by the grace of man.'

'We've got to get going from here before the rains come.'

'I'm off to set things in motion. Can you trust your fellows?'

'Dogs? As I trust myself! You saw yourself how faithful and devoted they were all along our path.'

'Keep your eye on those peasant mutts. They're cooking up something against us…'

'You're seeing things. They're the most faithful of the faithful. The shepherds won't even let you near the sheep.'

'The one who can stand up to me hasn't been born yet!' she yelped haughtily. 'I've seen somewhat going on among them and the herds at night. Some soft barking…'

That said, she sped away. As for Rex, he ran off to a rocky elevation that overhung the pasture lands, and stretching himself out, surveyed the world around him.

Like a gigantic, green shelf overgrown with trees, the piedmont fell away into a measureless valley thickly spread with the golden glow of the dawn.

Beyond the foothills rose the heaven-scraping wall of mountains, while from the side, far way, the skin of the sea sparkled with blinding flashes. A breeze, warmed by the rising sun, began to blow.

The sun was now high in the sky. The scattered herds were grazing, barely visible among the grasses. Their colours blended in with their surroundings — only the whiteness of the pigs lounging beneath the great cedars stood out sharply. They and the sheep — like pearls or stones scattered against the green slopes. From somewhere came the monotonous roar of a waterfall. Waves were playing on the far distant sea shore. Every now and then a drawn-out bellow resounded, but more frequently it was the chattering, friendly barks of dogs that disrupted the quiet.

Rex roved across the area with his eyes. It might seem that his gaze lingered longest on the immaculate blue above the mountain summits, where the eagles where wheeling, although he cast a glance behind him from time to time at that confounded pinewood, hanging on the edge of the horizon like a black storm cloud full of hail. But actually he was blind both to the area spreading around him and all visible forms. For his sightlines were blocked by the distress aroused by the stupid howls of the she-wolf. All the events that had occurred since they abandoned the world of man passed before his eyes. The images were as clear as they were when he first experienced them, but now he was reliving them at blinding speed. Not a single moan he heard then was missing now. He saw again all the corpses left behind; he relived all that marching on empty stomachs — the parades of starvation. All of this shook him with the force of a hurricane, though a perfectly silent one. He would shake those nightmares from him like water upon emerging from a pond, escape them, forget them, but that was impossible. They fed on his tormented heart. His hackles rose in terror and his teeth chattered. Again and again he whimpered and tore at the ground with his claws, but he was helpless before these memories clambering out of the caverns of his brain. Where are all those innumerable hordes? Miles, so many endless miles of roads paved with their bones glistened now like a horrid ribbon. And how many of those remaining will reach that promised land? Rex fell prostrate beneath a crushing burden.

Grief tore at his heart and at the same time something like a sense of responsibility for it all made itself known to him in waves of searing pain. He had believed in the songs of the cranes; they had driven him wild with their sublime, enchanting tales. Were they anything more than fairy stories? Can any such happiness really exist on the earth? Hammers, it seemed, were pounding within his skull, and each blow was more powerful than the last. And if it all were untrue? If all his elevated slogans and promises, which had incited the innumerable hosts to revolt, were just lies? And that promised land a mirage, an illusion? What will happen if, there, where he was leading them… when they got there at last and… No, no! His instinct of self-preservation cried out inside him. It must be just as he believed it to be, just as the cranes sang, just as his soul demanded it be! He had led the animals forth to their salvation, not their ruin. The way is difficult, many are they who suffer and die — but even so they are no worse off than they would have been, had they remained in slavery to man. He had shattered their fetters and led them forth to freedom! And they had followed him gladly, of their own free will — he did not force them to. They gripe, they curse him for their suffering. Well, suffering is the price one has to pay for it all. They'll learn how to live. The happiness won by suffering will not disappoint them. So many wild nations of animals exist, who would never exchange their freedom for the tutelage and care of man. They had declared war on injustice, and they must triumph! They are still blind, but there — beyond the mountains, on those paradisiacal fields of happiness, they will begin to see clearly. In the intoxication of their new life they will forget all about the past. The past be damned!

The storm within him was stilled. Every now and then a thunderbolt might crash, or lightning blaze from his eyes, but a proud peace now slowly rocked his heart.

His certitude was firm once again, and the ancient, steadfast faith once more nourished his fainting will.

He brooded a while longer there on the cliffs. Only when the dusk had deeply fallen, when the moon had sailed out onto the heavens and the cedars spread their long shadows over the meadows did he return to his den.

'The storks are coming. You can hear them clattering in the west,' the she-wolf snarled sleepily.

'It's them the cranes are waiting for. The cranes and us, too.'

All grew silent. The night embraced the earth with the silver wings of light.

The dawn had just made white the crowns of the trees and shone upon the still misty eyes of the waters when a loud threshing noise was heard from the west — something like an approaching storm. Soon, endless streams of birds could be seen flashing against the paling skies. They soared on in gigantic wedges like clouds shimmering and gravid with lightning. They flowed down from over the dead forests in a slanted descent, and the rattle of their clacking sifted down on the piedmont with the dry rushing of wood-chips.

'The storks! The storks!' voices seethed from side to side of the multitudes of animals.

And all the beasts leapt to their feet, lifting their heavy polls in the direction of that black and white cloud, which was tumbling ever lower. With thousands of bellows, they greeted their old friends. A joyful clacking came in reply, and the rushing whirlwind of innumerable wings boomed so low overhead that the sharp outstretched beaks and red legs flat against their bellies were clearly visible. The strong wind that arose from the beating of their wings set the very trees to sway.

At the same time, the chirping of small birds sifted down from on high, and whole swarms of them fluttered down with sweet trills from behind the backs of the storks. They alit on all the cedars, bushes, and all high places, with whole groups of them descending amidst the herds. For their part, the horde of storks, having circled the foothills, turned left, toward the wide wetlands shining from afar beneath the still white surface of the yet sleepy waters. There they alighted, and the clacking of their bills did not cease for a long while amidst the screeched greetings of the cranes and the plopping of the waters. Again and again swarms of storks took flight for a short jaunt before alighting again.

The herds were quite aroused by the arrival of the storks. Many of them chased after them. An inexplicable joy enflamed their hearts and lifted their spirits. A sort of happiness had flowed over them all as soon as the storks were seen. The horned tribes couldn't restrain themselves from constant bellows of joy. The horses gambolled wildly, whinnying, and thumping with their hooves. The dogs nearly went mad, barking until hoarse at the swallows and larks perched on the tree branches. An extraordinary rejoicing reigned. It was as if a holiday had been declared on the pasture lands. The animals even forgot to eat — constantly glancing toward the lowlands, toward the waters shining with the flames of the dawn. 'Storks! Storks!' the varied voices continued to cry. Something drew them all irresistibly towards them. How might it be otherwise, seeing that they had flown in from those skies over there? From the animals' distant fatherland. From their fields, their villages, their thatched roofs! With them, they brought some different, intoxicating air. That dry, wooden clacking sang to them with enchanting echoes of the past. For did they not graze together on the same meadows? Had that clacking of theirs not resounded above their thatched roofs for as long as they could remember? Even the pigs melted at the memory of how those long, hard beaks would steal food from their troughs. More than one of them recalled the sharp pain of being struck by those beaks… Now and then on the stubble fields their ears would be filled with the laments of the partridges when their eggs and young were stolen by them. A memory flashed in the mind of each one of them, and each one of them was shot through suddenly with a haunting longing for the past. Again they smelled the village smoke, the yards, the fresh fodder. The bellows of yearning were made louder by the accompaniment of the chirping of swallows wheeling crisply above their heads, as they always had done…

Rex was knocked off balance. He knew those storks well indeed. They had their nests in the old larch by the manor house, and from time to time they would filch potatoes from his bowl. Sometimes, for fun, he'd chase them around the fields. How many memories had arrived along with them!

'It's cold back there now, snowy. But they're heading in our direction!' he said aloud, his voice husky with emotion.

Only the she-wolf looked upon their arrival with disdain and indignation.

'Garbage-pickers! Frog-eaters! Just the proper company for dogs, who hunt the trash-heaps!' she barked sneeringly. 'I can understand the cranes. They live by their own laws and far away from people, but that band there — those farmyard bandits — forever hungry and forever on the prowl to snatch a morsel! Those eternal chatterers, befouling all the trees, never-sated gullets! You can't get away from them. They see everything and babble it far and wide. And how brave they are, well, we'll soon see.'

She did indeed, dragging back two she'd hunted down in broad daylight.

'I took these two while all the rest were looking on. They'll be shaking their beaks at me for months on end.'

Rex interrupted her gaily:

'They'll be flying off with the cranes in a few days, and we'll be right after them.'

Those few days passed in a strange atmosphere of excitement, anticipation, and, it seemed, quiet counsel. At night, mysterious grumblings could be heard. What was more, the suspicions of the sensitive she-wolf were aroused by the fact that the dogs, even a couple of the shepherds, kept constantly close together, as if conspiring something. But she kept that to herself. Then, some downpours of rain came, and in the breaks between them, wild winds swept the piedmont. The nights became dark and loud. The vales were covered with impenetrable fog. Across the skies tumbled heavy, dun clouds, and the sun had a green tint that resembled the colour of a bad egg. The sea was lashed by tempests; waves howled at the strand, pounding in foaming surf that leapt towards the clouds. There was nowhere to shelter from the raging winds and torrential rains as the trees, tugged this way and that by the hurricane, shrieked terrifyingly, sweeping the earth with their branches.

Then one day the cranes sent word that they were ready to set out.

'We move on tomorrow. I'll let everyone know,' Rex ordered and, after having gnawed through some loins that the she-wolf had dragged up, he crawled in among the bushes and went to sleep.

It was broad daylight when he awoke. The rain was no longer falling and a wind chased off the last of the clouds.

'Let's go! Forward! Forward!' he howled on all sides and — suddenly — gaped at the surrounding areas with alarmed eyes. The foothills were empty. Nothing could be heard except for the loud babbling of the mountain waters rushing through the grasses.

'Where have they gone?' A wild howl emerged from deep inside him.

'The river flooded its banks,' the she-wolf explained. 'They had to escape the rising waters!'

She stood there surrounded by her sons. A few dozen of Rex's most faithful shepherds were running about, helplessly snuffling the ground.

'No trace of them anywhere. They must have set out before midnight.'

'How dare they! Without my express permission! How dare they, without my express command!' Rex said, feverishly agitated.

'Well, they dared all right. The stranger thing is, I didn't hear them. Inconceivable.'

'We'll catch them up. Forward!' he bayed, recovering his accustomed spirit.

They rushed on ahead, outracing the ever more quickly flowing waters. The piedmont fell away quite steeply. Here and there they had to avoid rocky drop-offs. Down below the sheer cliffs were some small lakes overgrown with trees.

'They must be lower down, past the waters. The brush is blocking them from our view.'

But they weren't there either. Gazing round, they noticed with astonishment that past the waters the trail took a sharp right turn and led along further, parallel to the mountains.

'They're lost. The poor wretches! They wanted to go round the steep declivities, and then they mistook their road,' he lamented.

'But at least they're moving. Usually, they wouldn't cover so much ground in two whole days.'

'And we'll have to step on it, too.'

They galloped on. The traces of the herds' passage became visible on the broad expanses before them: the grasses were trampled into the earth, bushes were broken. Tufts of wool and fur had been caught against the low cactuses. Their path took them across numerous streams, rocky dykes, and sandy dunes. It was cut off at last by the white hills of broken chalk. Past these stretched some immense lowlands — grey, sad, and sunburnt. Here and there some white patches flickered, and copses of gigantic trees could be seen.

'That's where they've paused to rest!' one of them barked, looking toward a place where swarms of birds were wheeling. Soon, they caught sight of some blue wetlands, where the waters were ringed with feathery palm-trees, like eyelashes, and widespread green pasturelands.

'They're lying in the shade,' the dogs howled before tearing forward.

Rex, outpacing them all with frenzied leaps, was the first to fall in among the herds.

'Blind, are you?!' he bayed angrily. 'Instead of heading straight toward the mountains, to the east, you, like the stupid sheep you are, went off in the other direction! And without my orders?'

Not a single voice was raised in reply. And this made him so furious that, racing about like one possessed, he barked out his ire upon them all. Giving in to his nature, here and there he snapped at them with his fangs, butting them with his head and angrily pawing the ground.

Thousands of weary eyes were trained on him. Exhausted by the road and the heat, drowsing they were — and here comes this one, disturbing their needed rest! The spot was well-chosen: the sparkling-clean waters breathed forth a coolness, the palms cast a sweet shade, the grasses were succulent and soft, and a slight breeze rocked them as they drowsed luxuriously, as if it were singing them to sleep.

His rage subsiding somewhat, Rex began to command in no uncertain terms that, as soon as they had rested, they would return to where the cranes were waiting for them.

'And from there we'll head straight for the mountains. It's the last leg of our journey. Wide passes, through the meadows, along a river. Only three more rests, and it's the end of our road.'

'No! We're not going back! You can go if you want to! We've parted company!' The bellows came thickly, like a thunderclap.

Rex spun round in a circle, as if he had been hit by a stone. He couldn't believe what he was hearing.

'It's a flat road, just through the fields!' he went on. 'No troubles at all, and then the end of all our travelling…!'

'Liar! Liar!' barked all the mongrels suddenly, poking their heads out from among the pigs.

The she-wolf raced straight toward them with her sons. The dogs fought back with fury and determination, especially as the old sows rushed to their aid. An immense chaos erupted.

Then Rex, having lost the last bit of self-control remaining to him, began to whimper almost humbly. He pleaded with them, trying to appeal to their reason; he made promises, urged them, begged them to hold out. Despair could be seen in his eyes, brimming and overflowing with tears. An abyss appeared at his feet, into the unplumbable depths of which tumbled all his dreams, crumbling to dust just like that confounded pinewood, burying him beneath the punk of obliteration. He had given them his all — and now? He doubled his strengths, stumbling now and again, hardly breathing, but pulling himself back up and fighting, with the last of his strength and consciousness, against the universal idiocy, resistance and cowardice. He was betting his all now, fighting for all that belonged to him.

'You're killing yourselves! You're condemning all your future generations to destruction! You'll perish in these wilds, consumed by hunger, torn to pieces by wild animals, burnt to a crisp by the sun! Just a little more courage, brothers, a little more patience, a little more faith! We've suffered so much, and we're so close now to happiness, the happy end! And you prefer to waste away here?' He lost his voice, having screamed himself hoarse.

Then a mighty breeding bull, with a powerful poll and short horns, pushed himself forward through the crowds.

'Shut up, you tyrant, you!' His bellow made the very palms to shake. 'You whimper like a scolded puppy, but no one believes a word you say anymore. We're not going any-where with you. We don't want to keep dropping like flies. Run off yourself after the jabbering of the cranes! Chase those ideals of yours and keep trying to grab the tail of the wind. You murdered us with your villainous promises. It's time to put an end to this insanity and heed again the voice of reason. From time immemorial we've been ruled by man, and from time immemorial he's cared for us. What have you made of us, except homeless vagabonds run wild? Wretches that were are, we fell victim to this freedom of yours. For the sake of freedom, you made us abandon a solid life in our fatherland. You kept us in line with stupid mirages. Because it's a barefaced lie that just beyond those mountains there lies that promised land of yours, that paradise of freedom and happiness. It's not true! There's no such place anywhere there's no people, no barns, no fields sown with grain to yield ready fodder for the winter time. You knew this all along, and yet you led us on and sold us off to death.'

'You want to return to the yoke? To slavery? To the whip?' he bayed, sad unto the death.

'We want to live!' The words burst forth from thousands of throats. 'We want to live!'

Then he heard the she-wolf yelp. She was defending her-self desperately against the snouts of the sows and the fangs of the dogs. Rex leapt to her aid, but before he made it to her he was himself surrounded by a forest of terrible horns.

'Death to the tyrant! Death to the betrayer! Death to the murderer!'

At this he sat down and, sweeping his eyes around him without fear, he howled for one last time.

Just a moment later, on a shoreline bordering turquoise waters, beneath the swaying palms, lay a great, bloody stain on the sand lit up by the sunlight piercing through the flickering shadows.

In a wild fury, they had literally torn him to pieces with their hooves.

Their bellows of triumph announced to all the world the death of the tyrant and the regaining of freedom!

Liberated from chimeras, the herds began to wander about the empty spaces in an indefatigable search for man. But they didn't even know where to begin looking for him, so they moved on in the direction of better fodder — wherever the fancy took them. They wanted to return to their fatherland, but who among them remembered in which direction it lay? Who could lead them back there?

And so they stumbled on through the immeasurable desert spaces, scorched by the sun, slain by hunger and thirst. They were buried beneath the shifting sands, carried off by wild beasts, and yet in no way could their unappeasable, horrid longing for their masters be slaked.

And then, after many, many days of wandering, as if they'd coursed through the world entire, those at the head of the ranks suddenly pulled up short, bellowing, falling prostrate to the earth:

'Man! Our master! Man!'

There at the edge of an impenetrable jungle, beneath the shade of a wide spreading palm tree, sat a family of apes.

The gigantic male, stunned at their sudden arrival, tore himself up to his full height.

At the sight of him, all of the herds fell down in humility and sent up a heaven-shattering roar:

'Be our master! Rule over us! We are your faithful chattel! Don't desert us!'

The terrified ape rushed up the palm and, throwing coconuts at those closest to him, spluttering with rage, jabbered something no one understood.

But from below, the continual beseeching arose toward him:

'Be our lord! Rule us! We are yours! Master!'

Kołaczkowo
17 VII 1924

BIBLIOGRAPHY

SOURCE TEXTS:

REYMONT, Władysław Stanisław. *Bunt*. Gdańsk: Wimana, 2018.

REYMONT, Władysław Stanisław. *Bunt*. Warszawa: Gebethner i Wolff, 1924.

REYMONT, Władysław Stanisław. *Bunt*. Warszawa: Wydawnictwo Tygodnika Ilustrowanego, 1934.

SECONDARY SOURCES

BOROWY, Wacław. 'Reymont,' *The Slavonic and East European Review*, Vol. XVI, No. 47 (January 1938): 439-448.

DAVIES, Norman. *God's Playground: A History of Poland*. Vol. II: '1795 to the Present.' New York: Columbia University Press, 1982.

DOROSZ, Beata. 'George Orwell's 1984: The Polish Chapter in Light of the PIASA Archives,' *The Polish Review*, Vol. 61, No. 4 (2016): 57-66.

DYBOSKI, Roman. 'Żeromski and Reymont,' *The Slavonic Review*, Vol. IV, No. 12 (March 1926): 552-561.

HARDY, Thomas. *The Complete Poems*. New York: MacMillan, 1982.

JEFFERS, Robinson. *Selected Poetry*. New York: Random House, 1959.

KWIATKOWSKI, Jerzy. *Literatura dwudziestolecia* [Interwar Literature]. Warsaw: PWN, 1990.

ORWELL, George. *Animal Farm / 1984*. New York: Harcourt, 2003.

ORWELL, George. *A Life in Letters*, ed. by Peter Davison. New York: WW Norton, 2013.

ABOUT THE AUTHOR

Władysław Stanisław Reymont (1867–1925) was a Polish novelist of the realist period (the period of 'Organic Work,' as it is known in Poland, for its rejection of revolutionism and its dedication to preserving Polish culture among the three partitions by work among the people), and, especially, the Young Poland period, often equated with 'Polish Modernism.' He preferred to work as a labourer than to follow his parents' wishes into higher education, training as a tailor and labouring on the railroad. His fame as a novelist is based on two works, the epic *Chłopi* [The Peasants, 1902–1908] and *Ziemia obiecana* [The Promised Land, 1897–1898]. In 1924 he received the Nobel Prize in Literature. *Bunt* [The Revolt of the Animals, 1922, 1924], his last major work, was suppressed by the Communist régime of the People's Republic of Poland on account of its blatant rejection of Marxism and satirising of revolutions.

ABOUT THE TRANSLATOR

Charles S. Kraszewski is a poet and translator, creative in both English and Polish. He is the author of three volumes of original verse in English (*Diet of Nails*; *Beast*; *Chanameed*); two in Polish (*Hallo, Sztokholm*; *Skowycik*) and a farcical novel about the end of the world as we know it (*Accomplices, You Ask?*). He translates from Polish, Czech and Slovak into English, and from English and Spanish into Polish. He is a member of the Union of Polish Writers Abroad (London) and of the Association of Polish Writers (SPP, Kraków). In 2022 he was awarded the Gloria Artis medal (III Class) by the Ministry of Culture of the Republic of Poland.

DRAMATIC WORKS

by Cyprian Kamil Norwid

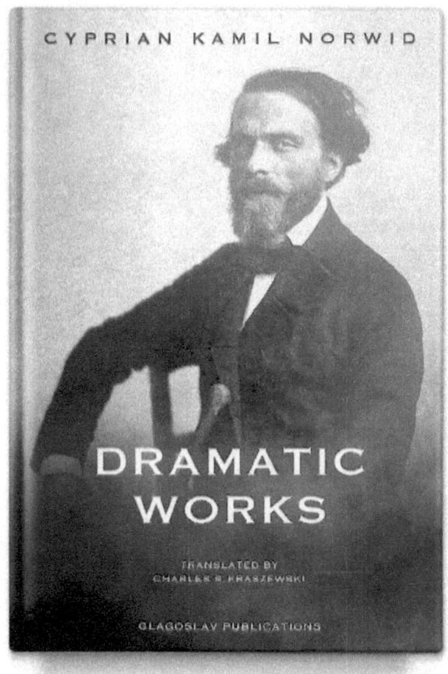

'Perhaps some day I'll disappear forever,' muses the master-builder Psymmachus in Cyprian Kamil Norwid's *Cleopatra and Caesar,* 'Becoming one with my work…' Today, exactly two hundred years from the poet's birth, it is difficult not to hear Norwid speaking through the lips of his character. The greatest poet of the second phase of Polish Romanticism, Norwid, like Gerard Manley Hopkins in England, created a new poetic idiom so ahead of his time, that he virtually 'disappeared' from the artistic consciousness of his homeland until his triumphant rediscovery in the twentieth century.

Chiefly lauded for his lyric poetry, Norwid also created a corpus of dramatic works astonishing in their breadth, from the Shakespearean *Cleopatra and Caesar* cited above, through the mystical dramas *Wanda and Krakus, the Unknown Prince…*

Buy it > www.glagoslav.com

A BURGLAR OF THE BETTER SORT

by Tytus Czyżewski

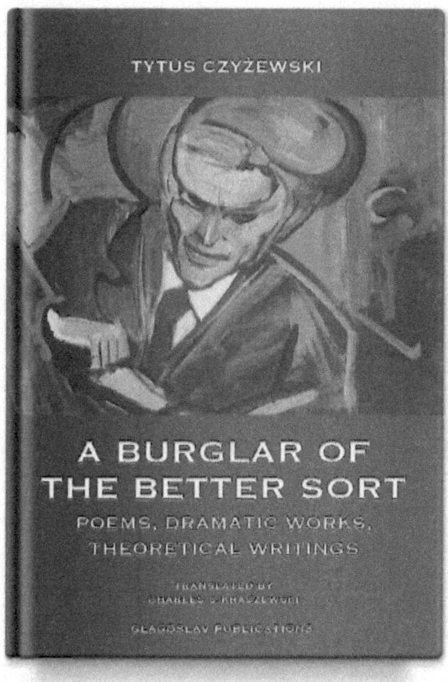

The history of Poland, since the eighteenth century, has been marked by an almost unending struggle for survival. From 1795 through 1945, she was partitioned four times by her stronger neighbours, most of whom were intent on suppressing if not eradicating Polish culture. It is not surprising, then, that much of the great literature written in modern Poland has been politically and patriotically engaged. Yet there is a second current as well, that of authors devoted above all to the craft of literary expression, creating 'art for art's sake', and not as a didactic national service. Such a poet is Tytus Czyżewski, one of the chief, and most interesting, literary figures of the twentieth century. Growing to maturity in the benign Austrian partition of Poland, and creating most of his works in the twenty-year window of authentic Polish independence stretching between the two world wars, Czyżewski is an avant-garde poet, dramatist and painter who popularised the new approach to poetry established in France by Guillaume Apollinaire, and was to exert a marked influence on such multi-faceted artists as Tadeusz Kantor.

Buy it > www.glagoslav.com

THE MOUSEIAD AND OTHER MOCK EPICS

by Ignacy Krasicki

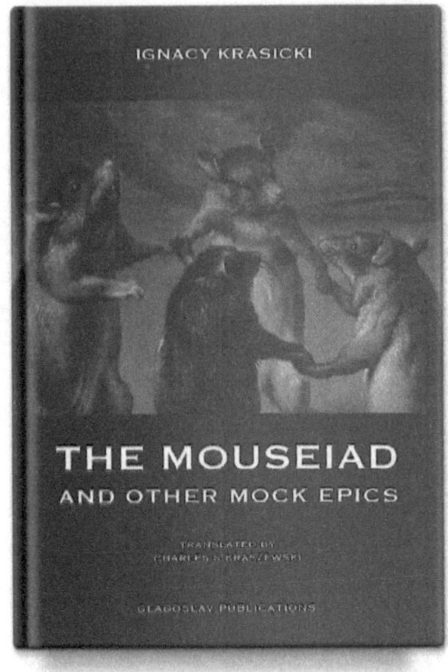

International brigades of mice and rats join forces to defend the rodents of Poland, threatened with extermination at the paws of cats favoured by the ancient ruler King Popiel, a sybaritic, cowardly ruler... The Hag of Discord incites a vicious rivalry between monastic orders, which only the good monks' common devotion to... fortified spirits... is able to allay... The present translation of the mock epics of Poland's greatest figure of the Enlightenment, Ignacy Krasicki, brings together the *Mouseiad*, the *Monachomachia*, and the *Anti-monachomachia* — a tongue-in-cheek 'retraction' of the former work by the author, criticised for so roundly (and effectively) satirising the faults of the Church, of which he himself was a prince. Krasicki towers over all forms of eighteenth-century literature in Poland like Voltaire, Swift, Pope, and LaFontaine all rolled into one. While his fables constitute his most well-known works of poetry, in the words of American comparatist Harold Segel, 'the good bishop's mock-epic poems [...] are the most impressive examples of his literary gifts.' This English translation by Charles S. Kraszewski is rounded off by one of Krasicki's lesser-known works, *The Chocim War*, the poet's only foray into the genre of the serious, Vergilian epic.

Buy it > www.glagoslav.com

ABSOLUTE ZERO

by Artem Chekh

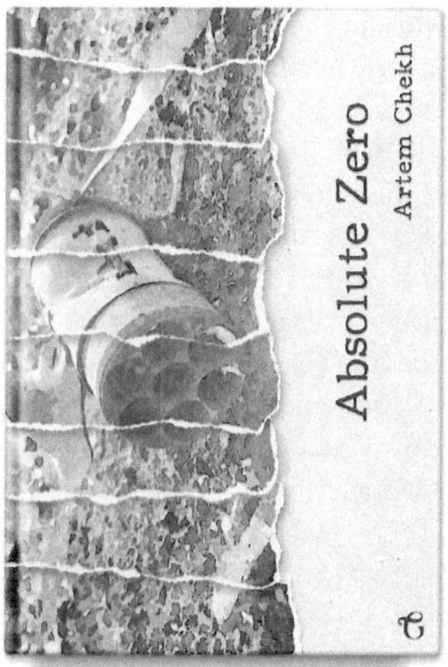

The book is a first person account of a soldier's journey, and is based on Artem Chekh's diary that he wrote while and after his service in the war in Donbas. One of the most important messages the book conveys is that war means pain. Chekh is not showing the reader any heroic combat, focusing instead on the quiet, mundane, and harsh soldier's life. Chekh masterfully selects the most poignant details of this kind of life.

Artem Chekh (1985) is a contemporary Ukrainian writer, author of more than ten books of fiction and essays. *Absolute Zero* (2017), an account of Chekh's service in the army in the war in Donbas, is one of his latest books, for which he became a recipient of several prestigious awards in Ukraine, such as the Joseph Conrad Prize (2019), the Gogol Prize (2018), the Voyin Svitla (2018), and the Litaktsent Prize (2017). This is his first book-length translation into English.

Buy it > www.glagoslav.com

- *A History of Belarus* by Lubov Bazan
- *Children's Fashion of the Russian Empire* by Alexander Vasiliev
- *Empire of Corruption: The Russian National Pastime* by Vladimir Soloviev
- *Heroes of the 90s: People and Money. The Modern History of Russian Capitalism* by Alexander Solovev, Vladislav Dorofeev and Valeria Bashkirova
- *Fifty Highlights from the Russian Literature* (Dutch Edition) by Maarten Tengbergen
- *Bajesvolk* (Dutch Edition) by Michail Chodorkovsky
- *Dagboek van Keizerin Alexandra* (Dutch Edition)
- *Myths about Russia* by Vladimir Medinskiy
- *Boris Yeltsin: The Decade that Shook the World* by Boris Minaev
- *A Man of Change: A study of the political life of Boris Yeltsin*
- *Sberbank: The Rebirth of Russia's Financial Giant* by Evgeny Karasyuk
- *To Get Ukraine* by Oleksandr Shyshko
- *Asystole* by Oleg Pavlov
- *Gnedich* by Maria Rybakova
- *Marina Tsvetaeva: The Essential Poetry*
- *Multiple Personalities* by Tatyana Shcherbina
- *The Investigator* by Margarita Khemlin
- *The Exile* by Zinaida Tulub
- *Leo Tolstoy: Flight from Paradise* by Pavel Basinsky
- *Moscow in the 1930* by Natalia Gromova
- *Laurus* (Dutch edition) by Evgenij Vodolazkin
- *Prisoner* by Anna Nemzer
- *The Crime of Chernobyl: The Nuclear Goulag* by Wladimir Tchertkoff
- *Alpine Ballad* by Vasil Bykau
- *The Complete Correspondence of Hryhory Skovoroda*
- *The Tale of Aypi* by Ak Welsapar
- *Selected Poems* by Lydia Grigorieva
- *The Fantastic Worlds of Yuri Vynnychuk*
- *The Garden of Divine Songs and Collected Poetry of Hryhory Skovoroda*
- *Adventures in the Slavic Kitchen: A Book of Essays with Recipes* by Igor Klekh
- *Seven Signs of the Lion* by Michael M. Naydan

- *Forefathers' Eve* by Adam Mickiewicz
- *One-Two* by Igor Eliseev
- *Girls, be Good* by Bojan Babić
- *Time of the Octopus* by Anatoly Kucherena
- *The Grand Harmony* by Bohdan Ihor Antonych
- *The Selected Lyric Poetry Of Maksym Rylsky*
- *The Shining Light* by Galymkair Mutanov
- *The Frontier: 28 Contemporary Ukrainian Poets - An Anthology*
- *Acropolis: The Wawel Plays* by Stanisław Wyspiański
- *Contours of the City* by Attyla Mohylny
- *Conversations Before Silence: The Selected Poetry of Oles Ilchenko*
- *The Secret History of my Sojourn in Russia* by Jaroslav Hašek
- *Mirror Sand: An Anthology of Russian Short Poems*
- *Maybe We're Leaving* by Jan Balaban
- *Death of the Snake Catcher* by Ak Welsapar
- *A Brown Man in Russia* by Vijay Menon
- *Hard Times* by Ostap Vyshnia
- *The Flying Dutchman* by Anatoly Kudryavitsky
- *Nikolai Gumilev's Africa* by Nikolai Gumilev
- *Combustions* by Srđan Srdić
- *The Sonnets* by Adam Mickiewicz
- *Dramatic Works* by Zygmunt Krasiński
- *Four Plays* by Juliusz Słowacki
- *Little Zinnobers* by Elena Chizhova
- *We Are Building Capitalism! Moscow in Transition 1992-1997* by Robert Stephenson
- *The Nuremberg Trials* by Alexander Zvyagintsev
- *The Hemingway Game* by Evgeni Grishkovets
- *A Flame Out at Sea* by Dmitry Novikov
- *Jesus' Cat* by Grig
- *Want a Baby and Other Plays* by Sergei Tretyakov
- *Mikhail Bulgakov: The Life and Times* by Marietta Chudakova
- *Leonardo's Handwriting* by Dina Rubina
- *A Burglar of the Better Sort* by Tytus Czyżewski
- *The Mouseiad and other Mock Epics* by Ignacy Krasicki
- *Ravens before Noah* by Susanna Harutyunyan

- *An English Queen and Stalingrad* by Natalia Kulishenko
- *Point Zero* by Narek Malian
- *Absolute Zero* by Artem Chekh
- *Olanda* by Rafał Wojasiński
- *Robinsons* by Aram Pachyan
- *The Monastery* by Zakhar Prilepin
- *The Selected Poetry of Bohdan Rubchak: Songs of Love, Songs of Death, Songs of the Moon*
- *Mebet* by Alexander Grigorenko
- *The Orchestra* by Vladimir Gonik
- *Everyday Stories* by Mima Mihajlović
- *Slavdom* by Ľudovít Štúr
- *The Code of Civilization* by Vyacheslav Nikonov
- *Where Was the Angel Going?* by Jan Balaban
- *De Zwarte Kip* (Dutch Edition) by Antoni Pogorelski
- *Głosy / Voices* by Jan Polkowski
- *Sergei Tretyakov: A Revolutionary Writer in Stalin's Russia* by Robert Leach
- *Opstand* (Dutch Edition) by Władysław Reymont
- *Dramatic Works* by Cyprian Kamil Norwid
- *Children's First Book of Chess* by Natalie Shevando and Matthew McMillion
- *Precursor* by Vasyl Shevchuk
- *The Vow: A Requiem for the Fifties* by Jiří Kratochvil
- *De Bibliothecaris* (Dutch edition) by Mikhail Jelizarov
- *Subterranean Fire* by Natalka Bilotserkivets
- *Vladimir Vysotsky: Selected Works*
- *Behind the Silk Curtain* by Gulistan Khamzayeva
- *The Village Teacher and Other Stories* by Theodore Odrach
- *Duel* by Borys Antonenko-Davydovych
- *War Poems* by Alexander Korotko
- *Ballads and Romances* by Adam Mickiewicz
- *The Revolt of the Animals* by Wladyslaw Reymont
- *Liza's Waterfall: The hidden story of a Russian feminist* by Pavel Basinsky
- *Biography of Sergei Prokofiev* by Igor Vishnevetsky

More coming . . .

GLAGOSLAV PUBLICATIONS

www.glagoslav.com